BLOOD OF YOUR SISTERS

By the same author

Dark Armada
Covenant of the Poppies
Atoll
Hell's Arena
Firestorm
Snowtrap
Glimpse of Forever
Hell Seed
Nightdive
Flameout
Cold Route to Freedom
On a Still Night
One Sword Less
Bitter Autumn
Adapted to Stress

Writing as Lindsey Grey

Smoke from Another Fire

Blood of Your Sisters

Colin D. Peel

St. Martin's Press
New York

A THOMAS DUNNE BOOK.
An imprint of St. Martin's Press.

Library of Congress Cataloging-in-Publication Data

Peel, Colin D.
Blood of your sisters / Colin D. Peel.
p. cm.
"A Thomas Dunne book."
ISBN 0-312-15065-2
I. Title.
PR6066.E36B57 1997
823'.914—dc21 96-48768
CIP

First published in Great Britain by Robert Hale Limited

First U.S. Edition: March 1997

10 9 8 7 6 5 4 3 2 1

Gone are those three, those sisters rare
With wonder-lips and eyes ashine.
One was wise, and one was fair,
And one was mine.

Ficke

BLOOD OF YOUR SISTERS

One

Experience had told him the view from the ridge would be like this – another pockmarked moonscape of gravel and sunbaked soil littered with the debris of the diggers who had chosen to sweat out a few weeks or a few months here. Already, in the distance, he could see men crawling across the field like so many ants travelling to the water's edge and back again. There were hundreds of them, working along a two-mile stretch of the river under the usual blanket of dust.

Stepping out of his LandRover into the liquid heat of another African morning, Mark Rayner found that the sight was more familiar than it was depressing. All along the Cuango River, from Cafunfo in the north where the drought had exposed huge areas of the alluvial plains, to the gravel beds further south where some of the biggest finds had been made, the picture was the same.

He'd got used to it, he realized. And, in the last two weeks, he'd seen enough diggers labouring with a rifle in one hand and a shovel in the other to know that coming this far down-river by himself had been a mistake. This was *garimpeiro* territory, a place you didn't visit unless you had someone to watch your back and a good map of the way out.

The whole damn province was like it, Rayner thought. Law and order hadn't just broken down in Angola, in the diamond areas of Lunda Norte, if there ever had been any law, it had vanished without trace when the *garimpeiros* moved in.

For a moment he wondered whether to risk a drive down to the river. Despite rumours about a white man working in the area, there was no reason to suppose the man was Janson. Even if he was here, there was probably little chance of him offering to help, Rayner decided. In the aftermath of the civil war, people who came to places like this only came to help themselves.

He reached into the LandRover for his binoculars, steadying them against the door while he scanned across the flood-plain terraces by the river. The heat-haze made it difficult to pick out anything that was markedly different about the field, but the scattering of corrugated-iron shacks, plastic sheeting and tents seemed normal enough and, as far as he could determine, there was no sign of the fortified enclosures he'd encountered elsewhere.

A low-grade field? he wondered. Or one relying on some kind of collective security to guard against a raid by government troops?

The answer came almost at once. He was putting the binoculars back into the glove box when he sensed there was someone behind him.

Rayner turned round slowly, taking care to keep his hands in the open.

It was a young African, a boy in his late teens. He carried the gutted carcass of an antelope on his shoulder and held a rifle in his hand.

Rayner didn't say anything until the boy spoke to him in Portuguese.

'Do you understand English?' Rayner kept his eyes on the rocks behind the LandRover.

The boy nodded.

'I'm by myself,' Rayner said. 'Tell your friends.'

The boy turned his head slightly.

From behind the rocks two other men emerged – unsmiling men who made no attempt to move any closer.

'You come to trade?' The boy dropped the antelope onto the ground.

'No. I'm looking for someone. A guy called Janson.'

The boy responded by going round to open the rear door of the LandRover. Rayner stayed exactly where he was, neither looking at the men nor the boy.

After a few minutes the door slammed shut and the boy reappeared carrying a box of Winchester cartridges and two cans of coffee. He placed them carefully on the ground beside the antelope.

'OK.' Rayner wasn't sure whether he was paying for safe passage or information. 'What about Janson?'

The boy pointed toward the river. 'Where the water is yellow,' he said.

'Hang on.' Still moving slowly, Rayner retrieved the binoculars, placing them on the hood of the LandRover. 'Show me.'

It took the boy some time to align the binoculars to his satisfaction. When he had finished he indicated Rayner should look.

'That's where Janson is?' Because one eyepiece was out of focus, all Rayner could see was a blurred rectangular hole and what looked like a green tent.

'By the yellow water.' The boy repeated his directions before collecting the cartridges, the cans and the antelope.

'How do I get down there?'

'It is better you wait. Today, maybe tomorrow, Kabinda comes. Afterwards, then you find a way.'

'Who's Kabinda?

The boy turned to go before Rayner had finished asking the question. A moment later the ridge was once again deserted. The exchange of goods for information had taken less than five minutes, an uneventful meeting that might or might not have provided a lead. There was no way of knowing, he thought. Just as there was no way of knowing whether his visitors would return with reinforcements and why the boy had mentioned the name Kabinda.

He sat down and tried to decide what he should do. Having come this far without discovering anything worthwhile, he was reluctant to discount the possibility of Janson being here, just as he was unwilling to wait a couple of days because of the boy's remark. But it had hardly been a warning, Rayner thought, more of a suggestion. And the sooner he found out whether this was another wild-goose chase the quicker he'd know what the chances were of getting paid.

In the end it was the money that persuaded him to climb back into the LandRover and start searching for a way to get closer to the river. It was always the damn money, Rayner thought. Gold in South Africa, diamonds in Angola and money everywhere else.

He shifted down into second, making the wheels spin to get rid of his irritation as he headed north along the ridge towards a group of trees. The minute he reached them he saw his mistake. Besides being no closer to the river, the end of the ridge was precariously steep and too rocky for him to attempt a descent.

Rayner turned the LandRover round, driving back through his own dust in the opposite direction until he was certain he had exhausted all the possibilities. By then, frustration had taken the place of his irritation. If he hadn't known before, he knew now. There was only one way down to the river, and that was by foot.

Once resigned to the prospect of a hike to the mining area, he worked steadily to safeguard the LandRover, removing the distributor cap and the rotor arm before hammering a steel pin into the sand to act as a ground for his electric-fence energizer. Electrifying the bodywork wasn't foolproof, but in open country like this he knew it would work well enough provided he wasn't away too long, and Rayner had no intention of being away too long.

By ten o'clock he was ready to leave. Picking up his rifle and his pack, he took a final look along the ridge, then started off down the slope towards the distant river flats.

To begin with, it was hard going. As well as being steep, the east face of the ridge was treeless and covered in a layer of loose soil. Half sliding and half running, Rayner kicked up a cloud of dust that was guaranteed to announce his arrival to anyone who happened to be watching – even when the slope began to flatten out he was unable to move without leaving a track behind him to show where he had come from.

At the bottom of the ridge he encountered the usual combination of silt and gravel, the weathered remains of the diamond-bearing kimberlite that had been washed down-river a million years ago. The stuff was easier to walk on, but Rayner didn't notice.

Ahead of him a number of men were gathering. He counted five of them, Africans who had temporarily stopped work to take up another job. Rayner knew exactly who they were. This was the proper advance guard, *garimpeiros* who were paid by the other diggers to check out new arrivals.

He took off his pack and stopped walking, waiting for them to draw closer so they could hear the sound of his rifle bolt when he chambered the first round.

Only one of them came forward. Although the man was shirtless like the others, the upper part of his body was free of sweat and there was no dust in his hair.

Rayner greeted him with a nod.

'You bring ivory for Kabinda?'

The question was a give-away, Rayner thought. Instead of speaking in French or Portuguese, the man had used English. And Rayner's pack was manifestly too small to contain ivory.

'Are you the one who looks for Janson?'

'Yeah.' Rayner nodded again, confident now that he was right. Word had already reached the area and, even though the mention of Kabinda was as mystifying as it had been before, at least this time it hadn't been followed by a warning.

The man turned his head to spit. 'Janson says you stay maybe one day.'

'Maybe.' Confirmation of Janson's presence at the field was an anticlimax. Rayner found he was neither pleased nor relieved. The atmosphere here was the same as it was everywhere else, an all pervading distrust of strangers whether they were Europeans or Africans. He could detect it in the eyes of the man in front of him, just as he could anticipate seeing it in Janson's.

'For one packet of cigarettes I take you.' The African held out his hand.

Rayner's finger strayed to the safety catch of his rifle. 'I'll find him myself, thanks,' he said.

The African grinned. 'You trip over a nice diamond, you tell me where.'

'Sure.' Rayner picked up his pack and walked straight ahead without looking at him.

Already the other men were dispersing, responding to some unspoken command to allow the stranger access. Because he had passed the test? Rayner wondered. Or because there was another white man here who had said it was OK?

He made himself relax the grip on the rifle. The stock was slippery in his hand and, in his mouth, mixed with the grit, there was an all too familiar taste.

Swearing under his breath, Rayner used the words to push away the feeling that he should be somewhere else. It had been like this for the last four days, a growing awareness of the futility of what he was doing and the urge to get the hell out of Africa altogether.

He walked for another fifteen minutes before he encountered the first large concentration of *garimpeiros,* a ragged band of diggers scrambling about in their gravel pits with scoops and sieves as though their lives depended on it. The men were filthy, either half naked or dressed in tattered shirts and dirty shorts, seemingly oblivious to everything except the need to tunnel further or dig deeper in the search for the one elusive stone that would make them rich forever.

Ten feet away an old man emerged from a hole in the ground, hauling a sieve full of gravel behind him. He could hardly carry it, but he staggered off barefoot towards the river to wash his find without giving Rayner a glance.

In his trip down the Cuango, Rayner had seen the same thing a hundred times, a reminder, if he needed one, of what Felix had told him in Johannesburg the night before he'd left. Illicit diamond mining was like compulsive drinking, gambling or sex, Felix had said. And you didn't retire until you were dead. Rayner hadn't believed him then, but he did now.

He picked his way between the pits, some of them shallow scrapings while others were excavations ten feet deep in which men were hacking their way through a layer of gravel and rocks with crowbars and shovels. The nearest thing to hell, Rayner thought. Felix had said that too.

Unlike the view from the ridge, at ground level the man-made hills of tailings made it difficult to see any distance at all, forcing Rayner to navigate from memory. He tramped on steadily eastwards towards the river, intending to walk north once he'd found it until he located Janson's tent.

It was hardly a plan, but Rayner had already decided it was better than looking for a section of the river that was running yellow. Until he'd lost sight of it altogether, the whole Cuango had appeared to be discoloured for miles and, this close to the water, the directions from the boy were useless.

Nearer the river the pits were closer together. These were more extensive, a number of them employing winches to haul up the bucket loads of gravel from the diggers labouring below ground. Here and there, Rayner came across individual guards, men leaning on their rifles with cigarettes hanging between their lips. Some nodded, some didn't but, without exception, every one of them stared at the white man who had ventured on to their area.

Rayner kept his head down, walking across the wasteland with his rifle slung across his shoulders until he reached the river-bank. Then he turned left and began searching for a green tent among the corrugated iron shacks. 200 yards up river, on the edge of a pit the size of a tennis court, he found one.

Sitting outside was a large, fleshy man in his early forties with a paunch and a round face burned almost black by the sun. He wore a bush hat, a red shirt patterned with dust and a pair of jeans cut off above the knees.

'Ross Janson?' Rayner said.

'Who the fuck are you?' Janson spoke with a thick South African accent. He made no attempt to shake hands.

'Rayner. Mark Rayner.'

'What do you want?'

Rayner met his eyes. 'Are you just naturally an ignorant bastard, or are you having a bad day?'

'You don't have good days in a place like this. How do you know my name?'

'Felix Osterman gave it to me.'

'Do you work for Osterman?' Janson's manner became marginally less hostile.

'Sort of. '

'I hear you've been looking for me.'

Rayner nodded.

'How do I know you're not full of shit? Maybe I've never heard of this guy Osterman.'

Rayner put down his rifle, then slipped off his pack and rummaged around inside it until he found the envelope. He gave it to Janson without saying anything.

The South African took less than thirty seconds to read the card inside. 'Do you know what this is?' he asked.

'No.'

'Listen.' Janson began to read. 'On surrender of this card to my office in Johannesburg, I Felix Osterman hereby guarantee the bearer a quantity of cold beer to be not less than ten dozen cans provided free over a period of one month following his return to South Africa.'

Rayner tried unsuccessfully to conjure up the image of a cold beer. The heat was rising off the ground in waves, and his mouth was so dry it was impossible to imagine a glass of cold water, let alone a beer.

Janson was smiling. 'Hey, I'm sorry,' he said. 'You kind of forget your manners after you've been up here for a while.' He stuck out his hand.

'It's OK.' Rayner shook hands with him. 'Look, I'm pretty dry. You wouldn't have anything to drink, would you?'

'Sure. Come on in out of the sun.'

It was as hot inside the tent as it was outside, but the shade made the air seem cooler. After removing his boots, Rayner sat down on an upturned bucket waiting while Janson dropped chlorine tablets into a jug of water. The tent contained a camp-bed, a butane cooker, a supply of canned food and a large quantity of toilet rolls. A lever-action rifle lay on the bed and there was a revolver in a holster hanging from the tent pole nearest the door.

Janson handed him a mug of water. 'How much scotch do you want in it?'

'Just enough to taste, thanks.' Rayner held out the mug, noticing that Janson's hand shook when he poured from the bottle.

'All right.' Janson sat on the edge of the bed. 'What are you doing here?'

'Working. For Felix – or for his company. Felix and I have sort of known each other since he was up in Zaire on the Brazzaville project. I ran into him in Johannesburg a few weeks ago, and he talked me into doing this freelance job for him. It's no big deal – just a quick, dirty trip to see if I can help De Beers find out what the hell's going on up here. I started in Cafunfo a fortnight ago and I've been working my way down-river ever since. Felix said if I couldn't get any good leads I should look for you.'

'That's a crock of shit.' Janson drank from his mug. 'De Beers know damn well what's going on. They're worried about how many diamonds are being illicitly mined in Angola. And they're worried about controlling the market to keep the prices up. They'll buy from anyone. We've had De Beers buyers come through here.'

'I know. Felix told me. It's more complicated than that. De Beers aren't stupid. They don't like illicit mining, but they know they can't stop it. Their problem is that there aren't any Angolan diamonds for them to buy. They're all disappearing and turning up somewhere else.'

'Shame,' Janson said. 'Go on.'

'According to Felix, to stop a worldwide collapse in the price, and to protect other producers who sell through De Beers, in 1992 his company spent the thick end of four hundred million US dollars soaking up illicitly mined stones from Angola. When the damn things began turning up on the market again De Beers tried to do the same thing but it hasn't worked.'

'Because the stones are being sold to someone else,' Janson grunted. 'For a better price than De Beers wants to offer. Felix must know that.'

Rayner nodded. 'He's tried to find out if there's another group operating in Central Africa, but he's going round in circles. De Beers know they're being outbid, but they don't know how or who by. They don't understand how another buyer can pay more for them when they've controlled the world market for over sixty years. It doesn't make sense.'

'So Felix sent you to sniff around?'

'I'm on a retainer, and a bonus if I get a lead on what's happening.'

Janson finished his drink. 'Why you? You're an American, aren't you? What the hell would you know about rough diamonds?'

'I don't know a damn thing about diamonds. I don't have to.' Rayner controlled his annoyance. 'I'm getting paid for information.' He held up his hand to stop Janson interrupting. 'And if you want to know why me, I'll tell you. Because I can make my money without digging holes in the ground in some godforsaken place like this, and because I'm good at what I do. That's why.'

'Yeah.' Janson was amused. 'Charlie told me.'

'Who's Charlie?'

'You've already met him. He was upset because you wouldn't give him any cigarettes.'

'Does he work for you?' Rayner asked.

'When he feels like it. He'd probably work for you if you paid him. Why don't you ask him?'

Rayner didn't answer. He wasn't sure whether he trusted Janson or not. Like all the Europeans in the diamond areas, the man displayed the usual streak of hard-nosed self-sufficiency, but there was something else about him that made Rayner uneasy.

'Well, my friend.' Janson stretched. 'What's it worth for me to tell you why De Beers is getting screwed?'

'Not a lot.' It was time to improvise, Rayner decided. 'I hear this guy Kabinda is due here today or tomorrow; I'll ask him.'

Janson laughed. 'I wouldn't do that if I was you. You don't even know who he is.' He paused. 'How about this? I'll tell you what Felix wants to know for ten per cent of your bonus.'

'I didn't say how much bonus I'm getting.'

'I don't care. You don't look like the kind of guy who'd be poking around Lunda Norte for chicken feed – not by himself.'

Rayner considered the offer. If Janson really had the

information, this was a quick way to end the assignment, a way to get back home for the spring with enough cash to stay there – maybe even enough to start over.

'Well?' Janson was waiting.

'Fifteen thousand rand.' Rayner stood up. 'Take it or leave it. But only if I'm satisfied – and I decide whether I'm satisfied or not.'

'Let me show you something.' Reaching inside his shirt, Janson withdrew a small leather pouch. 'I've been up here nearly seven weeks. This is what I've got for my trouble so far.' He tipped the contents of the pouch into his cupped hand.

The rough stones looked like pieces of round frosted glass. There was no sparkle to them, and none of the brilliance Rayner had expected to see.

'Here.' Janson handed him one that was the size of a peanut. 'Rub it between your finger and thumb. See how oily it feels?'

It didn't feel oily to Rayner, but he didn't say so. 'How much can you sell this for?' He held it up to the light.

'Depends. It's a nice one though with no yellow in it – real gem quality. Seventy-five per cent of Angolan diamonds are like that. You'd be lucky to find one as good up in Zaire. If you did, it probably came from Angola in the first place. Most Zairean alluvial deposits are industrial quality.' Janson reached out and touched the diamond with his finger. 'As far as I can see it doesn't have any inclusions in it. That means it'll be worth a fair bit in the hands of the right person.'

'How much?' Rayner repeated his question.

'Up here, a few hundred rand. In South Africa, if I find a dealer who likes it, more than you're offering me for information.'

Rayner gave back the diamond. 'Does that mean you're not interested?'

'No. I'm interested.' Janson grinned. 'I just thought you'd like to know you're getting your money's worth.' He poured the stones back into his pouch. 'Do you want to talk now, or have a look round my claim first?'

'How about now?' As well as having seen enough diamond pits to last him several years, Rayner wanted to get on with it.

'OK. You'd better sit down again and have a proper drink. This is going to take a while.' After Janson had refilled the mugs, this time with neat scotch, he made himself comfortable on the bed and lit a cigarette.

Outside, the clanging of picks and shovels was continuous, the sound of men tunnelling and burrowing into the terraces all along the river. It made Rayner wonder how anyone could ever get used to the noise, let alone the dirt and the unremitting heat.

'I'll give you some background first,' Janson said. 'Probably the same stuff you heard from Felix, but from a digger's point of view. This whole scramble for diamonds began late in 1992 after the Angolan Government made the mistake of changing the law. They passed legislation allowing Angolan citizens to start trading in uncut stones so the market would soak up all the rough diamonds that people had been hoarding illegally over the years. What that did, of course, was make it a hell of a lot easier for everyone to unload illicitly mined diamonds. That's why the country's crawling with people – all doing what I'm doing. You've got Angolans, Zaireans, South Africans and Lebanese dealers tripping over each other to get rich quick.'

'And are they?' Rayner interrupted. 'Getting rich, I mean.'

'Some. The ones who know what they're doing. It's the rest of them who are causing the problem for Felix.' Janson drew on his cigarette. 'I'm not surprised De Beers are hurting. A year ago they sold eighty per cent of the world's rough diamonds – now it's all turning to shit for them. It's like Felix said; to begin with, his cartel managed to buy up most of the illicitly mined diamonds in Angola. Then, all of a sudden the stones started going somewhere else. The *garimpeiros* found a better market – or at least around here they did.'

'And you know where this market is?' Rayner looked at Janson over the rim of his mug.

'I know how it works. It isn't a diamond market at all. That's why De Beers can't find it.' Janson paused. 'It's an ivory market. One of the four curses of Africa – along with gold, diamonds and slaving.'

'I don't understand,' Rayner said.

'I didn't think you would. You have to start by realizing there's no such thing as an ivory market anymore – not a legal one. It doesn't exist except for some tusks coming out of countries that cull their elephants, or the tusks from animals that die of natural causes. What does exist is an underground market worth around a billion US dollars a year. That's one hell of a lot of money – enough to interest some pretty smart people and make ivory poaching a way of life right across Africa.'

'What's ivory got to do with diamonds?'

'Ah.' Janson sat up. 'That's the clever bit. You see, the ivory poachers have a problem. They've got governments hunting them down like rats, and anyone unlucky enough to get caught carrying tusks winds up in jail and the keys are thrown away. The market is as good as it ever was in places like Japan and Hong Kong, if only the poachers could get the stuff out of Angola. But that's exactly what the poor bastards can't do because they haven't got the resources, and because they haven't got the business contacts overseas.'

Rayner still didn't understand. He was about to say so when Janson began speaking again.

'Now, imagine you're an international businessman. You can buy cheap, blackmarket ivory in Angola, and multiply its value twenty times over by shipping it to Hong Kong. The other thing you can buy in Angola is cheap diamonds. So what do you do? You set up an outfit that offers higher prices for rough diamonds than De Beers and the other buyers are prepared to pay. That gets you into a whole bunch of illicitly mined stones. You keep any of the real good ones and sell them in Antwerp – the rest you trade for ivory. Have you got the picture?'

'Yeah.' Rayner was thinking. 'You're saying someone's buying up Angolan diamonds and exchanging them for ivory because of the huge profit they can make from selling ivory overseas.' He paused. 'You can't really multiply your money by twenty times, can you?'

'Sure you can. I've told you. The whole thing's illegal – everything about it. There's a worldwide ban on importing or exporting the stuff.'

'And this businessman knows how to get it out of the country,' Rayner said. 'And into somewhere else.'

Janson nodded. 'He has his fingers in the diamond market a little bit too – for any exceptional stones he comes across while he's trading – otherwise he might just as well buy the ivory outright. This way he's too small a player in diamonds for anyone to track him down. He unloads all the ordinary stones onto the poachers. Ivory poachers are really happy to be paid in diamonds. They can sell them anywhere, and it's a lot easier and safer to carry a few stones around than it is to transport bloody great elephant tusks from one place to another.'

'What happens to the diamonds?' Rayner said.

'They'll turn up eventually – God knows where. The poachers probably trade them for food or ammunition out on the coast. That may be what is upsetting De Beers.' Janson grinned. 'If you make a living chainsawing the tusks off dead elephants you're not going to have much interest in the world price of diamonds or protecting the diamond industry, are you?'

'So everyone's happy,' Rayner said. 'Except De Beers, the diamond market and the elephants.' He swallowed a mouthful of scotch, wondering whether Janson had volunteered the information because he was a friend of Felix's or because of the 15,000 rand. Not that it mattered one way or the other, he thought. The explanation was believable enough, and apart from finding some way to back up the story, his job was over.

'Well?' Janson queried. 'Do we have a deal?'

'I guess so. Does this smart international businessman go by the name of Kabinda?'

'Maximilian Kabinda. I'm not sure how smart he is, but he's smarter than you and me. He's got half of Angola by the balls. He's into everything, including the slave trade.'

'Is he an African – an Angolan?'

'Don't know ' Janson blew out some cigarette smoke. 'But he's black. Black and powerful.'

'And he's due here today or tomorrow?' Rayner said slowly.

'Not today. If he was coming today the ivory would be coming in already and I haven't seen any sign of it. Maybe tomorrow or the next day.'

'Why does he use this area?'

Janson shrugged. 'Probably because it's far enough down-river from Cafunfo for him to feel safe. There haven't been troops around for months. You can cross the river here too – it gets shallow right on the edge of my claim.'

'Where the water runs yellow?' Rayner grinned.

'Right. The ivory poachers come from both sides of the Cuango. Every couple of weeks or so they turn up to trade. Don't ask me how they know when to come – I can't tell you. It's the same with the *garimpeiros*, even the ones who come by river. They always get the day right.'

'Have you sold diamonds to Kabinda?' Rayner asked. 'Good ones, I mean.'

'Don't be bloody silly. I can take mine to a proper dealer or straight to a manufacturer in South Africa.'

'And you've never thought of exchanging your low-quality stones for ivory?'

'What the hell would I do with elephant tusks? Even if I knew what they were worth, I couldn't get them out of the country.'

'How does Kabinda do it?' Rayner could see Janson was becoming irritated by the questions.

'No idea. I don't want to know.' Janson's hands were shaking again. He stubbed out his cigarette. 'You don't want to know, either.'

Despite Janson's expression, there was one more question Rayner had to ask. 'If De Beers want to put Kabinda out of business, how do they find him?' he said.

'Why don't you let Felix worry about it? That's what he gets paid for.'

Rayner unzipped his pack and pulled out his camera. 'Suppose I hang around until this character turns up,' he said. 'Could I get a photo of him?'

Janson frowned. 'So you've got something to show Felix? To make sure you get your bonus?'

'It's better than going back to Johannesburg just to tell him what you've told me. If I have a picture he's more likely to believe the story. Maybe he'll recognize the guy.'

'Look,' Janson said. 'Kabinda doesn't travel by himself. You don't walk up to him and take his photo. You're the wrong colour for a start. He'd just as soon blow your head off as have a piss. This is the wild west, Rayner, not New York City.'

Rayner took out his telephoto lens and fitted it to the Pentax.

Janson was unimpressed. 'I've told you,' he said. 'Don't push your luck.'

'Tell me if I could get a couple of shots – from a distance. I don't have to get close.'

'Maybe. As long as no one sees what you're doing. I mean no one. You don't want to trust diggers anymore than you'd trust Kabinda.'

'Fine.' Rayner put the camera away. 'Is it OK if I stay here until he comes?'

'Hundred rand a night, bed and breakfast.'

Rayner began to swear, only stopping when he saw Janson was laughing at him.

'Take it easy.' Janson was still amused. 'Sure you can stay. You're welcome. I'll see if Charlie can rustle up something for you to sleep on.'

Over the course of the afternoon, Rayner had cause to thank Charlie for providing him with more than a bed. By evening, in addition to an ex-army cot, Charlie had delivered two cans of Pepsicola and an unopened bottle of mineral water. The supplies had cost Rayner six packets of cigarettes, but in the circumstances he thought the deal was pretty good.

He had also begun to think that a night spent close to the river might be a welcome change from sleeping alone in the back of the LandRover. Standing now in the dusk outside the tent, the diamond area was a less unfriendly place than it had been earlier. In the last half-hour, because the diggers had stopped for the night, the dust in the atmosphere had largely disappeared and, although the ground was still warm, the air on his face was already much cooler. It made Rayner wonder what truly cold air would feel like again and whether the winter would be over by the time he got home. For a second he thought about Wendy too, remembering the snowstorm and how icy the wind had been on the night she'd said goodbye in Boston.

But that had been another time, Rayner thought. Another time, and somewhere so far removed from the flood-plains of the Cuango river it might as well be on another planet.

It was not until eleven o'clock on the morning of Rayner's third day at the field that Charlie came to announce the arrival of the ivory traders.

After waiting for so long Rayner was wary of another false alarm.

Shading his eyes he looked towards the river. 'Are you sure?' he said.

'Not from there. The first trucks are from the north.' Charlie was evidently pleased to be the bearer of good news. He was also unusually well dressed. Today, in addition to boots, he wore socks, a moderately clean shirt and a fresh pair of shorts.

'Are you selling?' Rayner asked.

Charlie shook his head. 'Janson says the price will be better in Mocamedes or Lobito. After I work for one more month I go there.'

Janson emerged from the tent. He inspected Charlie with

interest.

'We leave now?' Charlie said. 'You have told Rayner he is to come with me?'

'Hang on.' Rayner was suspicious. 'I don't need a minder. I can handle this by myself.'

'You don't know where to go,' Janson grunted. 'Charlie'll take you after he's got rid of that shirt. You're supposed to look like diggers – both of you.'

'Aren't you coming?' Rayner asked.

'What the hell for? I've got better things to do.'

Rayner wondered if he was supposed to be paying Charlie for his trouble, and whether Janson was deliberately exaggerating the need for caution. Charlie slipped off his shirt. 'We walk together,' he said.

'OK.' Rayner went into the tent to collect his rifle and his pack with the Pentax in it.

'Leave the gun.' Janson followed him inside. 'And make sure you keep that bloody camera out of sight.' He hesitated for a moment. 'Listen, Rayner, I wouldn't hang around out there any longer than you have to. And stay this side of the river.'

'For Christ's sake,' Rayner said. 'I'm only going to take some pictures.'

'Yeah.' Janson picked up a shovel. 'Have a nice day.'

Janson's instructions about avoiding a river crossing were unnecessary. Almost as soon as Charlie started escorting Rayner across the field it became obvious where today's trading was going to take place. There were dust trails everywhere. On the far side of the river two rusty Toyota Landcruisers were preparing to enter the water and, in the distance, a convoy of vehicles was zigzagging its way towards some trees at the north end of the ridge.

Observing from the top of a small mountain of gravel, Rayner was able to see that a number of the *garimpeiros* were on the move as well. They too were travelling north, following the river, but making no attempt to cross it.

'There.' Charlie pointed at what looked like a grassy plateau about a half a mile away.

Rayner squinted through the haze. 'Is that where we're going?'

'Kabinda has been there before. From the border with Zaire there is a track. Sometimes it is used by the army, sometimes by Kabinda.'

'Let's go then.' Rayner slid down the gravel, waited for Charlie to join him, then set off at a brisk walk.

At the outskirts of the main field Charlie changed direction, insisting that they should head away from both the river and the plateau. The reason for his strategy became less clear when they drew closer to the trees. There was a bank of them, scrubby, chest-high trees growing in a line from the plateau to the north end of the ridge not far from where Rayner had parked the LandRover.

Rayner was uneasy. 'Look,' he said. 'The cover's no good. The trees aren't big enough. What's wrong with just keeping our heads down and walking along with everyone else?'

'Some of the *garimpeiros* are friends of Kabinda. And you are a stranger here.' Charlie displayed a row of white teeth. 'I show you a better way.'

Charlie was right. Concealed in the grass, only a short distance inside the trees, Rayner came across the source of the moisture for the vegetation; a muddy stream carrying whatever water was left in the ridge down to join the even muddier water of the Cuango.

The stream was narrow and barely running but, in other years when the rains had come, it had carved out a ditch through the soil that was nearly four feet deep.

'You understand?' Charlie queried.

'Yes.' Rayner nodded. 'How close will we be able to get?'

'We see.' Jumping down into the water, Charlie started half walking and half crawling towards the river.

Rayner followed, squelching along behind through a layer of mud while he tried to keep his pack dry.

As well as being infested with insects, the ditch was foul-smelling and thoroughly unpleasant. It made Rayner wonder if the precaution was really essential and, if it was, why the hell he'd bothered coming to start with.

After they had been crawling for about a quarter of a mile, Charlie stopped. 'You look,' he whispered. 'But be careful.'

Rayner wiped the mud out of his eyes then peered cautiously over the bank. He was confronted by a scene of bustling activity.

In the time it had taken them to make their way down the stream, the plateau had turned into a place of business. 200 yards away, men carrying military assault rifles strapped to bloodstained elephant tusks were emerging from vehicles parked among a flotilla of canoes drawn up on the river bank.

The *garimpeiros* were here too, already beginning to assemble in a line that extended from one side of the plateau to the other.

'Jesus,' Rayner murmured. The whole scene had an air of unreality about it.

'This is close enough?' Charlie asked.

Rayner nodded. He was staring at the man in the centre of the plateau, a man sitting in a white chair beside a gleaming white Mercedes truck. Behind the chair a servant held a sun umbrella and a battery-driven electric fan while two armed guards maintained a disinterested watch over the proceedings.

The proceedings were uncomplicated. As soon as trading began Rayner was able to see how easily the transactions were carried out. He watched for several minutes, intrigued by the informality of the market. Except it wasn't a market, he realized. This was a one-man operation, an operation controlled exclusively by the man who was the centre of attention – Maximilian Kabinda.

Rayner fitted the telescopic lens to his camera and used it to obtain a better view, seeing how each digger proffered a selection of diamonds for Kabinda to value. What was clearly an intense inspection for quality was followed by equally intense bargaining over price until Kabinda motioned for the next digger to approach. Then, at some arbitrary point, Kabinda would hold up a hand to indicate that he had accumulated sufficient stones to begin purchasing ivory. That was the sign for one of the poachers to step forward and engage in similar negotiations based this time on Kabinda's assessment of ivory quality.

Kabinda himself was a good-looking man of about thirty. He wore sunglasses, a leopard-skin hat and a tailored safari suit with a handkerchief tucked into his jacket pocket. His expression was as impassive as his hand movements were casual and unhurried. Janson's smart international businessman, Rayner thought. Someone who knew exactly what he was doing.

'You have finished?' Charlie was becoming nervous.

'I haven't taken any photos yet.' Aligning his viewfinder on the growing heap of tusks beside Kabinda, Rayner pressed the shutter release button.

'OK,' Charlie said. 'Now we go.'

Rayner had no intention of leaving until he had obtained a

sequence of photos that would show how the trading was conducted. He started to concentrate on what he was doing, but had taken only three shots when he heard the roar of an engine. A second later an army truck swung out of the trees. It was moving fast, cutting a swathe through the grass. Soldiers spilled out of it on both sides before the vehicle came to a halt – Angolan army regulars who moved quickly to surround Kabinda and his guards.

Charlie tried unsuccessfully to pull Rayner down into the ditch.

'Cut it out.' Rayner shoved him away. Unlike the *garimpeiros* and the ivory poachers who were vanishing in all directions, Rayner was busy looking through his lens, unwilling to abandon his position without knowing what Kabinda's reaction would be. Only afterwards, when everything had gone wrong would Rayner wish he had listened to Charlie.

Rayner knew it would go wrong the instant he saw the girl. She'd climbed out of the army truck, a slightly built European in her twenties who was even more out of place here than the well-dressed African.

Kabinda ignored her, just as he was ignoring the presence of the troops. He remained where he was, speaking into a handheld radio transmitter as though nothing had happened.

'Who the hell is she?' Rayner whispered.

Charlie shrugged his shoulders.

Marching up to Kabinda, the girl presented him with an identification card, waiting with her hands on her hips while he read it.

Kabinda returned the card with a slight bow of his head.

To Rayner, the unreality of the scene was total now – a man sitting on a chair in one of the most lawless places on earth, politely inspecting the girl's credentials inside a circle of armed troops. He was fascinated, unable to drag his eye away from the viewfinder.

When the girl went to examine the pile of elephant tusks Rayner understood why the troops were here.

He saw her motion to some of the soldiers who began unloading jerry cans from the army truck.

Rayner knew what was in the cans. Gasoline – gasoline to burn the ivory.

Charlie knew as well. 'This is not good for Kabinda,' he said. 'The soldiers will show him he is not to do this trade.

After they make a fire they take him away with them, I think.'

Rayner's premonition of disaster was increasing by the minute. Kabinda was too relaxed, too controlled for a man who was about to see thousands of dollars worth of his ivory go up in smoke.

Carrying a can of fuel, one of the soldiers clambered awkwardly up the pile until he was standing on the top.

He died there, almost cut in half by a sudden burst of gunfire. The sound of the can clattering to the ground was followed by an unnatural silence right across the plateau.

Rayner could feel his heart beating. He put down the camera and sank lower into the ditch.

The soldiers had turned their backs on Kabinda now, nervously searching the trees for the gunman. But there wasn't one gunman, there were dozens of them – men hidden in the grass waiting for Kabinda's second signal.

It came soon enough, the instruction to open fire on the soldiers in what amounted to wholesale slaughter. The noise was awful, and the spectacle of men dying where they stood was almost too much for Rayner.

Towards the end, a handful of soldiers attempted to return the fire, but then they panicked, abandoning their weapons in a futile scramble to escape. Rayner watched them die, saw wounded men executed while they were on their knees, and saw more than one survivor despatched with a knife. It was butchery on a scale he had never seen before. He was sickened by it and he was scared.

In the centre of the plateau Kabinda's men had seized the girl. She was struggling while her wrists were being tied to a long rope attached to the truck.

For a second, Rayner considered leaving the safety of the ditch. Whether a white man would be gunned down as readily as the soldiers had been, he didn't know. Nor did he know what he would do if he lived long enough to reach Kabinda.

Charlie brought him to his senses. 'You not watch anymore.' Charlie gave the camera to Rayner. 'Now you understand how it is in Lunda Norte, I think. It is better we go at once.'

'What about the girl?' The taste was back in Rayner's mouth.

Charlie lowered his eyes, clearly worried that Rayner might do something irrational. Rayner was equally worried. But, unarmed, with only Charlie to back him up, he knew he would be powerless against Kabinda's men. It was the helplessness and the dreadful feeling of impotence that finally drove him to take more photographs.

He lay the camera on the bank and began squeezing the button on the Pentax as though it was the trigger of his rifle, continuing even when the girl's screams made his hands so unsteady he could barely see through the viewfinder.

While the ivory was being loaded into Kabinda's truck the girl had been stripped. On her back now, fighting and screaming like a tethered animal at the end of the rope, she was being systematically raped by three of Kabinda's men.

Rayner couldn't stand it any longer. Teeth clenched he started climbing from the ditch. He was less than half-way up the bank when he felt Charlie's arms around his knees.

'No.' Charlie hauled him back in. 'You leave this to Janson.' He pointed.

From nowhere, the solitary figure of a white man had appeared on the plateau. Rayner watched in astonishment as Janson carefully picked his way around the bodies of the soldiers and sauntered up to the Mercedes truck where Kabinda was standing with a gun in his hand.

What Janson was doing, Rayner couldn't imagine. There was no reason for him to be here any more than there was a reason for him to take such a risk. Unless he was crazy, or unless Kabinda had been expecting him.

Janson was offering something to Kabinda. Rayner could guess what it was – diamonds. Because the South African was on a private selling mission for himself? Or because he could no more stand by and watch the girl being raped than Rayner could?

The minute Kabinda and Janson began walking towards her, Rayner was sure he had the answer. Retrieving the Pentax, he looked again through the lens, taking more photos while he watched Kabinda pull the girl to her feet and cut the rope.

Then the unthinkable happened. At point-blank range Kabinda shot Janson in the stomach.

The girl took the only chance she had, running for her life towards the river. But she had travelled fewer than fifty feet when a bullet from Kabinda's gun caught her between the shoulders. Her body flipped in the air and came to rest face down in the grass.

Unaware now of Charlie's grip on him, Rayner was numb, enraged by what he'd seen to the point where he was finding it difficult to breathe.

The anger didn't go away. For the entire time it took Kabinda's men to finish loading the ivory and set fire to the army truck, Rayner fought against his rage. Even after the white Mercedes had left the plateau and Charlie finally released him, it was several minutes before he was sufficiently controlled to speak.

'I have to see if she's dead,' he muttered. 'And Janson.'

Charlie was uncertain. 'Maybe Kabinda's men stay behind in the trees,' he said.

'I don't care.' Rayner slithered out onto the grass, stood up and began walking towards the smoke from the burning truck.

He walked slowly, ignoring the dead soldiers, going to the girl first, but knowing before he turned her over that it was useless. Although her body was warm to touch and her eyes were open, she had died at once. Janson, though, was alive.

'Small calibre bullet.' Janson coughed. His face was grey and blood had begun seeping through his shirt. 'How's the girl?'

Rayner shook his head. 'It was pretty quick.'

'Not quick enough.' Janson sat up. 'Her jacket's there. Bring it over, will you?'

Rayner picked it up. He thought that for a man who'd just been shot, Janson's priorities might be wrong.

'WOPES.' Janson read out the letters. 'Jesus Christ. What were they doing sending out a girl?'

'Who's they?'

'Never mind.' Janson coughed again. 'You'd better dig a hole for her.'

'There isn't time. If I don't get you out of here I'm going to have to dig two holes. How bad is it?'

'I don't know. Feels like the bullet went right through.'

'My LandRover's up there.' Rayner pointed to the ridge. 'What do you think?'

'Ask Charlie to go back to the tent. Tell him to collect the guns and the first~aid kit from under my bunk and meet us at the base of the ridge. I can get that far.'

'Then what?'

'Then I pay Charlie to help you get me up to your LandRover, and I pay you to take me to Malanje or Luanda.'

'I don't want your goddamn money.' Rayner looked at him. 'It's a hell of a drive.'

'What do you care? If I don't make it, you get these.' Janson reached inside his shirt for the pouch. 'But you miss out on the two-carat bastard Kabinda took.'

On the way back to the stream to give Charlie his instructions, Rayner made himself two promises: the first was a promise never to return to the Cuango River region of Angola, and the second, a resolve to kill Kabinda on sight if he ever came across the man again.

The promises were irrational. Rayner knew they were, just as he understood his need for them at the moment. Not until he was in a very different environment thousands of miles away would he come to realize that these self-same promises were all he had to ease his anger, and help him come to terms with the horror of what he had witnessed here today.

Two

Felix Osterman removed his glasses and started polishing them with a tissue. He said nothing, apparently undisturbed by Rayner's account of how the girl had died.

Rayner too was silent, reluctant to finish the story or fill in the gaps because he knew it would only bring the whole thing back again. Not that there was anything more to say, he thought. It was over and, now he'd told Felix, perhaps the memory would begin to fade.

He went to the window and looked down into the street below. It was crammed with cars and people, an environment as foreign to him as the office was with its walls, doors and ceiling. Rayner knew the feeling would go away after a few days, just as it always did; but right now, the streets of Johannesburg were unfamiliar to him and less friendly than the dirt roads of Angola had been. His usual short-term inability to adjust? he wondered. Or because Wendy had been right? Because there really was some flaw in his make-up that prevented him from ever feeling quite at home anywhere.

Felix interrupted his thoughts.

'Sorry.' Rayner turned round. 'What did you say?'

'Janson.' Felix put his glasses back on. 'What happened to Janson?'

'I don't know. By the time Charlie and I got him to the LandRover he was in pretty bad shape. I strapped him down in the back and headed for Malanje, but it took damn nearly nine hours to get there. You know what the roads are like, and I was driving in the dark. I stopped once in a while to see if he was still alive, but there wasn't a hell of a lot I could do for him except keep going.'

'Did you leave him in Malanje?'

'No.' Rayner shook his head. 'About thirty miles out we ran into some kind of roadblock. I think they were UNITA guerrillas, but they had medical supplies, and there was a French doctor with them. He'd been working up in one of the villages, trying to help the children. I wasn't sure if he could do anything for Janson, but he said he thought he could. Next thing I know, Janson's being loaded into a truck on a stretcher. The doctor worked on him for about half an hour, and then told me they were taking him to hospital. They wouldn't let me talk to him or tell me where the hospital was – maybe because they found his diamonds. For all I know, they took the lot and left the poor bastard in a ditch somewhere.'

'You didn't try to follow the truck?' Felix asked.

'I tried.' Rayner paused. 'And had my windshield shot out to show me it wasn't a real good idea. I don't know whether Janson's still alive or not. If he is, I owe him fifteen thousand rand.'

'I wouldn't worry about the money.' Felix opened a drawer in his desk and took out what had once been a tube of toothpaste. The tube had been slit open and the contents removed. 'This came a couple of days ago,' he said. 'Addressed to you, care of me.'

'With toothpaste in it?'

'Full up.' Felix smiled. 'I hope you didn't mind me finding out what else was inside.'

'Diamonds,' Rayner said slowly. 'From Janson.'

Felix lay a folded velvet cloth on his desk. 'Two nice ones.'

Rayner stayed by the window, wondering why he didn't feel grateful, and why he didn't want to see the stones either.

'I'll give you a fair price,' Felix said. 'How about I just add it on to what we owe you?'

'No.' Reluctant as he was to examine the diamonds, Rayner had no intention of selling them. 'I'll take them with me, thanks.' He returned to the desk and sat down. 'Did they come by mail?'

Felix shook his head. 'Someone from an airline delivered them. We don't know who. I don't think there's any doubt that Janson is alive and kicking, but I wouldn't bother trying to find him to say thanks.'

Rayner smiled. 'You can do that for me. I'm heading back to the States.'

'Oh.' Felix seemed disappointed. 'I was hoping I could

interest you in a follow-up for us. Now we know what's going on, De Beers can't afford to sit around hoping this problem will solve itself – not if we're going to recover our market share in a hurry. We've lost enough damn time and money as it is.'

'Good luck,' Rayner said. 'Do you know where to start?'

'Up until last night we didn't. After you briefed me on the phone yesterday I called a meeting to discuss our options. It took us until eight o'clock to decide what we already knew. You see, our hands are pretty much tied, Mark. We do have a buying agreement with them, but we don't have a choice. The new Angolan Government are the only people who can handle this.' Felix paused. 'But they need to be persuaded, and we need someone – apart from ourselves – to present them with the right information so they can act.'

'I'm not in the persuading business.' Taking the film canister from his pocket, Rayner stood it upright on the desk. 'Give this to the Angolans. Be careful where you have it developed, though. There's some nasty stuff on it.'

Felix ran his fingers down his tie. 'Look, Mark,' he said, 'don't think I'm being picky, and don't think we're not grateful for everything. We think you've done a hell of a good job, but it's not enough. You have to understand, De Beers has to be careful. We're an international organization and we can't be seen to be telling governments what to do, anymore than we can afford to interfere in things that are none of our business.'

'And ivory isn't your business,' Rayner said.

'You know it isn't. It doesn't matter whether ivory trading is illegal or not. The Angolans don't take kindly to foreign corporations reminding them of problems they already know about – especially if the company has South African connections like ours. I'm afraid we have to find a way of getting Luanda to do the job without De Beers being involved.'

'You want someone to do your dirty work,' Rayner said.

'I wouldn't call it dirty work. Stopping Kabinda would do everyone a favour. Anyway, I thought perhaps you'd be the right person. It'll be difficult of course. Your photos might be unpleasant, but they won't necessarily prove Kabinda is trading ivory in Angola. They could have been taken anywhere. That's why we believe a semi-formal approach from a witness is the answer – from someone who's actually seen what's going on. We'd be happy to arrange everything, of course. And pay you well for your trouble.'

'Thanks, but no thanks.' Rayner wasn't entirely sure what was on offer, but he was in no two minds about whether to turn it down.

'You won't go back?' Felix said.

'I sort of promised myself not to. Janson called Lunda Norte the wild west, but it's worse than that. You didn't see the girl being raped and killed. I did. Just like I saw Kabinda massacre the soldiers.' Rayner hesitated. 'Maybe if someone paid me to go back and put a bullet through his head I might do it. I've had a few bad nights because of him – you know, because of what he did to the girl. The damn thing won't go away.'

'Do you know who she was working for?'

Rayner nodded. 'I do now. Janson told me afterwards. World Organization for the Protection of Endangered Species or something. He said they were a bunch of international do-gooders.'

'They are. But not in the way Janson meant. WOPES has a lot of support here in South Africa. They're saving thousands of animals right across the continent – not just elephants. Kabinda's probably more of a problem to WOPES than he is to us.'

'So tell the Angolan Government they've got a mad bastard who's running around killing their troops, and raping European girls from WOPES. They'll have to find him. You don't need to mention diamonds or ivory.'

Felix shook his head. 'As soon as you gave me Kabinda's name on the phone we started digging. Kabinda isn't Angolan. He's a respectable businessman operating out of Zaire. He runs a company called Kinshasa Copper that has offices in three countries. You can guess where – Belgium, Japan and Hong Kong. And you can guess how difficult it's going to be for the Angolan Government to arrest someone like that. They'll need persuading.'

'They can nail him the next time he crosses the border.' Rayner pushed the film canister across the desk. 'Once the Angolans have seen the photos they won't bother to arrest Kabinda. He probably won't even make it out of his truck. That's how things work up there.'

'Are you sure I can't change your mind?'

'I'm sure.' Rayner picked up the cloth containing the diamonds and put it in his pocket. 'Look, Felix, if you'd asked me a couple of months ago I'd have done it. But not now. I'm sort of screwed up. I need to get back home.'

'We're expecting you to dinner tonight. I told Susan you'd be coming. She said you'll need re-civilizing.'

Rayner grinned. 'She's right. But I'm not sure I'm very good company right now. Anyway, I don't know if I'll still be in town. There might be a plane tonight.'

'Well, you'd better phone her one way or the other.' Felix paused. 'If I have questions, how do I get hold of you in the States?'

'Call Wendy. Wendy Armitage. You've got her number and her address. She'll know where I am.'

Felix looked at him. 'You told me she was married.'

'That was a while ago. We're still friends. It's kind of complicated.'

Felix slid an envelope across the desk. 'There's a bit extra in there,' he said. 'To cover what you lost selling the LandRover in Luanda. Don't spend it all at once.' He stood up. 'You've already decided you're not coming to dinner, haven't you?'

Rayner nodded. 'Tell Susan I'm sorry. Say next time I'm in Johannesburg.'

'I'm not even going to ask when that'll be.' Felix put out his hand. 'One of these days you're going to wake up and find you've been on the road so long that you can't stop. You don't know the difference between one place and another now, do you?'

'Sure I do. Some are hot, some are cold, some are dry and in other places it rains all the time.' Rayner shook hands. 'I hope things turn out OK in Angola.' He walked to the door and let himself out of the office without saying goodbye.

Outside in the corridor he stood for a moment, considering whether there was any truth in what Felix had just said. Then he went to the elevator and started rearranging his thoughts so there would be no need for him to think about very much at all.

Except for the way she spoke the words, the dream was always the same. Feeling her bare skin warm against his hands, he turned the girl over on the grass and saw her eyes flicker open. At the same time he saw the bullet exit wound between her breasts, a tiny, red-rimmed hole from which had leaked a single bead of blood. And always, as he reached out to touch the blood, she whispered his name – sometimes accusingly, but more often as though she was pleading for his help. Both versions had the same effect on Rayner and, in both versions, his reaction was the same: he walked away, leaving her to die.

On this occasion he couldn't remember her tone of voice. All Rayner knew was that he had again woken up with his heart banging and, that for the third time tonight, he'd been back on the plateau in Angola.

He sat up, switched on the bedside lamp, and started pushing buttons on the telephone.

A click on the line was followed by the noise of someone dropping the receiver on to the floor. A second later Rayner heard Wendy say hello.

'It's me,' he said.

There was no answer.

'Wendy?'

'Are you calling from Africa or South America or somewhere?'

'No.' Rayner tried tc sound casual. 'I'm home – down the road at the cottage.'

'Oh God. When did you get back?'

'Yesterday.'

'Do you know what time it is?'

Rayner inspected his watch. 'Yes, I do. Listen, seeing as I've woken you up, if I come over would you make coffee? I need coffee.'

'My mother's here for the weekend. I'll get her out of bed and ask her to fix some, shall I? She'll be really pleased at three o'clock in the morning.'

'I lied,' he said. 'It's not the coffee. I want to see you.'

'Now? In the middle of the night? When you haven't called me for weeks. You're crazy.'

'I've got a rental car. Suppose I pick you up?'

'I don't want to be picked up, thank you. If I wanted to come, I'd drive myself.'

'OK.' Rayner grinned to himself. 'See you in ten minutes, then.' He replaced the receiver, already anticipating what she would look like, and imagining how she would greet him. Rather as he'd hoped, talking to her had made the dream less real. Wendy was real, not some half-imagined girl his mind would not allow him to forget, not some distant event on the other side of the world over which he'd had no control.

As usual, his attempt to rationalize the girl's death was not altogether convincing but, by tidying up the bathroom and clearing up two days of accumulated mess in the kitchen, Rayner was able to maintain a more balanced perspective on his dream until he saw the flicker of car headlights in the driveway.

He met Wendy at the door. Her hair was much longer than he remembered it, curving round her face so he couldn't see her expression properly in the dark.

'Hi.' She stood on the doorstep. 'What am I doing here?'

'Don't I get a kiss?' Rayner could smell her perfume.

Standing on tiptoe, she brushed her lips across his cheek, then pushed past him and walked into the lounge.

Rayner followed, watching her as she slipped off her coat.

'Don't do that,' she said. 'I don't like it.'

'I'll make the coffee.' He went to the kitchen.

She put her hands in the pockets of her skirt and leaned back against the doorframe. 'I hate you,' she said. 'I didn't realize until I was on my way here. I've always hated you – since I was fourteen years old.'

'Summer of eighty-one,' Rayner said. 'Right here at Sandy Neck on the beach, when we made the pact.' He took two cups from the cupboard, placing them side by side on the bench in front of him.

'Do you really remember?'

He turned round. 'Of course I do. I remember every damn thing about that day.'

'Oh. So you figured you could phone me at three in the morning because of the pact?'

'Right.'

'Even though you've been sleeping your way round the world with God knows how many different women.'

'I didn't get married,' Rayner said. 'Not like you.'

She smiled at him. 'I didn't get married for long.'

Rayner poured the coffee and passed her one of the cups. 'You look great,' he said.

'And you look terrible. Your eyes are funny.'

'Yeah. I had a lousy flight, and I haven't been sleeping much either.'

'Poor Mark.' She put down her cup before moving to stand in front of him. 'Do you want to make love? Is that why you called?'

He shook his head. 'I want to tell you something. I need to talk.'

'All right.' She carried her coffee into the lounge and sat down beside him on the sofa. 'I'm ready.' She took his hand. 'What is it?'

He began by describing the diamond field, trying to paint a picture for her of the *garimpeiros* on the river terraces so she would understand it was a place where her own experiences were meaningless and where life was valued differently. And this time, instead of the summary he had given Felix, Rayner told the story step by step, giving her the background to the events on the plateau before he went on to describe Janson's attempt to save the girl, and how Kabinda had gunned her down while she was still running. For the best part of thirty minutes Rayner spoke continuously, using words to clear the memories from his mind in the hope of preventing a recurrence of the dream.

Before he'd stopped talking he knew the idea was flawed. If anything, describing the events had made them more vivid and even more disturbing.

'You're hurting me.' Wendy pulled her hand away.

'Christ, I'm sorry. I shouldn't have unloaded this on to you. I was just trying to get it out of my head – to get things straight.'

She nodded. 'You know what's wrong, don't you? You believe you should have saved her. She was white, you're white. She wasn't an African miner or an ivory poacher. She was a European woman, and you saw her raped and killed – right in front of you. Your whole upbringing says you can't let something like that happen. But you did. You had to – because there was nothing else you could do. You couldn't even try to stop it.'

'Janson tried,' Rayner said.

'And nearly died. If it hadn't been for you he would have done. Mark, don't you see? It's guilt. You feel guilty, but you're wrong. You didn't have a choice.'

'Maybe I did.'

She reached out and took his face in her hand to make him look at her. 'You've seen terrible things before – in Kenya – you told me, remember?'

'They were different. I shouldn't have told you about those either.' He grinned. 'Great isn't it? Every time I fall over and graze my knee I go running to you so you'll make it better –

big sister Wendy.'

'Sister?' She raised her eyebrows.

'Sure.'

'I'd better go then. I shouldn't have asked if you wanted to make love, should I?'

'Ask me again.'

She smoothed down her skirt. 'Don't you want to know why I hate you?'

'I already know. Same reason I hate you. I always have to come back here because of you, and you always have to be here because of me. You've messed up my life, I've messed up yours.'

She nodded again. 'We could stop.'

'I don't think so.' Rayner pushed her backward on to the sofa.

She didn't move, keeping her eyes on his while he ran his fingers through her hair. Her breath was on his face now, and her perfume was all around him. He could feel her trembling, as eager to kiss him as he was to kiss her.

It was happening again, Rayner realized. Just as it always did. And to doubt it would ever be different was as stupid as believing either of them could ever stop. He'd returned because of Wendy, because of all the other summers, and because he'd known for a long time now that there would never be anyone else who could make him feel like this.

For May the weather was still uncharacteristically cool. Because of it, at the weekend there had been few cars on Highway 6 and, to Rayner, it seemed that Cape Cod remained deep in winter hibernation. Even in Provincetown, where he had taken Wendy to lunch two days ago, the atmosphere had been sleepy, although a handful of summer homes had shown signs of activity and there had been a sprinkling of tourists on the streets.

Largely as a result of the quietness, over the last week Rayner had started to unwind. He was also becoming more accustomed to the temperature. For much of the time he still felt cold, but by splitting logs in the day and burning them at night in the cottage fireplace, he had managed to shed the thickest of his two sweaters, and had stopped shivering when he went to the beach each morning.

Today, Rayner's trip to the beach had been postponed. An hour ago Wendy had telephoned to say he should expect a visitor, and that she had no intention of competing with anyone having a name like Cristabel. Whether she was put out or simply teasing him, Rayner wasn't sure. Nor was he sure he knew anyone called Cristabel.

Deciding it was pointless waiting for someone who might not arrive, he went outside to inspect the wood-pile. To begin his morning's work he chose one of the pine logs that had so far resisted his efforts, bringing the axe down steadily, time after time in the same place, until he had opened up a split. The log was beginning to yield when a green BMW turned through the gate.

Rayner made a final swing of the axe, burying the head of it in the log before he turned to greet his visitor.

'Full of knots.' The girl who had climbed out of the car came over to examine his work. 'You want to use a wedge or a proper splitter.'

Even if Rayner had known what to say, he could not have replied. In front of him was the girl in Angola, the girl who had died on the plateau. Except that she was very much alive, and standing right here on his lawn.

'Cristabel Castela.' She handed him a business card. 'I work for the World Organisation for the Protection of Endangered Species in New York. Are you Mark Rayner?'

He nodded, unsettled more by her resemblance to the dead girl than he was by the knowledge that events in Africa had somehow already caught up with him.

'I was given the number of a Wendy Armitage,' she said. 'I telephoned her last night to ask if she knew how I could find you. I'd have called you but your number's not listed.'

'Have you just come from New York?' Rayner asked.

'I flew to Boston and picked up a rental.' She pointed at the BMW. 'Miss Armitage said you'd be here. It's not inconvenient, is it?'

'No.' Rayner tried not to stare. 'Look,' he said, 'this probably sounds stupid, but there's something I have to ask you.'

'Don't bother.' Her manner was brisk and off-hand. 'Françesca Castela was my sister. Is that what you wanted to know?'

'It was your sister in Angola?' Because she'd used the past tense, Rayner assumed she knew what had happened.

'Yes. You're the person who photographed her, aren't you?'

'I didn't know her name,' Rayner said quietly. 'I'm sorry.'

'So am I. Perhaps if you hadn't been so busy taking snapshots she might still be alive.'

Rayner was shaken by the comment. He was also annoyed. 'You don't know a damn thing about it,' he said.

'Are you going to ask me in, or do we talk in your driveway?'

'Depends. If the only reason you've driven all the way from Boston is to make smart remarks, I might not want to talk to you at all. I've got this pile of wood to chop.'

Had she been less hostile and less like her sister, Rayner would have found her attractive. She had the same tawny-coloured skin, her mouth and her eyes were the mouth and eyes of the dead girl and, despite his efforts to control his imagination, he could also see a bullet wound between her sharply pointed breasts. 'Shall I take my clothes off? Or is this just a check to see if you want to photograph me as well?'

Rayner grinned, more amused now than he was irritated. 'I didn't mean to be rude,' he said. 'You're very like your sister – to look at, I mean.'

'I know.' She followed him into the cottage and sat down on the kitchen stool.

'OK,' Rayner said. 'What can I do for you?'

'Do you know why I'm here? Hasn't anyone from South Africa been in touch with you?'

'No.'

'Oh.' She thought for a moment then opened her briefcase and took out several sheets of paper. 'About a week ago these arrived in our New York office. They're photocopies of the pictures you shot in Lunda Norte. A man called Osterman sent them. He works for De Beers in Johannesburg.' She paused. 'Of course, you know who he is, don't you?'

Rayner remained silent.

'We received a letter from Mr Osterman at the same time. It was about the ivory trade in West Africa. He said he thought we should know that one of our field people in Angola had been killed by African guerrillas who are controlling the ivory business there. Osterman apologized for the content of the photographs, but said they could help identify the man responsible if WOPES wanted to file an official complaint with the Angolan Government.'

'Was that the first you'd heard about your sister's death?' Rayner asked.

She nodded. 'I didn't actually find out until a couple of days after the letter came. Stuart Lynch told me – he's the New York section head. He recognized my sister from the photos.'

So De Beers had made their decision, Rayner thought. They were going to use WOPES. And to help WOPES along, Felix had provided them with Wendy's phone number.

'What else did Osterman say in his letter?' Rayner said.

'Quite a bit. He gave us the name of the African who murdered my sister and the address of a company in Zaire.' Laying the photocopies on the bench she ruffled through some other papers. 'Kinshasa Copper. We've heard of the company before, but not in connection with ivory. I think it was animal skins or parrots.'

'And Osterman suggested you talk to me?'

'Yes. He said you might be willing to make a formal statement that we could use – because you saw what happened and because you took the photos.'

'There were other people there.'

'Dead people.' She glanced at him. 'All those soldiers. Would you make a statement?'

'Sure. If it'll help you get Kabinda.'

'Can we have the negatives then, please? All we have at the moment are the photocopies from the prints you left with Mr Osterman.'

'I didn't leave any prints with Osterman,' Rayner said. 'I gave him the film. He was going to have it developed.'

'Oh, I see.' She began writing in a notebook. 'Mr Lynch would like you to make your statement in New York. It has to be done in front of a public notary, and we need to have your signature properly witnessed. Is that OK?' She glanced up suddenly and caught Rayner's eyes. 'Is something the matter, Mr Rayner?' Her expression was cool.

'No, I'm sorry.' He was embarrassed. 'You know it wasn't easy in Angola. It wasn't how you think it was.'

'You don't know what I think. It's none of your business, is it?' She closed her notebook. 'Were you searching for diamonds in Africa? Are you a prospector?'

'No.' Against his better judgement he picked up one of the photocopies. It showed Kabinda standing beside his truck watching the girl kicking at the end of the rope.

Rayner placed the sheet of paper face down on top of the others. 'When do you want me to come to New York?' he said.

'Stuart Lynch will call you. I've written down your number.'

She stood up and gathered her papers together. 'Is any time all right for you?'

'Sure. I'm not going anywhere.' Rayner decided to attempt a recovery. 'Can I fix you some coffee before you go?'

'No thank you, Mr Rayner. I think we've both been embarrassed enough, don't you? Thank you for your time and for offering to help. If Mr Lynch believes we have a case, we'll be approaching the Angolans through diplomatic channels so it's possible you could hear something from Washington before we get in touch with you again.'

'What happens if you don't go ahead?' Rayner said. 'Are you just going to let Kabinda carry on his ivory business?'

She smiled slightly. 'There are two ways of preventing the exploitation of an animal species. In the case of elephants you can have a controlled management programme to cut off the tusks so the animals have no value to the poachers, or you can stamp out the international market for ivory. Kabinda doesn't kill elephants, and he doesn't sell products made from ivory either. He's a middle man – or at least in Africa he is.'

'So?' Rayner said.

'So the best way to protect elephants is to enforce existing trade bans, and launch a world-wide campaign against ivory products. Once the public starts to realize that over a hundred elephants are slaughtered for each ton of ivory, the market will dry up.'

'Putting Kabinda out of business will do, will it?' Rayner said. 'What about your sister for Christ's sake?'

'I think that's a question you could have asked yourself while you were watching her being raped, Mr Rayner. Goodbye.'

She walked from the kitchen without giving him the opportunity to reply, leaving him in no doubt about how distasteful she found his company.

He remained in the cottage until her car had gone, wondering whether her accusations were right. That they could be, was disturbing enough; that there was nothing he could do about it, made it worse. The two promises he'd made himself seemed hollow now, a way to avoid thinking about what he could have done or what he should have done.

Turning on the tap over the sink, he sluiced handfuls of water into his face. Then he went outside and began attacking the wood-pile.

By two o'clock, surrounded by wood chips and pieces of

shattered timber, Rayner was less disconsolate. But his efforts had not been without cost: one of his hands had been rubbed raw by a section of the axe handle that was rough and splintered, and both his hands were hurting.

Too tired to continue, he took the axe into the kitchen with him, and wrapped a layer of tape around the handle while he drank a can of beer.

He was outside again, sitting on a log, opening his second can, when Wendy arrived. Instead of parking her car under the cherry tree she drove right up to him, not stopping until the front bumper touched his leg.

'Are you trying to tell me something?' Rayner smiled at her as she got out.

'You bet I am. Did she come?'

'Yep. Been and gone. We didn't hang around.'

'And who precisely is Cristabel Castela?'

'Just a friend.' Rayner kept a straight face. 'You know.'

'But not a terribly close friend.' She eyed the heap of logs. 'Not if you've split all this since she left. You're not that good.'

'You don't know half of it,' Rayner said. 'We didn't get on very well.'

'Good.' Wendy sat on the hood of the car. 'Tell me.'

Rayner explained, describing the interview, but omitting the girl's parting remark.

'What did she look like?'

'I've told you. They're sisters – or they were – both working for this WOPES outfit. That's what made the whole thing so weird.'

'I meant was she pretty? Did she have nice legs? What was the colour of her eyes?'

'Jesus, I don't know.' Rayner frowned. 'She was probably Portuguese or something. She had dark hair and her skin was a sort of light brown colour.'

'Mm. OK, are you going to take me out to dinner tonight?'

'No. I thought we might go to the beach. I didn't go this morning. We could pick up a pizza and take it with us.'

She smiled at him. 'Mark, this isn't mid-summer.'

'I want to do it anyway.' Rayner brushed the woodchips out of his hair.

'You're not working this afternoon, are you?'

She shook her head.

'Stay then. I'd like you to – until we go out.'

Leaning forwards she kissed him on the mouth. 'I intended

to,' she said. 'In case your friend came back.'

At low tide in the moonlight, the beach was less attractive than it was in the daytime. As well as being deserted and colourless, the sand was cold to sit on, and the sea breeze had begun to freshen.

'I knew you'd freeze.' Wendy snuggled closer to him on the blanket.

'I'm OK.'

'I'm still not sure why we've come.'

'I wanted to.' He tried to see her eyes in the dark. 'A month ago I'd have paid a thousand dollars for half an hour on this beach on a night like this.'

'Because you grew up here? Or just because it's cool?'

'Both, I guess.'

She folded the empty pizza box in half and put a rock on top of it to stop it from blowing away. 'You were the one who had to go back to Africa. You said it was time, remember?'

Rayner hadn't forgotten. Neither had he forgotten what Felix had said about him being on the move too long.

'Come on.' He stood up and pulled her to her feet. 'Let's go home and light a fire.'

She walked beside him to the car without saying anything. On the drive back to the cottage, Rayner was equally disinclined to talk. The visit of Cristabel Castela had spoilt things, he thought, a reminder of how small the world had become, and why it was impossible to separate any one part of his life from any other.

Because Wendy's car was still in the driveway, Rayner parked alongside the cherry tree.

'I can't get out.' She began sliding across the seat.

Rayner wasn't listening. He was looking at the cottage, at the light shining from the upstairs window.

'What's wrong?' Wendy took his arm.

'Did you leave the light on?'

'Can't remember. Why?'

'I don't think it was on when we left,' Rayner said. 'I'd have noticed. It was dark.'

'Mark, this is Sandy Neck. Your parents' cottage has been empty for months. It hasn't been broken into for all that time, so why would anyone break in now? Anyway, there's nothing worth taking. You know there isn't.'

Except for the diamonds, Rayner thought. She'd forgotten about Janson's diamonds. He went to the front door and used his key, knowing the moment he entered the cottage that someone had been here. Empty drawers and the contents of the hall cupboard were strewn across the floor, and there was a light on in the kitchen.

'Go back to the car,' Rayner whispered. 'Now.'

'They won't still be around.' Wendy was nervous. 'They'll have heard us.'

A noise behind him made Rayner turn round.

Framed in the doorway was the figure of a man. He was black, thickset and unshaven. In one hand he carried a length of steel pipe.

Rayner's heart began to thump.

'Easy now.' Another man appeared from the kitchen. 'Don't be a hero.'

Trapped in the hall, knowing he had to get Wendy out fast, Rayner prepared himself to rush the man at the door. But before he could move, the door was kicked shut.

The man from the kitchen stepped into the light so Rayner could see his gun.

'Mark.' Wendy's voice was strained now.

'It's OK.' Keeping her close to him, very slowly Rayner began picking his way around the drawers, approaching the kitchen door until he was close enough to see the man properly.

'Who the hell are you?' Rayner said.

'In here.' The man moved the muzzle of his revolver. He too was black but, in contrast to his companion, as well as being much taller, he was cleanshaven and well dressed.

Rayner eased Wendy into the kitchen. She was holding on to him, breathing quickly.

'Are you Rayner?' The man leaned against the sink bench.

'What's it to you?'

'We don't want no trouble.' The man glanced at Wendy. 'You don't look like a lady who'd want any trouble. Why don't you tell your friend?'

Wendy remained tight-lipped.

'If you want to talk, you talk to me,' Rayner said quietly.

'Where's the film?'

Because the question caught him wrong-footed, for a second Rayner wasn't sure how to answer.

'The film. The one you shot in Angola. Where is it?'

'I haven't got it.' Rayner struggled to think, knowing he couldn't afford to waste time trying to guess what the hell was going on.

The man looked at him. 'I can leave you to have a nice evening or I can tear this house to pieces and let my friend down the corridor show this lady a good time. You decide.'

Although he could not have known it, by threatening Wendy the man had made a mistake. Rayner felt himself begin to tense. There was a dangerous taste in his mouth and the memory of what had happened on the plateau had started burning like a flame inside his head.

'Well?' The man was waiting.

'Take it,' Rayner said. 'I don't need the damn thing. But if I ever catch you around here again you're going to wish you'd never come. Have you got that?'

'Yeah. I've got that. Give me the film.'

'Right in front of you.' Rayner pointed to the roll of tape on the bench. 'It's inside that. In the middle of it.'

'Show me.' The man motioned with his gun.

Rayner walked towards him. The tape was where he'd left it. So was the axe, leaning against the wall, half hidden by the wood basket.

He picked up the tape, pretending to push out the centre of it. 'Here.' Tossing the roll into the air, Rayner hit the floor. At the same time he saw the gun kick and felt a bullet zip past his face.

But he had the axe now, and the man was wild with his second shot. Rayner heard the bullet ricochet off something as he swung the axehead upwards in an arc. The back of it caught the man under the arm, slamming him against the wall. He collapsed, dropping the gun immediately.

There was just time for Rayner to grab it before the other man came bursting through the doorway. In his mind, Rayner was elsewhere now, responding automatically. He shot the man above the knee, watching dispassionately as his leg buckled under him.

Levelling the revolver, Rayner was a second away from finishing what he'd started when the sound of Wendy's voice made him ease his finger off the trigger.

'Mark,' Wendy called again. She was bleeding from the shoulder, supporting herself on the kitchen dresser.

He went to her at once, guessing what had happened.

'I'm all right.' She tried to smile. 'Aren't I?'

'Let's see.' He ripped open her blouse to find that the bullet had struck her below the collar-bone, but with barely enough energy to penetrate her skin.

'Is it bad?' She pulled her blouse together.

'Ricochet,' he said. 'Off the damn axe. It'll be OK.'

The man with the injured arm was groaning. He was lying on the floor beside his companion, trying unsuccessfully to move his hand.

Rayner ignored him, concentrating instead on his instructions to Wendy. 'Do you think you can drive?' he said.

She nodded.

'OK. Take your car. Go down the road to the Thompsons and ask them to call the police. Explain what's happened.'

'I can call from here.'

'I want you somewhere else – right now.'

'What about you?' she said.

'I'll be along. Go on.'

As soon as she'd gone, Rayner turned his attention back to the men. 'Right,' he said. 'This is the deal. You tell me who you are, and what the hell this is all about, and I don't use up the rest of these cartridges. That's fair, don't you think?'

'You're full of shit.' The stocky, unshaven man stared apprehensively at Rayner.

'Self-defence,' Rayner said. 'You broke into my house. Try me.'

The man with the injured arm mumbled something, but he was in too much pain to make any sense. Rayner pointed the revolver at his companion, and pulled back the hammer.

'OK, OK.' The man held his hands in front of his face as if to protect himself. 'Jesus, you'd do it too, wouldn't you? You're crazy.'

'Where do you come from?' Rayner said.

'We work out of Providence and New Bedford – cars mostly, sometimes electronic equipment – you know, CDs, video recorders and stuff.'

'Why do you want the film?'

'This guy called in. He gave us two grand on account, and said there was another three for us when we got back.'

'Did he give you my name? And my address?' Rayner already knew he was wasting his time.

'Not the address. He said for us to go to this place at Sandy Neck and find some woman called Armitage. We went to the

Armitage place, but there was no one home.' The man winced. 'We asked around.'

'Who's the guy who gave you the money?'

'He didn't say. Look, straight up – we don't know nothing about this fucking film of yours.'

Rayner didn't doubt it. He wasn't sure he cared much anymore either. Gradually, as his anger had gone, disgust had replaced the need for an explanation. On the kitchen floor was the result of his months in Africa – one man bleeding from a bullet hole in his leg, another nursing a smashed arm or a seriously dislocated shoulder. An overreaction, Rayner thought, because of Wendy? Or because Wendy had been a substitute for the girl he'd failed in Angola?

Swinging out the cylinder of the revolver, he emptied the cartridges into his hand and started reloading them one at a time until each chamber of the cylinder was full. When he had finished he began again, methodically loading and unloading the gun without looking at it.

Even after he heard the siren he continued, no longer preoccupied with what had just happened, but with the disturbing notion that he had either misjudged Janson's warning or perhaps, somehow, misjudged Janson altogether.

Three

The paintings in the downstairs foyer were reproductions of the originals he was looking at now, marvellous paintings of whales, rare birds, lions and tigers. The board room was more like an art gallery, Rayner thought, except that the world map on the wall and the WOPES logo over the door spoilt the effect.

'Would you care for coffee?' Lynch asked. 'I'll get Cris to bring it in – there may be a few things she'd like to discuss with you.'

'Coffee would be great. Thank you.' Rayner sat down at the end of the glass-topped table. Dictating the statement had drained his energy and he felt flat and disinterested. In the three days since the break-in at the cottage, he had managed to convince himself that a meeting with WOPES would allow him to unload some of the responsibility. Instead, it had been an anti-climax.

Lynch was speaking into a telephone. For a small man he had an unusually deep voice, more than deep enough to compensate for his lack of height and rather boyish features. So far he had said little, preferring to listen while Rayner had brought him up to date with the incident at Sandy Neck.

'Well.' Lynch put down the phone. 'I didn't expect we'd be discussing anything like this. What did the police have to say?'

'Nothing much. They're treating it as a straight-out burglary. The guys who broke in both had records.'

'I see.' Lynch seemed surprised. 'Did you explain about the film?'

'There was no point. I don't think the Massachusetts police have a lot of influence in Angola.'

'No.' Lynch smiled. 'Unfortunately I'm not sure we do either. I must say the whole thing is extraordinary. As far as I know, this is the first time the ivory underworld has been active here in the States. I think Kabinda could have overreached himself.'

'That's why I figured you ought to know what happened,' Rayner said. 'If Kabinda believes he's in a corner, he might make another mistake that'll make it easier for you to nail him.'

'I suppose we can't be sure Kabinda is behind this.' Lynch sat down at the other end of the table. 'Although I can't imagine who else it could be. Even so it's a bit strange, don't you think? How does Kabinda know you photographed him in Angola?'

Rayner shrugged. 'Maybe Janson mentioned it to someone. Or Charlie. For a packet of cigarettes Charlie would tell anyone anything.'

'Do you know where Janson is?'

'No idea,' Rayner said.

'What about Osterman? He wouldn't have discussed the film with the wrong people, would he?'

'Not a chance,' Rayner said. 'Felix knew it was sensitive. He wouldn't have told anybody.'

'Except us.' Lynch smiled again. 'I must confess we're a bit suspicious of De Beers' motives in writing to WOPES. I imagine it's because Kabinda is treading on their toes as well. Is that right?'

'You'd better ask Felix.' Rayner had no intention of being drawn. 'Francesca Castela worked for you, not for De Beers. Maybe they just figured you were the right people to approach the Angolan Government.'

'Maybe.' Lynch put his hands palms down on the tabletop. 'I hope their confidence isn't misplaced. Getting the Angolans to move on anything is pretty damn hard. Which reminds me – is it possible for you to ask Osterman to send the negatives? The photocopies he supplied aren't exactly the most professional way for us to present evidence. We're going to need the best information we can lay our hands on.'

'Sure. I'll phone him. Is that all you need?'

'Unless you have anything else that could help.' Lynch paused. 'It's going to be tough, even with the pictures. I'm sure you know what the politics in Angola are like. The United Nations spent all that time supervising the 1992 elections just so the Angolans could wind up with what's really a Marxist regime. I've talked to Washington about our problem, but they were non-committal. They did say the US recognizes the new Angolan administration though, so I suppose we won't have to work completely alone.'

Not completely, Rayner thought. But damn nearly. 'Look,' he said, 'if this is all too hard, just say so. Or are you hedging because of what Ms Castela said?'

'What was that?'

'I kind of got the impression that you're more interested in protecting elephants than in stopping Kabinda.'

'Yes. Well, in a way that's right, of course. We're all upset about what happened to her sister, but that doesn't mean we can drop everything to concentrate on an activity which isn't strictly part of our charter. We're funded internationally to protect any species which is endangered, but there are very clear guidelines about how we do that. We also have a great number of other projects, I'm afraid. In this rather sick world of ours, elephants aren't the only species under threat.'

'And Kabinda doesn't kill elephants,' Rayner said. 'Yeah, I know. He's a middle man.'

'You sound unconvinced, Mr Rayner. As though you think we intend to do nothing about Francesca's death.'

'I think you're underestimating Kabinda. He has offices in Hong Kong and Japan– or his company has. Aren't those countries the main outlets for ivory?'

Lynch raised his eyebrows. 'You know about Kinshasa Copper's offshore business?'

'Only what Felix Osterman told me. Maybe you should have a look at what products Kinshasa Copper is selling in the Far East.'

'Yes, perhaps we should. Tell me, Mr Rayner, do you also have some knowledge of the ivory business?'

'No. Why?'

'Just a thought.' Lynch stood up. 'I'll see where the coffee's got to.'

'Hang on,' Rayner said. 'There's something I'd like to ask you first.'

'Ask away.'

'It's about the Castela sisters. I'm just curious. How come they were both working for WOPES?'

Lynch smiled. 'I presume you've never heard of Adam Castela, then?'

'No. I haven't.'

'He was a hunter – a Portuguese-born Angolan. Later he became a game warden, and eventually a conservationist. Until he was killed in Namibia about eighteen months ago, he was one of the most influential people in Southern Africa. Castela spent the last half of his life protecting African wildlife. Does that answer your question?'

Rayner nodded. 'Did both his daughters work here in New York?'

'Only for around eighteen months or so. Francesca had been on assignment back in Africa for over three years – in Kenya, Tanzania and Zimbabwe. She was a lovely person – one of our most experienced people, even though she was very young.'

'Not experienced enough,' Rayner said. 'She should never have been in Lunda Norte.'

Lynch's reply was interrupted by the arrival of Cristabel Castela. She was carrying a tray.

'Good morning.' She glanced at Rayner. 'Is Miss Armitage all right?'

He nodded. 'Nothing serious.'

She placed the tray carefully on the table. 'You're a dangerous man, Mr Rayner. Don't you mind that wherever you go people seem to get shot?'

Rayner took a cup and saucer from her.

'Cream and sugar?' she asked.

'No thank you.' Rayner was making sure he didn't stare at her. Today she was wearing a white, open-necked blouse and had her hair tied back. It should have made her look less like her sister, but it didn't.

'Mark,' Lynch said. 'Do you mind if I call you Mark?'

'Go ahead.'

'Have you thought through the implications of what's happened?'

'Sure.' Rayner was tired of thinking through them. 'Janson told me the ivory business is worth a billion dollars a year. With that sort of money at stake, it's obvious Kabinda isn't running some tin-pot UNITA rebel group in Angola. He's too smart for that. I think he's operating internationally on a big scale – big enough to stop anyone getting in his way And, because he can't afford to have the Angolan Government on his tail, he knows he has to hush-up the mistake he made with the girl.' The moment he'd finished speaking, Rayner realized how poor his choice of words had been.

'She wasn't a girl.' Cristabel Castela's expression was icy. 'She was a woman. And her death wasn't a mistake, Mr Rayner. It was cold-blooded murder.'

'Yes, yes,' Lynch interrupted. 'Let's try to keep our personal feelings out of this, shall we? Mark, you don't need me to tell you that Kabinda must have contacts here in the US. That's the implication which concerns me – you as well, I imagine?'

'I can look after myself,' Rayner said quietly. 'Anyway Kabinda's out of his depth. This isn't Angola or Zaire. He'll forget all about me once he hears WOPES is involved.'

'So you intend doing nothing more about it.'

'I'm not sure what you mean.'

'I thought you might feel strongly enough to – you know – ' Lynch's voice faded.

Rayner grinned. 'Who have you been talking to?'

'No one really.' Lynch finished his coffee. 'Washington asked questions so we made a couple of phonecalls – just to check. I must say you seem to travel around a great deal.'

Rayner studied the paintings on the wall. 'I've never saved a lion,' he said. 'Or any elephants.'

'No,' Lynch said. 'I suppose you haven't. Different line of business.'

'Very different.' Cristabel Castela slid back her chair. 'I'm afraid I have a lot of work to do, and I'm sure Mr Rayner has more wood to split at home.' She stood up from the table.

Rayner reached the door before she did, making it impossible for her to avoid him.

'Goodbye.' He shook her hand, feeling her trying to pull away. He wanted to explain – to somehow make her listen to him – but she used all her strength, forcing him to release her.

When she turned to slam the door, her eyes were flashing and he could see that her cheeks were flushed.

Lynch was amused. 'I wouldn't bother,' he said. 'She doesn't like you much.'

'She won't give me half a damn chance.' Rayner put his coffee cup back on the tray. 'It might as well have been me who raped and killed her sister.'

'I'll let her read your statement. You never know, it might give her a better idea of how things were.' Lynch went to the door. 'I think we've finished here anyway. I'll arrange for Washington to contact Luanda. If the Angolans know we're filing a complaint, word should get through to your friend

Maximilian. That'll make him pull his head in.'

'And tip him off,' Rayner said.

'It'll stop the son-of-a-bitch believing he's running some kind of African based Mafia.' Lynch smiled. 'Thanks for coming, Mark. I'll wait to hear from you.'

It was nearly one o'clock when Rayner left the building. Frustrated by his failure to talk to Cristabel Castela, during the journey home his mood deteriorated further until he was finally ready to accept that, in the circumstances, her attitude towards him was understandable. At one point he had even managed to convince himself that it didn't matter what she believed. But when he arrived back at the cottage, he was still thinking about her, and still unable to forget her expression of contempt.

Taking a bottle of scotch with him into the lounge, Rayner sat down to consider whether anything had changed. Two days ago he had concluded that Cristabel Castela's visit to the cottage was responsible for the recurrence of his dream. Now he knew it wasn't the visit – it was her.

As long as she believed he had deliberately allowed her sister to die, and as long as his mind somehow refused to separate one sister from another, nothing was going to change.

Self analysis, Rayner thought, an exercise in futility that was of no help whatever. He swallowed a mouthful of scotch and started calculating what time it was in Johannesburg so he'd know whether to call Felix at home or at the office.

He chose the office, pushing buttons on the telephone while he decided how best to explain why he needed the film.

A woman's voice came on the line.

'This is Mark Rayner,' he said. 'I'm calling from the United States. Can I speak to Felix Osterman, please?'

'One moment.'

Rayner drank more scotch, waiting for Felix to pick up his phone.

But instead of Felix, it was someone else who answered. 'Mr Rayner,' he said. 'My name is Borger, Lewis Borger. I'm sorry, I have some rather bad news for you.'

Rayner's hand tightened on the bottle. 'How bad?'

'I'm afraid there's no easy way for me to say this – not over the telephone. There was an accident – two days ago.'

'What kind of accident?'

'I'm not sure how to explain, quite.'

'I'd like to know, please. I'm a friend.'

'Felix was found dead in his car – near Pretoria. The car was partly burned out, but the police say they've found bullet holes in it.' Borger hesitated. 'I'm not certain I should be telling you this.'

Rayner felt sick. 'Is his wife all right?' he said.

'Well, yes. As well as you could expect. I can give you her number if you'd like to get in touch.'

'It's OK, I know the number, thanks. Thank you.' Very carefully Rayner lowered the receiver. Then he went outside where it was dark, and cold, and where the wind coming up from the beach was carrying the first few flecks of rain with it.

Overnight the rain had soaked into the woodpile, washing tiny rivers of sawdust and woodchips across the driveway to mix with leaves that the storm had stripped from the cherry tree. But the leaves were already drying in the sunshine and, here and there, patches of the sawdust were beginning to blow away. A gust of wind brought a cloud of it into the porch where they were sitting.

'Ow.' Wendy had used the wrong arm to brush the chips out of her hair.

'Does the shoulder still hurt?' Rayner wondered if he should check the dressing or whether in her present frame of mind she would resent the inspection.

'What do you think? Doesn't it always hurt when you get shot?'

'Yeah.' Rayner was uncertain of what to say. She'd been like this since she'd arrived – distant and resentful – as though she was angry he'd told her about Felix.

'Are you going back to work tomorrow?' he asked.

She nodded. 'What are you going to do?'

'I don't know. I suppose I'll have to phone Lynch.'

'About Felix?'

'And to let him know he won't be getting the negatives.'

'Then what?' She glanced at him.

'I told you. I haven't figured things out yet.'

'Yes you have. It's written all over your face. You won't leave this alone, will you? You've got all this guilt about the girl in Angola gnawing at you. Then there's her sister in New York sticking pins in you. And now there's Felix.'

'You forgot something,' Rayner said.

'No I didn't. I don't think you care about my shoulder. It's no big deal to you, is it? That's why I didn't mention it.'

'How the hell can I leave this alone? Do you know what Cristabel Castela said? She said I don't seem to mind people around me getting shot. Now you're telling me as well.'

'I don't see why you should take any notice of what she says. Anyway, there's nothing you can do now.'

'No,' Rayner said. 'There's probably nothing WOPES can do either – or De Beers – not without the negatives. I should never have taken the damn camera with me to start with. If I hadn't – ' He stopped, unwilling to finish the sentence.

'Felix would still be alive.' Wendy finished it for him. 'Mark, for goodness sake stop it.' She stood up. 'I'd better go.'

'Why?'

'John's coming for lunch.' She looked at Rayner. 'You don't mind, do you?'

'Why's your ex-husband coming to lunch?'

'Because as soon as my dear mother heard I'd had a bullet taken out of my shoulder she insisted on coming to look after me, and then, yesterday, telephoned John to tell him what had happened. He's worried. Anyway, despite what you might think, we still like each other. Half the house is his remember? If it wasn't for John I couldn't afford to go on living there waiting for you to show up whenever you need me.'

'What's that supposed to mean?' Rayner stood up to face her.

'Look in the mirror. Your eyes are funny again.'

'There's nothing wrong with my damn eyes.'

'Yes there is. You're somewhere else – acting out some stupid idea of putting things right to make yourself feel better. You've forgotten what it's like to be a normal person.' She turned to go. 'And you've forgotten about us.'

Rayner stayed on the porch, watching her walk to her car. He remained there for several minutes after she'd gone, confused by the speed at which things were unravelling, and trying his best not to wonder whether Kabinda was still making a bi-monthly diamond run from Zaire. And then there was Wendy's ex-husband, Rayner thought, as well as Cristabel Castela and the need for him to be sure about Janson.

It wasn't until Rayner went indoors to make his phonecall that the clutter in his mind began to clear. He spoke to Lynch for the best part of twenty minutes, using the opportunity to repeat what he'd said about the possibility of the Hong Kong and Japanese offices of Kinshasa Copper being used as outlets for Angolan ivory. Although Lynch listened politely enough, it was evident that with the loss of the negatives his confidence had decreased further. By the end of the call it almost sounded as if he had decided it was fruitless for WOPES to go ahead.

Rayner was not surprised. Nor was he surprised by the pointed lack of communication from Wendy over the next three days. Knowing better than to push his luck, he resisted the impulse to go and see her, spending his time instead, either fishing off the beach or splitting wood. He also wasted an afternoon with the police in Hyannis, clearing up details on the break-in. By Thursday he had become more reconciled to Felix's death, finding that, like the dream, he was able to keep it in perspective as long as he was busy and avoided the temptation to consider by-passing WOPES altogether.

This morning, because there was a smell of summer in the air, Rayner's thoughts had returned to Wendy. Since the night of the storm the weather had improved considerably, each day dawning clearer than the last, persuading him finally that spring had given way to summer.

He left the cottage at 8.30, driving slowly to the beach, wondering if he'd be able to get a line out before the tide began to drop. Three other fishermen had arrived before him. They were already down by the water, busy assembling rods or baiting hooks. Rayner waved to them, pleased to have company on what would otherwise have been another day spent by himself.

He was untying his rod from the roof-rack when Wendy's car pulled off the road into the parking lot. She drove across to him.

'Hi. I didn't think you'd be here so early.' She spoke to him through an open window. 'You'd better pack up again.'

'Why?'

'There's a parcel for you. It was in my mail-box yesterday. I've just put it in yours.' She paused. 'But I thought I'd call by the beach in case this is where you were – so I could tell you. I'd have phoned last night, but it was late when I got home.'

'What kind of parcel?'

'From South Africa. From Felix Osterman. His name's on the outside.'

'Oh Jesus,' Rayner said. 'Is there a Customs sticker on it?'

She nodded. 'It says photographs. He must have mailed them before – '

Her voice tailed off.

Rayner refastened the lashing around the rod, not yet certain whether the news was good or bad.

'I'll go back with you,' she said.

'You don't want to see them. I'll call you later at work.'

'I'm not going to work. I'm going with you to the cottage.' She wound the window up, waiting for Rayner to lead the way.

On the return trip he drove more quickly, knowing the instant he stopped at the mail-box to collect the parcel that he'd made a mistake in not being firmer with Wendy.

It was a bubble-pack, a thin, innocent package with a row of South African stamps along the top. Rayner carried it into the kitchen and placed it unopened on the bench.

'Mark, they're only pictures,' she said. 'Go on.'

There were eighteen of them, seven inch by five inch colour prints separated by sheets of paper. The negatives were there as well, slipped into an envelope which also contained a letter.

Unlike the poor definition of the four photocopies Felix had sent to Lynch, the prints were of almost agonizing clarity. Worse still, Rayner had forgotten how close the telephoto lens had brought the images. His recollections were of what he had witnessed with his own eyes, not what he'd photographed through the lens of the Pentax. As a result, the photos seemed to be larger than life, a close-up record showing unnecessary detail.

He spread them out on the benchtop, forcing himself to arrange them in the right sequence without looking at each individual print too long.

Wendy, though, was looking. She was studying them, moving from one to another, her eyes widening as she came to a particularly graphic shot in which Kabinda's men were preparing to rape the girl.

'Only pictures,' Rayner said. 'Right?'

Wendy turned round. 'They're terrible,' she said. 'I've never seen anything so terrible.'

Rayner slid the letter out of the envelope. It was typed on De Beers letterhead, dated May 17th.

'What does it say?'

'I don't know yet. Hang on.' He skipped through it, searching for anything that could indicate Felix had been concerned for his safety.

'Well?' Wendy queried.

Rayner counted on his fingers. 'It was written seven days ago.' He checked the post mark on the bubble-pack. 'And mailed on the 18th. It doesn't say much. Just that he's sent some photocopies to WOPES in New York, and given them my name and your phone number. He asks me to call him if WOPES agree to lay a complaint with the Angolans – so he can tell his board of directors.' Rayner paused. 'I suppose I ought to contact De Beers and let them know WOPES will be going ahead.'

'Are you sure they will?'

Rayner nodded. 'Pretty sure.' He glanced at her. 'Do you think these will persuade Luanda?'

'I'm not supposed to understand how things work in Africa. You told me that.' She selected two of the prints. 'I'd have thought these would convince any government in the world.'

The first photograph showed Francesca Castela standing naked in front of Kabinda and Janson while Kabinda cut the rope from her wrists. Semen was running down her thighs, she was bleeding from a cut on her forehead, and her face was contorted in a mask of hate and terror. Rayner made himself look, wondering how he could have ever believed Janson's attempt to free her would succeed.

Wendy handed him the other print. In this one, Janson was on the ground clutching his stomach. Beside him, Kabinda was holding his gun in both hands, drawing a bead on the fleeing figure of the girl. The camera had caught her with one foot off the ground in the last second of her life.

Rayner put both photographs back on the bench. Now that he'd seen them he felt emotionless and strangely uninvolved.

'Is Cristabel Castela really like her sister?' Wendy said. 'You're sure you're not just imagining she is?'

Rayner was sure. 'I saw Francesca Castela afterwards,' he said. 'When she was dead. They could be twins.'

Wendy folded her arms. 'So what happens now?'

'Lynch can do what De Beers want him to do – a nice diplomatic approach to fix something that could be fixed easier with a bullet. Felix knew that better than anyone.'

'The Rayner solution,' she said. 'Judge, jury and executioner.'

'How the hell do you expect me to feel?'

'I don't know. You and I don't live in the same world – not any more.'

'How's your ex-husband?' In attempting to change the subject, Rayner had broached a subject he'd intended to avoid.

'All right. He wants to have the house redecorated.'

'His half? Or your half?'

''Stop it. Just stop it, please.'

Rayner went to the bedroom, returning with a packet of cigarettes in his hand. He gave the packet to her.

'What do I do with these?' she asked.

'Buy out John's half of the house, pay off the mortgage, redecorate. Whatever you want. I don't care.'

Removing some tissue paper, she tipped the contents of the packet into her hand. Rayner could see the diamonds nestled together in her palm like two glass pebbles. For a second he thought she was angry, but then he saw tears were rolling down her cheeks.

'What is it?' he said. 'What's the matter?'

'Oh, Mark. How can you ask me that? How? If you don't know, what's the point?' She put the diamonds back into the packet.

'I don't understand.'

She wiped away her tears. 'You really don't, do you? Mark, I don't want your diamonds. I don't want you to pay off my mortgage. For God's sake, can't you see what's happening to you?'

'Hey, look,' Rayner said. 'I'm not trying to throw money at you or anything.'

'Aren't you?' Wendy gave him the packet. 'I think it's best if we don't see each other for a while. And please don't call me. I hope things turn out all right now you have the negatives. Goodbye, Mark.' She walked away, leaving him standing alone in the kitchen.

Rayner crushed the packet in his hand. Then he went to examine his eyes in the bathroom mirror.

Unlike the paintings on the wall with their pastel shades, the photographs were too bright; garish rectangles of colour laid out in a line along the edge of the table.

'Dynamite.' Stuart Lynch used a magnifying glass to inspect one of them. 'I didn't realize you took this many.'

'Nor did I.' Rayner spoke from the far end of the room. 'I wasn't counting.'

'No, I guess you weren't.' Lynch picked up the envelope of negatives. 'If we were dealing with anyone except the Angolans I'd have no doubt these would do the job. Kabinda would be pretty nervous if he knew what we had hold of here.'

'He does know,' Rayner said.

'You didn't think to run off another set of prints – for safety reasons?'

'No.' The idea hadn't occurred to Rayner.

'That's OK. We'll arrange it. Now, I imagine you'd like to know how we intend to handle things.'

'I don't care,' Rayner said. 'Just so long as it works.' He hesitated. 'If it doesn't, I want you to call me.'

Lynch glanced at him. 'Does that mean you have some kind of alternative arrangement in mind?'

'I didn't say that. Maybe.'

'In that case I think you and I better have a talk.' Lynch opened a folder and began reading from it. 'Mark Edward Rayner,' he said. 'Date of birth April 3rd 1964, West Barnstable, State of Massachusetts. Anyone you recognize?'

Rayner said nothing.

'Military Service record.' Lynch turned the page. 'Discharged 1988, then the interesting bits – or they would be if they weren't mostly blanked out. Libya, Kenya, South Africa, Angola and what looks like two months in Iraq -- November 1990 – just before the Gulf War. All for the National Security Council, I presume. It's not exactly clear here.'

This time Rayner grinned. 'Probably because I don't exactly work for the NSC.'

'For who then?'

'A lot of people. Multinationals, private companies, newspapers sometimes. Mostly I freelance.'

'I see.' Lynch sat down. 'At the risk of boring you, I'd like to give you a few facts. In the 1920s, this country alone produced 60,000 billiard balls a year and about four times that number of piano keys – all from ivory. Up until the 1970s the world ivory consumption was enormous, even to the extent where, in some countries, it was traded like gold bullion. To give you some idea of the scale of the industry, between 1979 and 1987 Hong Kong processed tusks that represented the slaughter of nearly half a million elephants. Then, about five years ago, people started waking up to what was happening.'

'I know about the trade ban,' Rayner said.

'Forget trade bans. Trade bans are about politicians signing pieces of paper, not saving the lives of endangered animals. You can't even begin to imagine what it's like in the field. Whole herds mowed down by automatic assault rifles, tusks hacked and chainsawed from baby elephants while they're still alive, mutilated carcasses rotting from one end of Africa to the other. Trade bans only half work. If the butchery carries on at the present rate, we estimate that around a thousand elephants will die each week.'

'Why are you telling me?'

'Two reasons. If we're going to use these photos to shock the Angolans into doing something about Kabinda, I don't want anything or anybody in the way to screw things up.'

'What's the other reason?' Rayner said.

'When Cris visited you, I believe she explained how WOPES works to protect a species. And when you were here before, I remember telling you how restricted we are in the protection methods we can use.'

'Because of your charter.'

'Right.' Lynch nodded. 'When it comes down to it, our main job is to monitor and advise countries who have signed the Convention on International Trade in Endangered Species. That means as well as lobbying to get various animals on the endangered list, we prosecute countries who violate the Convention, and do what we can to educate the public. We also have staff in the field acting as observers or advisers – experts who are supposed to be backed up by the governments who employ them.'

'OK.' Rayner smiled. 'I've got the picture. You don't want me going off halfcocked, spoiling things for you. I understand. But that's not why I'm getting the lecture, is it?'

'No.' Lynch closed the cover on his file. 'I spend too much damn time talking to politicians, I'm afraid.' He paused. 'I'll be as direct as I can. First off, don't get the idea WOPES has gone soft on Kabinda. We haven't. We believe that Maximilian Kabinda is a major player in Angola. He's a buyer of ivory and he's an exporter of ivory – and the bastard killed one of our people. Sure that means we can talk to Luanda. But I'd like to do something else as well. If we had the right resources or the right person for the job, I'd like to find Kabinda violating the statutes of a country that has a real commitment to the Convention – a country with a half-way stable government where we have some proper influence.'

'Japan,' Rayner said.

'I know you've only been back in the States a few weeks, and I know it's probably not your line of work.'

Rayner didn't answer. He was thinking – about Wendy, about Felix and about the girl in the photographs. Walking over to the table, he studied the prints again.

'It'd be Hong Kong,' Lynch said. 'According to our statistics, three hundred tons of undocumented ivory were processed in the colony last year. You wouldn't have to go in cold, of course. We'd arrange for someone to bring you up to speed on the business once you got there.'

'I don't think so, thanks. I'm sorry.'

'That's rather what I thought.' Lynch collected up the photographs. 'Never mind. You can't blame me for trying. Come on, I'll take you to lunch. Let's talk about something more pleasant.'

Over lunch and for the remainder of the day, Rayner found himself increasingly preoccupied with a single thought. By rejecting the opportunity to uncover an African ivory operation in Hong Kong, he had committed himself to forgetting about Kabinda. And that was what Wendy had wanted him to do.

Arriving home late, he took the risk of phoning to tell her. But she was gone, her mother said, gone for a month to visit a friend in Salem. And, no, Wendy hadn't left a message for him, nor had she wanted him to have her number there.

That night Rayner took two things to bed with him, the bottle of scotch and the crumpled cigarette packet containing the diamonds. The diamonds were to remind him of why she had gone. The scotch was to help him forget and to assist him in making a decision. It took all night, but by dawn he had decided.

Two days later, on a soft summer afternoon, Rayner locked up the cottage and headed for the airport. But this time, unlike all the others, he was unaccompanied and, at the gate to the departure lounge, there was no one for him to wrap his arms around and no one for him to kiss goodbye.

Four

The streets of Johannesburg and New York had been crowded enough, but here in the seething mass of humanity that was Kowloon, Rayner was suffocating. He stepped off the sidewalk and began walking in the road where there were fewer people.

Yesterday, tired after his long flight from the States, he had ventured out from his hotel only once, late in the evening when a steady drizzle had forced the tourists to take refuge in the bars. This afternoon, though, there were sightseers everywhere. They were drifting from one shop to another, carrying cameras and plastic bags or emerging from restaurants into a sticky heat that even Rayner found unpleasant.

He continued heading south on Hankow Road, avoiding cars and bicycles until he was forced back on to the sidewalk by traffic coming from the bus station. Ahead, he could see the dome of the space museum now, the landmark he'd used before to locate the hotel entrance. He could see the hotel too, and the usual line of limousines and taxis parked outside it.

Rayner used the Salisbury Road entrance, walking into an airconditioned environment so cold that it made him shiver.

At the desk he collected his key and had started to walk away when a Chinese girl called to him from the office. She was waving an envelope.

He returned to the desk to see what she wanted.

'Mr Rayner, I have a message for you, a fax from New York. It came a minute ago.'

'Thank you.' He took the envelope from her.

'If you wish to send a reply, please ask for me. My name is Janine.'

Rayner returned her smile. 'I will,' he said.

He waited until he was upstairs in his room before he read the fax. It was from Lynch, to say that contact with Luanda had been delayed because of diplomatic difficulties. Lynch described the problem in detail, explaining how the US was engaged in a human rights issue involving thousands of Angolan women and children who had been sold to work in brothels or as labourers in Cuban sugar plantations. Two months ago Rayner himself had witnessed the horror of children being traded like animals to Cuban mercenaries, but although he knew that measures to stop it were long overdue, he couldn't imagine why Washington should believe the prevention of the Angolan slave-trade had anything to do with the ivory business. Not that he should've been surprised, he decided. Experience had taught him that no one could ever figure out what Washington believed.

Leaving the fax on the table beside the bed, he went to see if the housekeeper had restocked the fridge. She had, but only with two more miniature bottles of scotch – hardly enough for the evening, which meant he'd have to try one of the hotel bars.

He mixed the contents of one bottle with some soda, then lay down on the bed to study the notes he'd made. There were three pages of them, listing the type of ivory products he'd seen today, where he'd seen them, and the addresses of six manufacturers.

Although his list was on the thin side, he was not too discouraged. As well as starting from cold, it was early days yet, and he could remember plenty of other times when he'd begun a job with far less information and far less chance of success.

Already he knew that success depended on two things; discovering how the ivory was being brought into Hong Kong, and locating the place where Kinshasa Copper was storing it. As long as he could find that out, at least Lynch would be happy, he thought, even if it was still going to be difficult to implicate Kabinda. But for the moment Kabinda could wait. One step at a time, one day at a time until it all started to come together. Putting the notes aside, he started to consider his options, wondering what line of attack to adopt tomorrow.

By seven o'clock he was sufficiently satisfied with his decision to stop work for the day. After he had showered and put on a clean shirt, he sat down to finish the second bottle of scotch while he endeavoured to choose a restaurant from the hotel brochure.

He was interrupted by a knock on the door. Thinking it would be the maid wanting to turn down the bed, Rayner grabbed his jacket, intending to leave once he'd let her in.

He got no further than opening the door. It wasn't the maid. Instead, it was the last person he'd expected to see. Standing in the corridor was Cristabel Castela. She wore a tight smile and seemed to be slightly nervous.

Rayner's manners failed him. Too astonished to ask her into the room, he remained where he was with his hand on the doorknob.

'Good evening,' she said. 'Is this a surprise?'

'Yes.' He had absolutely no idea what she was doing in Hong Kong, let alone why she was here in his hotel.

'Didn't you get a fax?' she said. 'From Stuart Lynch.'

'It didn't say anything about this – about you.'

'You don't know then?' she said.

'Know what?'

'I'm your adviser. Stuart said he'd send a fax to tell you.'

'Why the hell would he do that?' Rayner said. 'He knows you wouldn't give me the time of day.'

'Is that what he said?'

'Kind of.' Rayner stared at her. 'Have I missed something somewhere?'

'Probably. May I come in?'

He stood to one side, holding the door open for her, noticing the faint trail of perfume she left behind her as she entered the room.

Choosing a chair near the television she sat down and crossed her legs. 'Isn't that the fax?' She pointed to the envelope on the table.

'I've told you. It doesn't say anything about you coming here.' He paused. 'Look, I don't want to be rude, but I don't think this is a great idea.'

'Oh. Shall I go away then?'

'Not until we've got this straightened out.' Rayner went to the fridge. 'What would you like to drink?'

'White wine, please, if there is one. Otherwise just mineral water.'

Rayner poured two glasses of wine. He took one over to her.

'Thank you.' She glanced at him. 'Perhaps it would be better if I apologized first. I can tell we're not going to get on very well unless I do.'

'Apologize for what?'

'I read your statement – the one you made in New York. Stuart asked me to. And I listened to the dictaphone tape too. You see, I made up my mind about you as soon as I saw those photocopies from your friend in South Africa.' She drank some wine. 'I do it all the time – make up my mind about people, I mean – when I don't really know them. Mostly I get it right.'

Rayner waited.

'I didn't realize you were hundreds of yards away in a ditch or something,' she said.

'You didn't ask.'

'And I didn't realize you thought Kabinda would let my sister go when Janson gave him those diamonds.'

'So what?' Rayner said. 'You still believe I sat and watched the whole damn thing without trying to stop it. You're right, I did. I watched it from start to finish.'

'I'm trying to say I was wrong. Short of committing suicide I can't see what else you could've done. I suppose there are times when this sort of thing happens.' She hesitated. 'In dreadful situations, I mean. When people can't do what they want to do.'

'It's never happened to me before,' Rayner said. 'Not like that. I hope to Christ it never happens again.'

'You told Stuart it should have been Janson who died instead of my sister.'

'No, I didn't. I said your sister was unlucky. There's a difference. She was shot with a small calibre bullet – a .32 or maybe even a .22. A couple of inches to the right and she'd still be alive.' Rayner put his glass down. 'I'm pretty sure it went through her heart.'

'Your hand's shaking.' She looked at him.

'I know. I don't want to talk about it. Do you mind?'

'No. I'm sorry. I'm sorry for how I behaved too.'

'It's OK.' Rayner was already struggling, half imagining he could see the bead of blood. It was bright red, lying directly under a button of her blouse.

'I don't think it is OK.' Her smile had slipped. 'This is going to be difficult isn't it?'

'Did Lynch tell you to come?'

'He asked me if I would. I know about ivory – a little bit. And I can speak Chinese. I said I thought we could probably work together as long as I apologized properly and didn't get in your way too much. I suppose I should have phoned you before I left, shouldn't I?'

'Yes,' Rayner said. 'Except you wouldn't be here if you had.'

'Mm.' She placed her glass alongside his on the table. 'I don't know what else to say. Do you want to fax New York and get me recalled?'

'I don't know yet.'

'What does it depend on?'

'I don't know that either.' Rayner's wariness had gone. She was still quite tense, he thought, but obviously anxious to create a good impression. She was also trying her best not to push too hard. 'Where are you staying?' he asked.

'Here. Room 238 downstairs.' She wrote the number on the back of the fax.

Rayner watched her, wondering if this was a way to exorcise the ghost of her sister, or whether he was being foolish to even consider allowing her to stay.

'Have you eaten?' he asked.

'Why?' She corrected herself. 'No, I haven't.'

'How about having dinner with me then? You can tell me all the things I don't know about ivory.'

'Thank you. That would be nice.' She stood up and went to the door. 'Can you give me time to change?'

'Pick you up in ten minutes,' Rayner said.

Over dinner, rather than asking questions about ivory, he avoided the subject altogether. Nor did she touch on the events that had brought him to Hong Kong. Instead, as if by mutual consent, their conversation revolved around other things – matters of less significance that should have allowed Rayner to break the tension. But try as he might, the barrier remained, an uneasiness that persisted throughout the evening.

It was only later, after he'd seen her to her room and said goodnight that he understood what was wrong. Discovering she no longer held him responsible for the death of her sister should have made things easier. But having dinner with Cristabel Castela had made it worse. Because, just as before, she was a reminder of what had happened, he realized. Because whenever he was with her, she brought back the image of her sister.

Rayner knew it was absurd, just as he knew that one way to get rid of the image was to get rid of Cristabel Castela. By phoning Lynch he could have her on the next plane out. A quick fix, Rayner thought, for a problem that might be better fixed by a jolt of common sense or by concentrating on what he'd come here to do.

For a while, before he went to bed, he considered whether or not to call New York, deciding in the end that he would wait until tomorrow before making up his mind. But by morning Rayner had decided to adopt a more positive approach.

Discovering there was no answer when he knocked on her door, he went downstairs expecting to find her in the breakfast-room.

She was sitting by herself at a corner table drinking coffee.

'Hi.' Rayner pulled up a chair. 'We'll try it,' he said. 'See how things go.'

'Oh. Did I pass the test? Or did someone twist your arm?'

'I didn't ask anybody.'

'So it's OK?'

He could see how pleased she was. 'To be honest I could use your help,' he said. 'You're going to be my short cut.'

'I brought some stuff with me but I don't know how much help it'll be.'

'We'll see.' Rayner stole one of her pieces of toast and spread a layer of honey on it.

'Why do you do that?' she said. 'Why do you drink black coffee with no sugar in it and then go and use all that honey on your toast?'

'Habit. If you live out of the back of a LandRover in Africa you don't carry milk and sugar with you. Anyway I like black coffee.'

'And you like honey?'

'Sure. In a hotel I do.'

She smiled. 'Hong Kong isn't much like the African veld, is it? Have you been here before?'

'Few times,' Rayner said. 'What about you?'

'I used to come quite often – when I visited my uncle and his wife. They live down the coast in Macau.' She paused. 'My family comes from Portugal but my father and my uncle Raoul were both born in Angola. My uncle went to live in Macau about fifteen years ago. You know, because it's still under Portuguese administration. He's incredibly rich.'

'Is that where you learned Chinese?'

She nodded. 'I learned English in Angola from my Portuguese father, and learned Cantonese in Macau from the wife of my Portuguese uncle. Crazy, isn't it?'

Unconsciously Rayner had been looking at the colour of her skin. She was wearing a sleeveless dress and had her elbows on the table holding her cup in both hands. 'What about your mother?' he asked.

She smiled again. 'You don't get a spring sun-tan in New York. My mother was a black African. Is that what you wanted to know?'

'I want to know whether to call you Cristabel or Cris.'

'I don't mind.'

'OK.' He signed his name on the restaurant check. 'Have you finished your breakfast?'

'Yes thank you.'

'Right. There are three or four places I want to go this morning and a couple more I'd like us to check out this afternoon. Then, if there's time, we'll have a quick look at the Kinshasa Copper office and see if they have a warehouse somewhere. Having you along to translate ought to speed things up a fair bit.'

'I might not be that much help,' she said. 'I'm fairly rusty.'

It took Rayner less than an hour to learn how big a help Crlstabel Castela was going to be. Her knowledge of Hong Kong was more extensive than she had led him to believe and, as he was to discover over the next four days, she was equally at home speaking in Chinese to ivory merchants in squalid, backstreet workshops as she was in down-town shops talking to salesmen about magnificent ivory figurines and carvings worth tens of thousands of dollars.

She had also provided Rayner with a crash course on the ivory industry. It had given him a fresh insight into the business, adding to what he could see with his own eyes. In workshops so dusty and so dirty that it was barely possible to breathe, Rayner had begun to understand why the demand for illicit tusks was on the increase. He had seen ivory chopsticks, fly whisks, rosary beads, toothpicks and dice. He had seen tusks with bullet holes in them stacked like firewood at the back of carving shops and he had seen countless thousands of bangles, necklaces, rings and trinkets being packaged for the Hong Kong tourist trade. And at every shop, warehouse or factory he was met with the same, impenetrable wall of silence.

Had he been working alone, his lack of progress would have been more demoralizing. But Rayner wasn't working alone.

Everywhere he went, Cristabel Castela went – never intruding unless he asked for her opinion, never questioning his decisions and not once suggesting they should try some other way of tracing the origin of all the tusks they'd seen. She was supportive, but also careful never to tread on Rayner's toes.

As a result, he had not only begun to enjoy her company, but on one occasion had even considered bringing up the subject of her resemblance to her sister. But then, because the timing had been wrong, he had veered away from it and had been reluctant to raise the matter since.

This evening though, perhaps because he'd drunk too much or perhaps for another reason, it could have been either of the Castela sisters sitting at the table with him in the half light of the hotel bar.

Ten minutes ago, by forcing himself to look elsewhere, Rayner had avoided the impulse to tell her. But that had been before they'd started on their fourth round of drinks and before she'd started asking all the questions about Wendy.

'What does Wendy do?' she said.

'Works for some real estate outfit in Hyannis.' Rayner tried to think of a way to redirect the conversation.

'And you've known each other for a long time?'

'We grew up together,' he said. 'Same school – the whole bit.'

'Childhood sweethearts.' She smiled. 'Why didn't you marry her?'

'Long story,' Rayner said. 'Anyway she married someone else – the guy who used to run her office.'

'Oh.' She finished her cocktail. 'Is that why you went to Africa?'

'No.' Already lightheaded from the scotch, he didn't want to talk about Wendy. He wanted to talk about something else.

'What's the matter?' she said. 'Why are you staring at me like that?'

Had he stopped to think or if the circumstances had been different, Rayner would never have made the mistake of telling her about his dream. But at this moment, sitting alone with her in the bar, it was easy.

When he'd finished speaking, she made no comment, only touching on what he'd said half an hour later when Rayner was about to say goodnight in the corridor outside her room.

'I have some pills that'll make you sleep,' she said.

'Guaranteed. No dreams, no nightmares.'

'Thanks.' He smiled. 'But the scotch'll do it.'

'Would you like some coffee? It's only ten-thirty.'

He shook his head.

'What about this?' She reached up and put her arms around his neck. Then very gently she kissed him on the mouth.

Her breasts were hard against him, two hard points pressing into his chest. Rayner could feel them through his shirt as she made him return her kiss.

She opened her mouth, teasing him.

Shoving her away, he forced her back against the door. She was breathing fast and her eyes were tightly shut.

'Look at me,' he said.

Her eyes remained closed. She said nothing.

Rayner shook her by the shoulders. 'Look at me.'

'No. Don't you want to take me to bed?'

He prised the room key from her fingers, unlocked the door and pushed her inside. In the hall she turned around to face him, still breathing quickly, but with her eyes open now.

'You're drunk,' he said.

'Oh no I'm not.' She removed her shoes first, then her skirt and finally the remainder of her clothes until she was naked.

To Rayner it seemed that everything about her was provocative, the way she stood, the curve of her hips, the shadow between her legs and, illuminated in the light coming from the bathroom, the outline of her tiny breasts.

He already knew he wanted to touch them. He wanted all of her – now – before she turned into someone else.

As if reading his thoughts, she stepped towards him, took his hands and placed them on her breasts. 'What do you think?' she whispered.

Picking her up, Rayner carried her to the bed. Somehow he knew there was still doubt, but when he kissed her this time, her response drove everything from his mind. Her whole body became alive, her stomach and her thighs as taut as her breasts, her mouth urging him to touch her everywhere until, moaning, she arched her back to receive him.

By then Rayner was lost. As well as being unable to think, he was insensitive to the past, no longer caring how the death of a girl in Angola could have ever brought him to seek such pleasure from her sister.

He took her slowly, waiting for some minutes after her cries had subsided before he pulled her hair away from her face to look at her.

'Hi.' She spoke softly. 'Was that nice?'

Rayner didn't answer.

'I wanted to show you I was sorry,' she explained. 'Because I was horrible to you when we first met. And to make your dream go away.'

'Suppose it doesn't go away?'

She smiled up at him. 'Then I'll have to try harder, won't I?'

Because the binoculars she'd bought were of such poor quality, Rayner was only using them when there was definite activity on the deck of the *Coloane* or on board the neighbouring fishing junk. For the hundredth time he swung the binoculars on to the cable hanging over the freighter's rust-streaked stern, studying it until his eyes began to water. Having to look through the misty windshield of the car made the job more difficult, the result of Cristabel running the airconditioning unit at full blast. He reached out and turned it off, waking her up in the process.

'Why don't you watch from outside?' She stretched. 'It's no more suspicious than having the car parked here on the wharf for hours on end.'

Rayner knew she was bored. For three days now they'd been observing the freighter, a long-drawn-out vigil that so far had yielded less information than their visits to the ivory workshops had done.

If it hadn't been for the occasional exchange of personnel between the *Coloane* and the big, three-masted junk that was berthed alongside, Rayner would have been equally bored. Yesterday, for a while, after the freighter had unloaded several tons of Angolan coffee and sisal on to the wharf for Customs inspection, his interest had been rekindled. Today, though, he'd started to wonder if his theory was right and whether they should have followed the trucks after all.

The trucks had arrived at the wharf earlier this afternoon to collect the coffee and the sacks of sisal, each vehicle bearing the logo and the name of Kinshasa Copper. Rayner had let them go, believing it was pointless tailing them across town to the warehouse at Hung Hom. If Kinshasa Copper was bringing ivory into Hong Kong, it wasn't being smuggled in openly, of that he was sure – just as he was certain the warehouse wasn't being used illegally to store elephant tusks. Which left the steel cable and the junk, he thought, and the knowledge that the longer he spent in the car with Cristabel, the less inclined he was to worry about the ivory.

Since the night they had first made love, Rayner had found it difficult to focus his attention on anything but Cristabel Castela. Disturbed by being so attracted to her that she seemed to be continually on his mind, twice in the last three days he had endeavoured to normalize their relationship. And both times, by teasing him for being serious, she had succeeded only in heightening his interest in her – an intense physical interest that refused to go away.

In the last half-hour, partly because of the dress she was wearing, and partly because he was tired of watching the freighter, Rayner had again been unable to stop thinking about her. She was half asleep, slumped beside him in the passenger seat with her skirt pulled up so high he could see the mole on her thigh. He wanted to touch her, to slide his fingers over her leg while her eyes were closed.

She saw him looking and quickly drew her skirt down. 'Kinshasa Copper,' she said. 'We're supposed to be working, remember?'

Rayner grinned. 'I don't know about we,' he said.

'This is your theory, not mine. Why don't you go and ask one of the men on the freighter to winch in the cable? Then you'll know.'

'I don't need to. All I need is to see the end of it transferred to the junk.'

Taking her notepad and a pencil from the glove box, she placed them on his lap. 'If you really want me to believe sitting here for three days has been a good idea, I think you're going to have to show me why this stupid cable is so important.'

'How many times do I have to explain? It's not the cable, it's what's on the end – what's under the water.'

'Draw it – this submarine thing.'

'I didn't say it was a submarine.'

'Whatever.' She put the pencil in his hand. 'Go on.'

Rayner sketched a crude picture of the freighter, pencilling the name *Coloane* on the side above the waterline. 'OK,' he said. 'Kabinda ships three things from Angola: coffee, sisal and ivory – all nicely packaged in the hold. Now imagine he also carries a special empty container. I'm not sure what it'd look like, but suppose it's a closed steel tube around fifty feet long and three or four feet in diameter – something like that.'

'You're making things up as you go along,' she said accusingly. 'Yesterday you said it had fins.'

'Just hang on. First of all, assume that at some time before the freighter gets into Hong Kong territorial waters the crew stack all the ivory in this tube, seal it up and chuck it over the side on the end of a cable. Then they tow the tube into harbour – like a torpedo on the end of a line. I only said it could have fins because fins would make it travel through the water at a more or less constant depth at a certain speed.' He drew the tube trailing along behind the freighter.

'It's a guess,' she said. 'You know it is. Based on nothing except how you think it could be done.'

Because he was certain it wouldn't make any difference, Rayner decided not to tell her how often smaller versions of the torpedo were used to smuggle cocaine into the Persian Gulf. 'Why's there a cable over the stern of the freighter?' he said. 'Why aren't any of the other ships trailing a cable? And why should the only freighter that's got one just happen to be delivering stuff to Kinshasa Copper?'

'I don't know.' She sat up and started brushing her hair. 'It's too complicated.'

'No it isn't. If anything goes wrong before they arrive, the crew can drop the cable and maybe collect the tube later. Don't forget half the ports in this part of the world have drugs passing through them. Kabinda knows there's a chance the authorities could board the freighter and sniff around.'

'So there's a steel tube full of ivory down there in the water somewhere?' She pointed with the handle of her hairbrush. 'And you think the *Coloane* is going to leave without it.'

'Sure. The junk will take over. All it has to do is tow the tube into some coastal estuary up in the New Territories – a nice local trip that won't attract attention from anyone.'

She shook her head. 'If Hong Kong Customs are looking for drugs, why wouldn't they think of it?'

'They might if the ship was coming from South America, but they're not going to look very hard at one coming from Angola. Central Africa isn't a major drug producing region. Anyway, Kinshasa Copper is a perfectly legitimate importer of products into Hong Kong.'

'It's still a guess though, isn't it?'

'What's wrong with that? It's a better lead than we've got

from anywhere else. The warehouse at Hung Hom looked like a waste of time, and the ivory carvers weren't exactly a lot of help, were they?'

Narrowing her eyes she pretended to be one of the old Chinese carvers they had visited in Tsuen Wan. 'Ah, Mr Rayner,' she said. 'How I wish I could assist you in your search. To do so would give me more pleasure than I receive from my wife on my birthday.'

Rayner laughed. 'We should've given him a ticket to one of those sampan brothels we saw moored in the typhoon shelter,' he said. 'It might have worked better than offering him money.'

'I don't think anything's going to work,' she said. 'Including this. What happens when the *Coloane* sails?'

'Depends. If she goes without the cable we're in business. I'll bet you anything you like the junk leaves the next day. If it does we can follow it.'

She raised her eyebrows. 'Suppose it heads out to sea?'

'Suppose it doesn't?'

'You're a very determined person, aren't you?' she said. 'You make me sit in a rental car for three days because of some crazy idea you have, and then you decide we might have to follow a Chinese junk up the coast. Don't you ever think you could be wrong?'

'Never.' Rayner gave her back the notepad and pencil. 'Trust me.'

'I still think we should have a proper look at the warehouse – inside I mean – not just drive past it like we did the other day. You said you know about burglar alarms. We could go tonight.'

'If we're not doing anything else,' Rayner said. 'It's all right for you, you've been asleep all day. I need to catch up.'

'Only because you had your dream again last night. It's no good saying you didn't – I know you did. You woke me up.'

Rayner was using the binoculars, avoiding the issue by watching a crewman throw a bucket of slops over the side of the junk.

She took the binoculars from him. 'Why won't you talk about it?'

'It's no big deal.'

'Really.' She smoothed down her skirt. 'How much longer are we going to stay here?'

'We'll give it a couple more hours.'

Today Rayner's determination deserted him. By five o'clock he was ready to head back to the hotel, as weary of watching as Cris was of sitting in the car. Whether or not the *Coloane* might slip anchor overnight, he didn't know. If it did, and if the junk disappeared as well, then he had wasted three days. But if both vessels remained at the wharf, there would be time tomorrow for him to decide what best to do. Until then he had other things to occupy him.

Arriving back at the hotel early, he had a single drink at the bar with Cris then excused himself and went directly to his room where he sat down to write to Wendy. It turned out not to be a letter but a note, a single page in an envelope addressed to her mother, with a request for it to be sent on to wherever Wendy was staying in Salem.

As soon as he'd finished writing, Rayner knew it was a mistake. Because of what was happening with Cris, his mood was wrong and the month with Wendy at Sandy Neck seemed now to be a month remembered from some other summer at some other time.

After mailing the letter at the desk downstairs he returned to his room where he spent the best part of an hour in the shower before lying down on the bed to think.

It was much later in the evening when a knock on the door dragged him out of a restless sleep.

Knowing it would be Cris, he went to let her in, pleased that she'd come to wake him up.

'Didn't you want to have dinner with me?' She looked disapprovingly at the rumpled bed. 'Or have you been entertaining someone else?'

'I was just tired.'

'Oh. Do you know how late it is?'

He inspected his watch. 'The restaurant's still open. Or we can use room service.'

'We don't need room service.' She put a paper bag down on the bed beside her. 'I've brought you a present – for your therapy.'

'What therapy?'

'Something to make your dream go away. It's part of a deal. I tell you a secret, then you tell me your secrets. You know, why we're here, why Wendy is so important to you, why you can't forget about Francesca.' She smiled. 'I promise it'll work.'

Two minutes ago Rayner had been asleep, yet already he

was uncomfortably aware of her being in the room with him. She was wearing a different perfume, but that wasn't the only thing different about her. It was her hair, accidentally arranged to remind him of someone else.

'Do you like strawberries?'

'Why?'

She patted the bed. 'Come here and sit down. I have a story to tell you.' Rayner sat, having no idea what this was all about.

'It's about my sister,' she said. 'I've never told anyone this before, but I think you ought to know what kind of person she was. You see Francesca was evil – the most evil person I've ever known. You didn't know that, did you?'

He shook his head.

'When we were children in Angola she started sleeping with men before she was fifteen. Black African labourers who worked for my father, white boys, migrant workers – anyone. She liked it because she believed it gave her power. I can remember her telling me about it, how she could make men beg to touch her, how she could drive them crazy by tying them up in the barn and then undressing in front of them and masturbating while they watched her. She was so pretty, men couldn't take their eyes off her.'

Rayner was intrigued. 'Didn't your parents know?' he said.

'My father did. He tried to stop her, but she used to laugh at him. I won't tell you the really bad things that happened, except to say that in the end he refused to have her in the house for days on end. It was my father who made Francesca go to work for WOPES. Because we both grew up on the game reserve, he thought that if she had a job in wildlife conservation she might get straightened out.'

'Why did you go with her?' Rayner asked.

'Because I wanted to. Not to be with my sister – because I've wanted to work with animals all my life. My father believed Francesca thought the same way.' She stopped for a moment. 'He never understood how much she hated the reserve and hated the animals in it. One day I saw her shoot over fifty monkeys – whole families of them – while they were in an enclosure. She enjoyed doing it.'

By now Rayner had a vague understanding of what she was attempting to do.

He remained silent waiting for her to continue.

She went on, 'When WOPES sent Francesca back to Africa,

she said she was going to get rich. She used to boast about it to me – about how simple it is to make money in the endangered species business.'

'Kickbacks,' Rayner said.

'Mm. First off you establish your power base, which is easy because you nearly always have government backing. Once you've done that, you get to know the poachers and they get to know how much they have to pay you to look the other way. It happens all the time. Fran was good at it.'

'Until she met Kabinda.'

She nodded. 'Francesca had only been in Angola for two months and I think the rules must be different there. Or maybe she'd decided to teach Kabinda a lesson because he wasn't paying her enough.'

'And Lynch doesn't know anything about this?'

'Nobody does except me. I should've told him, but I couldn't. I didn't want my father to find out what she was doing.' She paused. 'Perhaps he knew. I'm not sure. He never talked about it.'

'Hell of a story,' Rayner said.

'Do you know why I've told you?'

'If it's so I won't feel bad about not being able to save her, it won't work. She didn't deserve to die like that.'

'Remember what you said to me the other night about exorcising her ghost?'

'What about it?'

'All you remember is how my sister looked after she'd been raped and killed. I don't just look like her; we had the same genes.' Leaning across, she started to unbutton his shirt.

Rayner could feel her breath warm on his skin as her hands began straying, searching, forcing him to acknowledge what she already knew – that he wanted her again – more than he had ever wanted anything.

She let him push her back on to the bed and helped him to remove her dress. Beneath it she was naked. But when he tried to touch her she stopped him, making him wait while, from the bag beside her, she took a single strawberry and crushed it between her breasts.

Rayner watched her do it, seeing the bullet hole appear as if by magic. Again he went to touch her, but again she prevented him, this time because she was holding something else – a miniature cardboard carton. Slowly she lifted it above her, pouring out a thin stream of honey over her stomach and her thighs.

'Who am I?' she whispered.

It was a game, he realized. Some incredible game of make-believe designed either to drive him crazy or to make him forget her sister. Rayner didn't want to play it. But, no sooner had she closed her eyes and parted her lips in anticipation, than his ability to resist dissolved. She pulled him down on top of her, forcing his mouth on to hers, holding him tightly to her.

Despite the unreality of the fantasy she was creating, he couldn't help himself, answering her whispered demands, but not yet sure of what she wanted him to do.

It was only afterwards when she was lying still beside him that he began to comprehend.

'*Hao chi ma?*' she murmured to him in Chinese.

'I don't know what that means.'

'You don't have to.' Wriggling off the bed, she stood in front of him with her hands on her hips. 'Look,' she said. 'No bullet hole, no blood – nothing.'

'For Christ's sake,' Rayner said. 'Stop it. Come back here.'

'All right.' She returned to the bed, snuggling up against him. 'It's your turn now. Who are you, Mark Rayner? What makes you so special? Why are you here? Where are you going? And what are you going to do about me?'

He smiled. 'Rest of the therapy?'

'Mm. You don't have to feel guilty any more. Francesca's gone. It's me you have to worry about now. And that means I have to know everything about you.'

'Everything?'

She nodded.

Rayner told her; told her about endless summers with Wendy at Sandy Neck, about Libya, about Angola, about Janson, Felix, the break-in at the cottage and finally about his decision to take the assignment in Hong Kong. But long before he'd finished speaking she was asleep, cradled in his arms, lost in some secret dream of her own that she had yet to share with him.

In the narrow channel between Tung Lung island and the Fat Tong Kong promontory the water had been choppy rather than rough. But out here in the open sea where at times the sampan was barely moving, the hull was pitching heavily in the swell. Although Rayner knew that a change of speed would make the ride more comfortable, he was reluctant to gain on the junk and equally wary of falling too far behind as they had done earlier.

For nearly four hours he'd been doing this, trying to keep the sampan at what he thought was a safe distance without losing sight of the three lateen sails of the slowly moving junk ahead of them. Despite the unfavourable wind, it was continuing on the same bearing, about half a mile out from one of the tiny islands on the eastern seaboard – a part of the New Territories' coastline that was as foreign to Rayner as it was to Cristabel.

He shouted to her over the noise of the diesel, asking her where she thought they were.

Holding onto the bamboo rail she brought the chart to him and spread it out. 'There.' She pointed. 'Fan Tsang Chau. It's the only island this far out.'

Rayner studied the chart for a moment, wondering whether he should call it a day. As well as being a long way from anywhere, in a little over an hour it would be dark. And that meant they could forget about returning the sampan.

'Big adventure.' Cristabel had read his thoughts. 'Adrift in the China Sea in a rented sampan. Something I've always wanted to do.'

He smiled. 'You didn't have to come.'

'We didn't have to come.' She corrected him. 'Can you imagine what's going to happen if we run aground?'

Rayner pointed at a flotilla of southbound fishing boats and at a small, steelhulled lighter that was about to overtake the sampan. 'Plenty of help out here,' he said. 'We're not exactly alone, are we?'

'Not so long as you have a crew who can speak Chinese. I should be getting paid for doing this.'

'You are,' he said. 'WOPES are paying you. Anyway, we're not going to run aground.'

'I still think you're mad.' She waved to the captain of the lighter as it slowly overhauled them. 'Maybe I could hitch a ride back with someone who knows what they're doing.'

The sampan started wallowing in the lighter's wash, forcing her to grab the rail again. 'For all you know the junk isn't towing your torpedo anyway,' she said.

Rayner handed her the binoculars. 'Is the cable still there?'

She steadied herself while she looked. 'Yes. But we don't know it's the cable from the *Coloane* – not the same one, I mean. You were wrong about the freighter leaving first. Why shouldn't you be wrong about this?'

'Come on. Yesterday the cable's hanging off the stern of the *Coloane* and this morning it's over the side of the junk. How much of a coincidence do you want?' Rayner knew she was hoping for a reaction from him – or perhaps trying to persuade him to abandon the exercise altogether.

She put down the binoculars. 'I suppose we'll have to spend the night on board this thing.'

'I gave the guy five hundred bucks. He said it was OK if we weren't back until tomorrow.'

'You didn't tell me that.' She frowned. 'I'm not sure I'll be safe – not with you for a whole night.'

Since they had last made love their relationship had changed, he thought. She was more confident now, more likely to poke fun at him or question his decisions – either because she felt more comfortable when she was with him, or because she realized the effect she had on him, Rayner didn't know which. All he did know was that the attraction remained, a fascination he still couldn't explain and one that, in the present circumstances, was as stupid as it was dangerous.

To stop himself from wondering about tonight, he swung the wheel to bring the bow of the sampan closer to north and directed his attention back to the junk. It was sailing in the shadow of the cliffs, no longer out in the bright sunshine that had allowed Rayner to follow it so easily throughout the day. He could still pick out the distinctive pattern of the sails, but once the sun sank lower, it would be a different matter, he thought, especially if the captain decided to duck in behind one of the points along the coast.

Ahead of the sampan, the lighter too was hugging the coastline, travelling on the same course. Because of shallow water? Rayner wondered. He inspected the chart again, searching uneasily for reefs or a hidden sandbar.

When he looked up again the junk had vanished.

'They're going to the south of Sai Wan,' Cris said. She put her finger on the chart. 'Somewhere near here. That's why they've turned.'

Rayner opened the throttle wide, feeling the hull shudder as the sampan picked up speed. Already it was handling the swell better, pushing its bow north through the water towards the last place he had seen the junk. Using the wake from the lighter as a guide, he kept the sampan a constant distance from the shore, entering the shadow of the cliffs shortly after the lighter disappeared behind the headland.

Beside him at the wheel, Cris was silent. Her hair was blowing in the breeze and he could see her expression had changed. Because she was concerned about spending a night at sea? he wondered. Or was it just the wildness of the coastline that bothered her? This morning when they'd first started out she'd been cheerful enough, but since then, apart from the odd flash of humour, she'd gradually become more reserved. Even now, when with any luck their journey would soon be over, she was staring blankly into the distance as if still waiting for him to admit he had brought them here for nothing.

Rayner stopped worrying about her, listening instead to the throb of the diesel and watching for rocks as they drew steadily closer to the cliffs.

It wasn't until the port bow of the sampan cleared the headland that they suddenly spoke at the same time – not to comment on the junk or on the much calmer water, but on the fairy-tale picture that lay before them.

Less than half a mile to the west, nestled in a bay between two hills was a fishing village, a tiny coastal settlement of flat-roofed houses set amongst some trees. Sampans, fishing boats and skiffs lined each side of half a dozen rickety landing-stages, while still more boats were moored in clusters off the shore. Further away, at the north end of the beach near a long, low building, the lighter had dropped anchor. Beyond it, becalmed on a sea of glass, was the junk, its sails already furled for the night.

But more than anything it was colour that made Rayner cut his engine, one colour that had transformed the hills, the coastline and the sea into a crimson painting. From the headland to the far end of the bay, the cottages, the boats and the landing-stages were on fire, drenched in a blood-red glow from the setting sun.

Cris was spellbound, her reservation temporarily gone. 'Oh,' she said. 'Why haven't we got a camera? I've never seen anything like this.'

Rayner hadn't either. He let the sampan drift, looking north-west now towards the conical peak of Sharp Mountain.

It too was glowing, but only on the western flank. The rest of it was unlit, casting a huge shadow out over the neighbouring hills and valleys.

'It's air pollution,' he said. 'From the city. Look.'

Cris followed his finger, staring at the sun. It was going down at the head of the valley, sinking through a dull red haze behind the village to form a backdrop as unreal as the rest of the painting.

For three or four minutes Rayner watched the sun sink lower, unwilling to spoil the moment by restarting the sampan's diesel.

'What are we going to do?' Cris glanced at him.

'Moor out here somewhere. I don't want to risk going back to Kowloon in the dark. Not when there's so much coastal shipping about. Anyway we have to see if I'm right about the junk. Maybe that building belongs to Kinshasa Copper.'

'Maybe it doesn't. That's what you always say to me.'

He smiled. 'Well, we'll soon find out. For all we know, ten minutes from now someone's going to drag my torpedo ashore.' He pushed the button to start the engine, hearing it cough before it settled down into an uneven tickover. He left the throttle where it was, allowing the low engine speed to propel the sampan slowly towards the beach.

The sun had all but gone by the time Rayner decided he was close enough. Turning the bow of the sampan he headed north again, shouting at Cris to let go the anchor when they were about a quarter of a mile from the junk. It was already hard to see, a grey outline indistinct against the even darker hills behind it.

On shore now, only a few of the houses were burning lights, but out in the bay, most of the sampans were illuminated. A smell of cooking was coming from one of them and Rayner could hear the clatter of pots and the sound of laughter.

Cristabel came aft carrying their last vacuum flask of coffee. He could see she was ill at ease.

'Look,' he said. 'I know this isn't a nice airconditioned hotel with a proper toilet and a shower. I promise we'll head back in the morning.'

'Don't be silly. It's not the toilet or not having a shower. You forget where I grew up.'

'What is it then?'

'Nothing.' She gave him the flask. 'Except that I know more about places like this than you do. This isn't the African veld. This is the coast of China – in case you hadn't noticed.'

'It's the east coast of Hong Kong.' He tried to make her look at him but she walked away. Rayner let her go, wondering again what the hell was wrong with her.

It was his own fault, he thought. Although in the dark, the village was far less friendly than it had been at sunset, he knew that wasn't the problem. It was her refusal to accept his theory about the junk. This morning he'd endeavoured to make sure she understood the trip was a long-shot, but that was before they'd travelled thirty miles up the coast– before he too had begun to lose confidence.

So what should he do tomorrow? Rayner wondered, if nothing had happened by then and she held him to his promise.

He poured himself some coffee before going to join her under the awning, intending to lay the groundwork for a possible change in plan. But before he could speak, she was on her feet, pointing into the darkness.

'There's a boat.' She pointed again. 'Over there. I saw it.'

'For Christ's sake, take it easy,' he said. 'This is a fishing village. Three-quarters of the people out here live on their boats. It's probably just someone coming home in a dinghy.'

'It was bigger than a dinghy.' She seized his arm. 'Mark, I don't feel right about us being here.'

By now Rayner was ready to take her seriously. Straining his eyes, he scanned the water off the starboard bow, searching for ripples or for any sign of a passing boat.

He was still looking when there was the muffled sound of something bumping against the hull. A second later, as if from nowhere, the figures of two men appeared on the deck of the sampan. Four other men clambered over the side. They stood in a row under the awning.

'I told you.' Cristabel tightened her grip on Rayner's arm. 'Mark, I told you.'

Warily Rayner turned to face their visitors. 'Hi there,' he said. 'What can I do for you?'

There was no answer.

'Find out what they want,' he said quietly. 'Ask them in Chinese.'

She spoke to them, still holding on to him, her voice wavering as they made their move.

Rayner was half prepared, but they were quick and surefooted, and there were too many of them.

They rushed him – small wiry men – shadows coming at him two at a time. He kicked one of them in the groin and rammed his elbow backwards hard into the stomach of a man behind him. But, outnumbered, fighting in the dark, Rayner knew how slim his chances were.

In desperation he tried to grab a length of chain, only to trip, lose his grip on Cristabel and see her dragged away.

Shouting at her to jump, he lashed out at what he thought was the face of an assailant. It was a rifle butt, being swung by a man to his left. Rayner felt his fingers crack. At the same time he was driven to his knees by a blow to the head.

On all fours, believing he could still make it over the side, he gathered his strength. Then he started crawling.

Five

Overnight, one wall of the room had become so cold that beads of ice had formed on it. Since the sun had come up, the ice had started to thaw, but Rayner was still not yet thirsty enough to risk drinking from the puddle of water on the floor.

He used some of the water to wash the blood out of his hair, then held his injured hand against the wall, letting the coldness drain away the pain. When his fingers were numb he went again to the window and looked out through the grating.

On the beach, the torpedoes were being unpacked, two gleaming stainless steel cylinders resting one behind the other on the sand. They were longer than he'd expected them to be, but much more slender. And they had fins, short, stubby vanes protruding from their bodies like the control surfaces of a guided missile.

Last night in the dark, when Rayner had heard the winch grinding to pull them out of the water, he hadn't been sure how many of them there were or what they looked like, but this morning in bright sunshine, he could pick out every detail. He could see the towing eyes, the rear hatches lying beside the sealing gaskets, and he could see plastic tubes being slid out of the torpedo nearest to him.

Not far from his window, stacked on the concrete apron in front of the building, was the confirmation of his theory:.a growing heap of tusks sitting beside a half a dozen of the empty plastic tubes. In different circumstances Rayner would have welcomed the proof to show his theory had been right. Instead it meant nothing. Sick with worry about Cris and in considerable pain from his hand, he could think only of the need to somehow or other keep a hold on his nerve.

Men had brought him here from the sampan shortly before midnight. Since then, locked in the tiny room with its one cold wall, he'd been left completely alone without either food or drink. Twice he had been forced to urinate on the floor, and although he was less dizzy from whatever it was that had smashed him round the head, Rayner had no illusions about the seriousness of his predicament.

Going to the door, he inspected the lock again, trying to push aside the cottonwool inside his head. The door was made of steel and, as far as he could determine, impossible to open from the inside without a welding torch or a fairly large amount of high explosive.

He returned to the window, nursing his hand while he watched more tusks being removed from their protective plastic tubes. The tubes were black, shrink-wrapped in a clear film, and seemed to contain variable quantities of ivory. There were all kinds of tusks, some quite small, others that had been sawn in half to make them fit, and even a few short sections, each piece packaged in a bed of polystyrene beads. Although he'd noticed that beads were being stored in a fifty gallon drum, and seen how carefully the tubes were being handled, it wasn't until now that he realized why.

The torpedoes were not returning empty. On the apron, men were beginning to repack the tubes with a different commodity altogether.

The ache in his hand temporarily forgotten, Rayner looked out into the bay.

The backload for the torpedoes was coming from the little lighter they'd seen yesterday. It was in shallow water close to the beach, moored alongside a floating landing-stage that was serving as a platform for the men who were unloading the cargo.

There were ten or more workers, small Chinese men bent double under the weight of the wooden boxes they carried on their backs. They were bringing the boxes up the beach, lowering them on to the apron beside the tusks.

To make sure he wasn't imagining the whole thing, Rayner watched one of the boxes being opened, seeing how each gun was taken out individually still wrapped in its protective paper before it was inspected and the magazine removed. He knew exactly what kind of guns they were – Chinese copies of the AK47 military assault rifle – inexpensive, but highly prized copies of a weapon used by half the terrorists in the world.

If he hadn't understood before, he understood now. What he was witnessing was the real extent of Kabinda's business network. Not just ivory from Angola to Hong Kong. Not just the odd diamond from the Cuango River to Antwerp. This was something else – something he'd never considered – guns for the MPLA in Angola, guns for the National Patriotic Liberation Front in Liberia, for the rebels and guerrillas in Namibia, or for anyone who had the money to buy them.

Rayner started counting, watching the rifles being packed into the tubes twenty at a time before a cushion of polystyrene beads was added and the lids of the tubes were refitted. To guard against leakage, the men were using hot wax to reseal the tubes, melting a thick bead of it around the join. The operation was quick, simple and damn near foolproof, Rayner thought, a way of shipping guns into Africa that was as easy as shipping ivory into Hong Kong.

Already he had a rough idea of how many rifles were involved – somewhere around four or five hundred in each torpedo, he calculated – perhaps as many as a thousand for the consignment, a nice round figure, and a nice way for Kabinda to maximize the profit of the *Coloane*'s return voyage to Angola or Zaire.

Because of their weight, the tubes were being transported down to the beach on sleds. It took six men to haul a sled over the sand, but only three to slide a tube into the waiting torpedo. By nine o'clock, with all the ivory unloaded, Rayner estimated that more than twenty people were working to bring the rifles ashore from the lighter, repack the tubes and refill the torpedoes with their new cargo.

He continued to watch until he was forced back to the wall to freeze his hand. But the wall was warmer. Because the overall temperature in the room was rising? he wondered. Or because someone had switched off the refrigeration unit next door? It was some hours ago that he'd concluded the building was a fish processing plant. As well as smelling powerfully of fish oil and offal, he was almost certain that the cell shared a wall with an adjoining cold store. Rayner could also hear the constant drone of a diesel engine operating somewhere, a noise he thought was probably the source of the electric power needed to drive the winch and run the refrigeration unit.

Studying his fingers again he saw that three of them were

swollen now, one quite badly. Whether they were broken or dislocated, he didn't know. Either way, his right hand was damn near useless, a serious hindrance if he was going to escape – if indeed escape was possible at all. The room was utterly bare, with no light, no furniture – nothing with which he could attempt to force the grating out of the window.

Because the sun on the corrugated iron roof was making the room uncomfortably warm, he sat on the floor where it was cooler, thinking about Cris, wondering where she was and whether she was all right. How he had ever come to put her in this position, Rayner couldn't imagine. By underestimating the risk of tailing the junk, he had done what he'd promised himself he wouldn't do again. After Angola and Felix, and after the episode at the cottage where Wendy could have easily been killed, bringing Cris with him on the sampan had been plain stupid – another example of his inability to understand what he was dealing with. Weeks ago Janson had tried to tell him, tried to warn him. He hadn't listened then, and because of it, he had ended up here, discovering again what he should have known all along – Kinshasa Copper wasn't an African trading organization making money on the side by exporting ivory. Kinshasa Copper was big time, with links into South Africa, the US, Hong Kong, and with a line in automatic assault rifles that could stretch from Lagos to Cape Town.

But sitting on the floor feeling sorry for himself wasn't going to solve the problem, Rayner decided. And it wasn't adding a hell of a lot to his knowledge of the Kinshasa Copper ivory operation either.

Using the memory of Cristabel being dragged across the deck of the sampan to combat the pain in his fingers, he forced himself to go back to the grating.

The sun was still climbing, shining into his eyes and reflecting off the concrete. In the harsher light of morning, the village was no longer the fairy-tale village of yesterday evening. The houses were dilapidated with flaking paint and broken windows, while out in the bay many of the fishing boats were equally run-down. Even the sampans were rough, some of them looking barely seaworthy. Not a fishing village at all, Rayner thought, but a labour base for the building in which he was imprisoned.

For the next hour and a half he remained at the window, observing the activity outside until the working party started to disperse. Only a few men were busy now, tightening the last bolts on the hatches of the torpedoes or pulling empty sleds back to the building. At the landing-stage the lighter was preparing to leave, but it had one more job to do.

Rayner saw water boiling from its stern as it began to drag the torpedoes off the beach. They disappeared from sight like two seals sliding into the grey-green water, ready now for the junk to take over the task of towing them back to the *Coloane* in Kowloon.

By midday the operation was over. Once the cable had been transferred, Rayner watched the lighter head off to the north-east, leaving the junk to sail south, moving so slowly at first that it almost appeared to be standing still. Soon, all that remained to show what had taken place were skid marks in the sand, a handful of polystyrene beads and some pieces of plastic film blowing around the concrete apron.

In the sweltering heat of his cell, Rayner was drenched in sweat, leaning back against a wall that was now only a few degrees cooler than the air around him. Because he was beginning to dehydrate, he knew that if he continued to be imprisoned he would have to spend half the night licking or chipping ice off the wall in order to keep up his strength.

Despite conditions in the room, he had somehow managed to persuade himself that things were getting better. Over the last couple of hours, as the temperature had climbed to what he guessed was well over ninety degrees, his headache had eased. His hand too was less painful, still swollen and tender, but bearable providing he didn't try to use it. Even the pool of urine in the corner had evaporated, although the smell was as bad as ever.

Rayner had no intention of adding to the pool. Nor had he any intention of spending another night in the same circumstances. Cut off from Cristabel, neither knowing where she was nor how she was, he knew he had to find her and find her quickly.

He spent the afternoon considering the few options he had, deliberately discounting the possibility that he would be left alone in his cell for much longer. If they were going to kill him, Rayner reasoned, they wouldn't have bothered to lock him up. And if they weren't going to kill him, eventually someone would have to open the door.

The opportunity to find out if he was right came sooner than he expected – shortly after a game fishing boat had dropped anchor half a mile off shore and a launch had swung into the bay to draw up alongside the landing-stage.

There were two men on board the launch, one wearing a singlet and shorts, the other dressed in a dark business suit.

The man in the suit disembarked at once, passing only a few feet from the grating on his way by, but without looking up at it. Five minutes later, Rayner heard the sound of a key in the doorlock.

A young, sullen-looking Chinese guard entered the room first. In one hand he carried a chair, in the other he held a small, short-barrelled machine-pistol. Behind him was the man in the suit. He came in leaving the door ajar, wrinkling his nose in distaste at the smell of stale sweat and dried-up urine.

Rayner waited while the man removed his jacket and sat down on the chair. He too was Chinese, in his late forties, running to fat and with grey hair thinning at his temples.

'My name is Wu Kinwah,' he said. 'I believe you are the American who has been working in Africa. Is that correct?'

'What's it to you?' Rayner said.

'Mr Rayner, I have little time and I have no desire to waste it in bantering with you. There are some questions I should like you to answer. I suggest we conduct this conversation on a civilized level.'

'I've got some questions too,' Rayner said. 'If you want to be civilized you'd better let me see Cris.'

Wu smiled slightly. 'Let me explain something to you. Unlike me, you come from a western culture where personal freedom is valued, and where the lives of individuals are regarded as being important. Here, on the edge of the Chinese mainland, values are different. You must understand that in Hong Kong, neither you nor Miss Castela are of any significance either to me or to the operation of Kinshasa Copper.'

'Well that's fine. We'll be on our way then.'

'Mr Rayner, I have a job to do which requires me to acquire certain information. If I fail to obtain it from you, I shall obtain it from elsewhere. I am afraid that if you believe the unexplained disappearance of two Europeans in this part of the world is of any more consequence than the loss of Miss Castela's sister in Central Africa, then you are mistaken. Furthermore, if you continue to be flippant, I shall assume you are unwilling to co-operate. Is that clear?'

It could hardly have been put more clearly, Rayner thought. 'What do you want to know?' he said.

'Where are the prints and negatives from Osterman?'

'Somewhere safe.'

'And the copies you made?' Wu put the tips of his fingers together.

'I didn't make any copies.'

'Where is your friend Ross Janson at present?'

'He's not a friend of mine. I don't know where he is.'

'I see.' Wu stood up and put on his jacket.

'Hang on.' Rayner's heart was beating faster. 'I want to know about Cris.'

'Why do you?'

'Because it's part of my goddamn culture,' Rayner said. 'Why do you think?'

'I think you lie unconvincingly, Mr Rayner. You see, we are aware that both Castela sisters were employed by the World Organization for the Protection of Endangered Species. And, of course, we know you have given the photographs to WOPES in New York. By pretending otherwise you have persuaded me that I should regard everything you say with suspicion. Consequently I can see no point in prolonging our conversation.'

Rayner knew he was out of his depth. Wu was clearly annoyed and apparently prepared to leave almost before he'd got here.

'Look,' Rayner said. 'If you know about WOPES, you know Cris isn't going to be a problem. She's in the wildlife business, for Christ's sake. She doesn't know anything about ivory smuggling or arms deals. All she's trying to do is save elephants.'

'Like her sister,' Wu remarked caustically. 'Come come, Mr Rayner.'

'She's nothing like her sister. Just let her go. You'll have scared her witless already. She'll be too damn frightened to tell anyone anything.'

'Your argument is naive. It also overlooks the commercial nature of our business. My African colleagues learned a great deal from their Cuban friends, Mr Rayner. In the right market, Miss Castela has a financial value which we would be foolish to ignore or waste. Once this value has been confirmed by our associates in Thailand, or recognized by a buyer from one of the Arab states where the colour of her skin and the proportions of her upper body are less important, I can assure you she will not be a problem to us.'

To prevent himself from moving, Rayner rammed his damaged fingers into the wall behind his back. 'You do that,' he said, 'and I'll see you burn in hell – you and Kabinda.'

Wu sat down again and lit a cigarette. 'Why not see if you can persuade me to adopt a more sensitive approach to the problem of the girl?'

'How did you know I took the pictures in Lunda Norte?' Rayner spoke with difficulty.

'Do not be stupid. There are few secrets among the *garimpeiros* on the diamond fields, and Kinshasa Copper is a very large organization.'

'For Christ's sake,' Rayner said. 'The goddamn photos can't be that important. Not important enough to kill Felix Osterman and have me followed back to the States.'

Wu blew out a stream of smoke. 'The new administration in Luanda is ineffective, but if provoked sufficiently by the UN or a foreign government they could perhaps choose to interfere in our Angolan activities. Why should we not take steps to prevent such an occurrence?'

'By killing people?' Rayner said. 'You're out of your mind.'

Wu smiled again. 'Kinshasa Copper has investments in many countries. In two years it will be the most successful African-based and African-funded company in Zaire. And that, Mr Rayner, comes from the application of European business techniques in an African environment. No one is out of their mind. Quite the reverse. Now, do you have anything which you wish to say to me?'

'I can get the prints and negatives back from WOPES.' Rayner paused, searching for ways to make the lies sound more plausible. 'And you can have the copies I made for myself. I don't give a damn how successful Kinshasa Copper is or what business you're in. You can supply guns to half of Africa for all I care. And if you want to find Ross Janson, I can tell you where he is. He's in Cape Town staying with friends.'

'This is in exchange for the freedom of Miss Castela, I presume.' Wu met Rayner's eyes. 'Is that the arrangement you are suggesting?'

'I'll tell you what I'm suggesting once I know she's safe.'

'I see.' Wu rose to his feet. He handed the chair to the guard and spoke to him briefly in Chinese.

'Well?' Rayner said.

'I have another appointment.'

'Hold on a second.' Rayner tried to moderate his voice. 'What did you just say – to your friend here with the gun?'

Wu crushed his cigarette under the sole of his shoe before he spoke. 'I told him we have no further use for you. Goodbye, Mr Rayner.'

The reprieve, if it was a reprieve, could end at any time. Rayner had half expected to be shot where he stood. Instead, the steel door had clanged shut in his face, leaving him alone to consider a future over which he had no control.

That had been five long hours ago, but still not long enough for him to come to terms with what he believed was probably an order of execution. Why Wu had come here at all, Rayner couldn't understand. Nor could he imagine sweating more hours away in the cell waiting for the door to open again. What little confidence he'd had was gone, his hand was worse, and on top of everything, there was the awful question of Cris. For the moment, though, the only question that mattered was whether or not he could buy his way out of this, a question he knew could only have one answer if he was going to find her before she was taken from the building.

So he would have both hands free, and not have to reach into his pocket for the diamond, he removed his shoe and prised the smallest one from the cavity in the heel. He put it in his mouth, endeavouring to generate some saliva by rolling it around with his tongue while he rehearsed his speech again.

He was still sucking on the diamond when out in the bay there was the sound of voices and the noise of an engine being started.

Guessing that the launch was about to depart, he went to the grating. Although the sun was nearly gone, in the fading light he could see people in the cockpit. There were three of them – the man in the singlet who was casting off, Wu sitting on the transom lighting a cigarette, and beside him, staring back over her shoulder as the launch began to move away – Cristabel.

Spitting out the diamond, Rayner started shouting her name at the top of his voice, waving at the grating until the launch was no more than a red dot on a red horizon. Again, everything was the same colour, the same blood-red hue that it had been twenty-four hours ago when the sampan had first rounded the headland. But tonight there was no magic in the colour, and Rayner wasn't looking at a painting. He was looking at the last thing he wanted to see – the confirmation that he had failed Cris as thoroughly as he had failed her sister.

His despair was short-lived. The grinding of a key in the lock gave him just enough warning to prepare himself.

It was the guard, his face expressionless, standing in the open doorway holding the machine-pistol levelled at Rayner's chest.

'Do you speak English?' Rayner said.

'You come now.'

'Where are we going?'

'You come.'

'How about a deal?' Rayner took his hands out of his pockets.

The guard motioned with his gun.

'Take a look at this.' Rayner spat the diamond out into the palm of his left hand. 'This is an uncut Angolan diamond,' he said. 'A good one. I know you can take it anyway, but I can make you a better offer. Fix it so I can get back to the city, and you'll be a rich man. There are ten more of these waiting for you at my hotel.'

'You steal from Kabinda, yes?' The guard was uncertain, shifting his weight from one foot to another.

'Sure,' Rayner said. 'And from the ivory poachers. This baby's worth around twenty thousand Hong Kong dollars. Here.' He held out his hand.

The guard shook his head.

'Why not?' Rayner said. 'You're going to wind up with it one way or the other, aren't you?'

'You have more?' The man took the diamond cautiously, holding it up to what was left of the light filtering through the grating.

'I've already told you I have.' Rayner knew the idea wasn't going to work. Even in good light the diamond was unimpressive, nothing more than a glass bauble. He could remember his own reaction when he'd first seen one.

'Why should I believe this?'

'You don't have to. All you have to do is get me out to a

sampan. You can come with me to the hotel. Who the hell's going to know?' Rayner could feel the sweat running down inside his shirt. He was going to have to risk his injured hand – very soon – while the guard was still considering the offer.

'There is a man in Sai Wan. I ask him if this one is OK.'

Rayner stopped breathing, waiting for the right moment. He was almost too slow, nearly missing the only chance he was going to get.

Putting the diamond into the pocket of his jacket, the guard looked down.

Rayner hit the barrel of the gun so hard that it felt as though his hand had come off. The muzzle swung sideways, then up. At the same time, the heel of Rayner's left hand caught the man beneath the chin, slamming his head back against the door.

The door began to close. To prevent it from shutting completely, Rayner threw himself forwards, trying unsuccessfully to take the guard with him.

Unbalanced, Rayner was fighting now, only just managing to twist the muzzle of the gun away from him before the man got his finger back on the trigger.

The first bullets hit the wall, spattering fragments of lead into Rayner's face. But it wasn't the lead that terrified him, it was the noise, a dreadful shattering burst of sound that seemed to come from somewhere inside his head.

To escape a second burst, he wrenched on the barrel with all his might, tearing the gun free.

It wasn't over. The guard was young and fit, and he was scared. He came in crouched so low that if the gun had gone off it would have taken half his head away.

Rayner didn't fire. He used a foot, kicking the door into the guard's face.

Again the door began to swing. But on this occasion, Rayner was ready, standing not inside, but outside the room.

For a second, through the gap, there was a glimpse of a man with his cheek split open. Then the door slammed shut, leaving Rayner standing alone in a narrow corridor. He ran, knowing that if he'd chosen the wrong direction he could just as easily be trapped again.

At the end of the corridor was another door. It was open, leading into a large storeroom housing some machinery and some lengths of rusty steel racking. Behind him men were shouting to each other.

To his left lay the sea. He could see it through a window. But to his right was a better option: a wooden ramp connecting the storeroom to the outside world.

He hit the ramp awkwardly skidding on a slick of fish oil as a single shot rang out. Whether the skid saved him, Rayner didn't know. He knew only that somehow he had to make it to the trees.

Holding the machine-pistol in his good hand, he started to weave, heading away from the building over a dangerously open area of grassland.

There were two more shots, the bullet from the second one screaming off the ground somewhere near his shoe. Relying on the poor light, Rayner straightened up, sprinting the last few yards to safety.

For a minute he stayed in the protection of the trees, listening and watching for signs of pursuit while he struggled to regain his breath. He could detect nothing until some lights came on in the building making it easier for him to see the figures creeping towards him.

Six or seven men, Rayner decided, approaching warily because they'd guessed he had the gun.

To the west of the village, a dull glow in the sky told him it would soon be dark. Which meant that, unless he was stupid enough to try swimming out to the sampan, it would be much harder for anyone to run him down.

He left the trees, travelling inland away from the sea, away from the sampan and away from what he believed was the only chance he had of reaching the *Coloane* before it sailed with Cristabel on board.

From his lookout on the foothills of Sharp Peak, the water of the high island reservoir was shimmering in the sunlight like a mirror. Further away to the south, the sea was a different colour, more green than blue, stretching away into a dirty morning haze. Rayner could see fishing boats too, dozens upon dozens of them, trailing their wakes across the bays and inlets around the coastline.

Unlike yesterday, apart from the game fishing launch which was still moored in the bay off Sai Wan, there were no freighters or container ships anchored near the island. More importantly, there were no men on the track leading to the village. Because they'd given up? Rayner wondered. Or because they were going to try something else?

He stood up, searching again for a tell-tale dust cloud that would indicate the presence of a vehicle on a road somewhere. For three days he'd been looking, unwilling until this morning to believe there was no overland access to this section of the coast.

There were no roads. Villages, footpaths, tracks and trails, but no roads and no cars or trucks. And because there were none, if he was to get away, he would either have to walk out or he would have to requisition a boat.

Whatever he decided to do, Rayner knew he had to do it today. Even if the men from the village had abandoned the hunt, giving him more freedom to move in daylight, he could not continue to live like this. The search for food was consuming more energy than he was getting from the odd egg he could manage to steal from hen houses in the outlying villages, and unless he resorted to more ambitious means of acquiring provisions, Rayner knew his strength would not hold up.

In any other circumstances his position would have been laughable, he thought. In Africa, hundreds of miles from anywhere, he could have survived for months. Yet here, surrounded by villages and settlements, he was being forced to exist on dirty stream water, eggs and fish heads. He decided that the comparison was unfair. In Africa, for most of the time, no one had been trying to kill him, and in Africa there had been no need to worry about how tightly-knit the community might be in any particular part of the country.

While he was considering whether to risk another attempt to reach the sea he saw he'd been wrong about the search parties. At least one of them was out after all, starting later than they had done on previous mornings and with fewer men, but unmistakably a group he'd seen before. The men were already fanning out from the end of the north-west track to disappear one by one into the scrub.

Knowing they were too far away to bother him, Rayner lay down on the grass. He was thirsty, hungry and in danger of thinking about Cristabel again. Usually it was at night that he had the trouble, a sense of hopelessness which made him break out in a sweat if he allowed himself to believe she was already trapped on board the freighter. Only by holding two separate images in his mind had he been able to pretend the worst would never happen. The first image was of the past, of one of the nights they'd spent together. The second image was of an imagined event yet to take place either in Hong Kong or at some other foreign port where the *Coloane* was berthed. The scene was always the same – of Cris leaving the freighter, running toward him down a gangway to safety.

This morning the images didn't work. After three days in the New Territories, Rayner knew that believing he could save her, was probably as much of a fantasy as the trick he was using to keep himself going. In real life it depended on whether the *Coloane* had sailed. And, if it had, on how much longer it was going to be before he could telephone Lynch and contact the US Embassy.

He rubbed his finger over the gun, wiping away the corrosion where the salt air and the sweat from his hand had begun to rust the metal. It was an old 9mm Uzi with a folding steel stock, a good survival gun, Rayner thought, if the magazine hadn't been half empty and if he could have held the damn thing properly.

Spreading his fingers out in front of him on the grass, he inspected his hand again. As a result of his struggle with the guard, two of the fingers seemed to have improved. Compared with the bad one that was so painful he couldn't move it, his first and third fingers were straighter and less swollen. Because they were no longer dislocated? he wondered. Was it even possible that his second finger wasn't broken either?

Gingerly he put it through the Uzi's trigger guard and started twisting the barrel sideways. He was trying to summon the courage to increase the pressure when the ground exploded in his face.

Less than a second later the crack of a rifle told him where to look. A tiny puff of smoke gave away the gunman's position. He was hidden on a ridge above the tree line, six or seven hundred yards away to the south-east.

Spitting out a mouthful of dirt, Rayner was already on the move, running diagonally across the slope, cursing himself for being so careless. This was new; a long-distance sniping instead of armed men patrolling the beaches and the trails; a fresh approach to solve the problem of him holding the high ground with a short-range weapon.

He heard no further shots and saw no more puffs of smoke – either because the sniper had gone to ground, or because he'd gone altogether. Rayner didn't know which. But if the man had left, where the hell was he now? And was he in radio contact with someone else?

Crouching in the shelter of some rocks, Rayner scanned the hillside, searching for flattened grass, a glint of sunlight off the lens of a telescopic sight or the movement of a gun barrel.

Except for a lone seagull circling high above the ridge, there was nothing. The hills were empty, brown and green slopes so bare that if the sniper was still there Rayner should have been able to see him as easily as he could see the seagull.

It was a trap, he decided, designed to drive him in the most obvious direction – inland, towards the cover of the nearest rocks. Which meant he had made a mistake and that there was another gunman closer to him.

Still watching the ridge, Rayner started retracing his steps. He walked backwards, holding the Uzi with the muzzle high in case the second sniper was concealed on the slope above him.

Half-way to the lookout he saw part of the hillside move. The man was in a trench, almost perfectly camouflaged, exposing only his head while he did something to his sights.

This time Rayner took off straight downhill, trusting to speed and the increasing range to keep him alive.

Two rifles fired together. But he was flying now, putting more distance between him and the snipers with every second. He started counting yards, imagining the sights centred on his back, waiting for another bullet. It came late, zipping past his hip to carve a furrow in the ground ahead of him. From the closeness of it he knew it was better than a lucky shot. It was a shot from someone who even at this range might just be good enough to try again.

Fifty yards further on, Rayner's legs gave out. He slowed to a walk, urging himself on toward the remnants of a low stone wall.

Once he reached it he looked back. Above the ridge one of the snipers was standing up, his rifle held loosely in his hand. As if to acknowledge failure, he waved before disappearing to become part of the hillside again.

Slumped behind the wall with his eyes full of soil and sweat, Rayner was exhausted. Still in open country, still exposed to danger – particularly if there were more snipers elsewhere – he had no idea of what to do.

When he had recovered his breath he rammed the Uzi under his belt behind his back, then began to slither away in line with the wall, crawling downhill on his stomach. It took him nearly ten minutes to traverse sixty or seventy yards to the head of a scrub-filled gully. By then he was fairly certain there would be no more shots, and more confident about his position.

In the gully it was cooler. Because sunlight filtering through the leaves was casting a pattern of natural camouflage on the grass he also felt safer. But it wasn't camouflage or trees that he needed, Rayner thought. There were too many damn people hunting for him, men who were so familiar with the surroundings that they'd guessed what he would do and where he would go in his search for a road out. What he needed was to get the hell away from this part of the countryside altogether.

He used the gully for protection, half walking and half sliding down it until the ground flattened out on to the floor of a valley. To his right now, Rayner could see the sea again. Although it was closer than he'd expected it to be, he was reluctant to believe his luck had changed. He made his decision without thinking, knowing that his choice was equally likely to be right as it was to be wrong. Either he would find a boat or he wouldn't, and his luck would either improve or remain as lousy as it had been over the last two days.

Holding the Uzi in his left hand he started off toward the coast, keeping in the shade whenever he could, pausing to listen from time to time in case one of the search parties was active in the area.

It was past eleven o'clock when he arrived at the valley mouth. In front of him was the beach, a deserted sweep of yellow sand with a few houses standing at the north end where the scrub and grassland extended down to the water's edge. He counted five boats. They were tied up at a more than normally dilapidated landing-stage, floating in a patch of oil and dead seaweed above thirty yards off shore.

Further east, the sea-lanes were busier than they had been earlier. Two empty lighters were travelling south one behind the other; there was an ocean-going freighter steaming in the same direction and he could see numerous fishing boats working about a mile out from the headland to his right. The game fishing launch was underway too, cruising at its usual slow speed, trailing lines from twin cabin-mounted rods.

Keeping his eyes on the houses and on the landing-stage,

Rayner walked down on to the damp sand left by the retreating tide. He thought that two of the boats looked promising, one of them in particular, a twenty footer with a vertical exhaust stack and fresh green paint on the hull. Better still, there was someone on board, a man mending a net which was draped over the stern.

To avoid creating alarm, Rayner stuck the Uzi inside his shirt before he headed up the beach. Walking at an easy pace, he followed the high waterline, wondering how many of the houses were occupied and whether he should try offering his second diamond to the boat owner rather than scaring him by producing the Uzi straight away.

About 200 yards from the houses, Rayner made a final check, looking over his shoulder to make sure that the beach was still deserted. It wasn't. Men were spilling out of the valley – armed men – starting to run now they could see him.

Rayner didn't wait to see how many there were. He sprinted for the landing-stage, hearing the rifles open up behind him.

Although the fisherman on the boat had seen him, more immediate trouble was coming from somewhere else – from the sea – from the game-fishing launch. Travelling in a curve at the head of a ten-foot rooster-tail of spray, it was picking up speed as it approached the shore.

Rayner knew he had to buy some time. Bullets were burying themselves in the sand all around him, driving him to take shelter behind one of the houses. He lay on his back and made himself transfer the Uzi to his right hand. Then he rolled over and fired a single burst along the beach.

The men scattered, but kept coming, moving more cautiously until he hit the sand again, running as fast as he was able out on to the landing-stage.

Half-way along it, he fired another burst in the general direction of the beach before he swivelled round to confront the launch. It was on top of him, closing too swiftly for Rayner to follow it with the muzzle. He squeezed the trigger anyway, holding it back until the Uzi's magazine was empty.

More bullets smacked into the woodwork beside him. Simultaneously the launch ploughed into the centre of the landing-stage, splintering it to pieces.

Only the flimsiness of the structure saved Rayner from losing his footing as a whole section of the landing-stage disintegrated. Still the launch came on, smashing its way through a mass of shattered wooden slats and bamboo poles.

Just before the hull broke free, at the last moment Rayner grabbed at the cabin rail, hauled himself on board and hurled the Uzi into the face of the man in the cockpit. The gun missed, bouncing harmlessly off the windshield. At the same time the launch began to swing toward the shore.

But instead of beaching it on the sand, the man spun the boat into a turn, heading for the open sea.

'Hey stupid,' he yelled. 'Keep your fucking head down. We're still in range.'

It was Janson, braced against the gunwhale, gripping the wheel in both hands. On his face he wore a huge grin.

Six

Rayner turned the shower control onto cold, and redirected the water on to his face. The change in temperature had no effect. He still felt dull, and he knew the let-down was beginning to take hold. Until now it hadn't been too bad, but staying in the shower trying to make sense of everything had been a mistake. Wondering if Janson was going to be more forthcoming than he had been so far, Rayner turned off the water, wrapped a towel round his waist, and wandered out into the other room.

The South African was busy on the phone. On the table in front of him stood a line of beer cans, two packets of cigarettes and a large number of empty peanut packets. As soon as he saw Rayner he put down the receiver.

'Well?' Rayner said.

Janson shook his head. 'Like pulling teeth,' he said. 'I've just been talking to some prick who wanted to know why I wanted to know. You'll have to try something else.'

'If the port authorities know when the *Coloane* sailed, why the hell don't they know where it's going?' Rayner helped himself to a can of beer.

'Because it's none of their business. The freighter's not registered in Hong Kong, and it's not owned by Kinshasa Copper – not officially anyway.'

Rayner sat down at the table and took a long drink. He hadn't anticipated this. On the way back in the launch, in between shouting questions at Janson, he'd tried to convince himself that the *Coloane* could still be at the wharf. Discovering that it wasn't had been bad enough, but learning that the freighter would be hard to trace was something he hadn't expected. Another miscalculation, he thought, to add to all the others.

'What about the junk?' he said.

'What about it?' Janson lit a cigarette. 'How many Chinese junks do you think there are in Hong Kong? Look, you're too strung out to think straight. You don't even know she's on board the *Coloane*. The bastards could've taken her anywhere.'

'For Christ's sake,' Rayner said. 'I've told you where she's being taken.'

'Well, you've got it wrong. Wu might kill her, but he's not going to trade her. I guarantee it. He's not that stupid, nor is Kabinda. It's too dangerous for them. Wu was just using her to squeeze information out of you.'

Rayner used his uninjured left hand to crush the beer can. 'So where is she?'

'I don't know. But there's a hell of a difference between transporting black Angolans to Cuba, and shipping a European woman to Saudi or somewhere. You don't understand how Kabinda does business – I do.'

'I don't understand what you're doing in Hong Kong.' Rayner looked at him. 'Are you going to tell me what this is all about, or not? I don't want to sit here in your hotel room wasting time if you're going to carry on pretending this is just some kind of coincidence.'

Janson grinned. 'You don't have a choice. You're buggered. There's probably someone watching your hotel, you're so tired you can't keep your eyes open, and on top of that you don't know what you're doing. You're lucky to have got this far. Go off half-cocked again and you're going to be real dead. Take my word for it.'

'I'm not going to take your word for anything,' Rayner said. 'Not until I get some answers. Let's start with why you followed me to Hong Kong.'

'I didn't.' Janson dropped his cigarette into an empty beer can. 'Why the hell would I want to do that? Do you know what your trouble is? You think you're smarter than you are.'

'I'm smart enough to know you're not a diamond prospector. And you're not in the ivory business either, are you?'

Janson grinned again. 'You can have the whole story if you want – if you think you can keep awake long enough to listen.'

'I'm listening,' Rayner said. 'What about the food?'

'It's coming. I ordered while you were in the shower. Are

you sure you're OK?'

'I'm OK. I just want to know what's going on.' Rayner picked up another can of beer.

'Have you heard of the Afrikaner Resistance Movement? Or the Azanian Peoples Liberation Army?'

'South African terrorist groups?'

Janson nodded. 'The Afrikaner Resistance is an ultra-right paramilitary outfit. They were the people who gunned down Chris Hani in '93. He was the leader of the South African Communist Party, and one of the big names in the ANC. The Azanian Peoples Army is the military wing of the Pan-Africanist Congress. The Afrikaners are white, the Azanian Army are black, but they've both got one thing in common: they're half terrorists and half guerillas, pushing their own barrows, and pushing South Africa right up to the edge. No one likes them much – particularly people who believe that the country doesn't have to be the way it's been over the last twenty years or so.'

'And you're one of those people?' Rayner said.

'I guess so.' Janson lit another cigarette. 'If I wasn't, I suppose I wouldn't be here doing a job like this.'

'What job?'

'I work for SAMI – South African Military Intelligence. You didn't know that, did you?'

'Why didn't you tell me in Angola?' Rayner was only partly surprised.

'What sort of question is that? Some guy I've never seen before comes wandering out of nowhere with a rifle looking for information. What do you expect?'

Rayner didn't say anything. He waited for Janson to continue.

'If you'd take the time to think it through, you'd have got it figured out by now,' Janson said. 'This hasn't got anything to do with ivory – well, not much. This is major organized crime – run by the three directors of Kinshasa Copper – Kabinda, Wu and a guy called Victor Marle in Antwerp. They've found a way to bring Southern Africa screaming into the twenty-first century. You've already seen how.'

'I didn't know how until yesterday.' For the first time, Rayner had an idea of what might have brought Janson to Hong Kong. 'Are you after the guns?'

'Long story,' Janson grunted. 'I was sent to Lunda Norte way back in March, after a whole lot of Chinese-made AK47s started turning up in the hands of the Afrikaner Resistance Movement and the Azanian Army. We'd had our eye on Kabinda and Kinshasa Copper for a while, but we didn't know where the pipeline started. My brief was to watch Kabinda – to find out where he was buying the guns and trace the overland route he was using into South Africa. We figured the arms deals had something to do with Angolan ivory or diamonds – the rest of it we got wrong.'

'Because it wasn't an overland route, you mean?' Rayner said.

'We thought he'd be crazy to try ships. But that was before I saw those torpedo things yesterday.'

'If you didn't know about the torpedoes, what were you doing up the coast on a game fishing-launch? Why were you watching the village?'

'I wasn't watching the village,' Janson said. 'I was watching the guns. I've been waiting for them to come in from mainland China. I picked up on them a few days ago when they crossed the border into Hong Kong. Someone in Guanzhou told us what to look for, and when to look for it. I've been in Hong Kong for over three weeks, waiting. I got as far as seeing the boxes put on board that little lighter, then I had to borrow a boat in a hurry.'

Rayner understood now. 'So you followed the lighter,' he said.

Janson nodded. 'You were tracking ivory; I was tracking guns. If I'd guessed what was going on, I could've left the whole thing to you.'

'I was ahead of you.' Rayner managed a smile. 'Didn't you know about the freighter?'

'No, not until you told me on the way back here.'

'But you saw the torpedoes being loaded,' Rayner said. 'Why didn't you follow the junk when it towed them off the beach?'

'I was about to when your friend Wu turned up at the village – at least I figured that's who it was. I thought I'd hang around to see what he was up to. Then, of course, as soon as the bastard left, a whole lot of guns started going off. After that I decided I'd stay where the action was.'

'You could've done something when you saw Cris on the launch,' Rayner said. 'Instead of just watching Wu take her away.'

'How the hell was I supposed to know it was her? I don't

know what she looks like.'

'Yes you do,' Rayner said. 'She looks just like her sister.'

'The girl Kabinda shot, you mean? The pretty one with little tits?'

A knock on the door interrupted Rayner's reply. He finished his beer, waiting for Janson to tip the waiter and sign the bill.

'Help yourself.' Janson pushed the tray across the table. 'But leave the bacon sandwich. That's mine.'

Rayner could hardly bring himself to eat. Now the food was in front of him, he felt nauseous. He had also drunk too much beer.

'Are you happy now?' Janson attacked his sandwich. 'Have you got everything figured out?'

'What happened after I handed you over to that French doctor in Angola?' Rayner began to eat, chewing everything methodically before he swallowed.

'No big deal.' Janson unbuttoned his shirt to reveal a small, puckered scar on his belly. 'All I lost was a lot of blood. They pumped a couple of pints into me in Malanje and gave me an injection. There was a field hospital there – full of UNITA guerillas with their arms and legs missing – you know how it is in those places.'

'What about your diamonds?' Rayner spoke with his mouth full of fried chicken.

'Cost me a couple. I sold the rest here. Did you get the stones I sent to Felix?'

Rayner nodded. 'You know he's dead, don't you?'

'Yeah. It was pretty weird how I found out, though. Here I am sitting off Sai Wan in a borrowed boat looking through my binoculars at some poor bastard who's being hunted down in the hills, and I suddenly get this funny feeling I've seen him before.'

'I should've waved,' Rayner said.

'You didn't have to. But just to be sure, I got on the radio to these English friends of mine in Hong Kong and asked them to do some checking for me. They started by trying to contact Felix.'

'To see if he knew where I was?'

'Right.' Janson nodded. 'They spoke on the phone to some guy called Borger at De Beers who said Felix was dead. Borger gave us the number of a woman in the States who was supposed to know you.'

'And she told you I was here.' Rayner tried to picture Wendy talking on the phone to someone in Hong Kong.

'It wasn't that easy. She wasn't home – only her mother or someone. I'm not sure what the story is. It wasn't until the next day that we got a call back from the States.'

'From Wendy?' Rayner said.

'Yeah, I think so. She said you were working on an assignment for WOPES in Hong Kong, and that she had the name of your hotel on a letter you'd sent her. We didn't bother with the hotel. Soon as I heard you were in the neighbourhood I figured I wasn't dreaming after all.' Janson paused. 'Mind you, if I hadn't owed you a favour, I'd have left you where you were.'

Rayner smiled. 'And because I owe you fifteen thousand rand.'

'At least.' Janson finished his sandwich, wiping his mouth with the back of his hand. 'Who's Wendy?'

'A friend.'

'Like this Cristabel Castela is a friend?'

'Sort of.'

'But you're screwing both of them – depending on where you happen to be at the time?'

'It's not like that.' Rayner was too weary to explain.

'Tell me about this deal you've got with WOPES.'

'There isn't time,' Rayner said. 'I will later. I have to telephone New York and then see what the Embassy can do here.'

'Don't be bloody silly.' Janson passed him another can. 'It's four-thirty in the morning in New York, and the consulate is going to be closed by the time you've figured out what you're going to say to them.'

'I'll try anyhow.' Rayner wanted to get on with it.

'Wait until morning. Talk to me instead – in case there's something I can do overnight. Then you can get your head down while I make some calls.'

'I'm OK.' Rayner held up his hand. 'I've got this to keep me awake.'

Janson inspected it with interest. 'Bend your fingers,' he instructed. 'Curve them into mine – like this.'

Rayner winced, endeavouring to clench his fist.

'Shit.' Janson glanced at the door.

Too late, Rayner realized he'd been distracted. The crack of his fingers being wrenched out straight was accompanied by a bolt of pain shooting up his arm. He started swearing.

'Do you want some ice?' Janson asked.

Despite being able to move his second finger for the first time in days, Rayner was furious. 'It could've been broken,' he said.

'Sure. And I could still be in Lunda Norte and you could still be in Sai Wan.' Janson threw him a cushion. 'Now get some sleep. You can have the sofa. I'll wake you for breakfast.'

Breakfast would be too late, Rayner thought. Far too late. Another hundred or two hundred sea miles for the *Coloane* to sail on toward wherever it was going; another eight or ten hours to add to the three days he'd already wasted.

Intending to fetch the phone directory, he endeavoured to stand up, but found that the room had begun to spin. After failing on his second attempt he decided to wait for a few minutes. But by then, to his relief, he had discovered there was no need for him to call anyone. The *Coloane* had already berthed. And there, standing on deck at the head of the gangway with her sister on one side of her and Wendy on the other, Cris was waving at him.

The sunlight streaming through the window was already warm, reminding Rayner of the morning in his cell, when he'd watched the torpedoes being loaded.

He transferred the telephone to his other ear and contained his impatience. Either because Lynch was disguising his concern or because he didn't understand, it was hard to tell how much of his optimism was contrived.

'How long will it take?' Rayner asked.

There was a crackle on the line. 'I can't answer that,' Lynch said. 'Ask me after I've been in touch with Washington. What's the name of the ship again?'

'The *Coloane*.' Rayner spelt out the letters. 'Janson thinks it's headed for the coast of either Namibia or Angola. We don't know that for sure, though.'

'OK.' Lynch said. 'I'll see what I can do. Don't get your tail down. If Cris is on board, the minute we can get a fix on the ship we should be able to do something by radio to guarantee her safety. Is there anything else I need to know?'

'I don't think so.' Rayner took a cup of coffee that Janson passed to him. 'I'll check the warehouse here as soon as I can.'

'In case they've still got her in Hong Kong, you mean?' Lynch sounded doubtful. 'Do you think that's a good idea?'

'It's better than doing nothing. If you're going to talk to Washington, I don't have to contact the Embassy. I can have a look round while I'm waiting to hear back from you.'

'Are you sure you don't want to come home?' Lynch said. 'I can probably get you on a plane today.'

'I'm sure.'

'How do I get in touch?' The confidence was back in Lynch's voice.

'Hang on.' Rayner checked the number on the phone, but changed his mind. 'I don't know where I'll be,' he said. 'I'll call you in a couple of days at your office.'

'All right.' Lynch hesitated for a moment. 'Listen, Mark. I'm sorry as hell. If I'd had any idea things would turn out like this, I'd never have asked you to get involved. Should I arrange for some more money?'

'No,' Rayner said. 'Just find the freighter. I'm relying on you. So is Cris.' He put the phone down.

'I'd just as soon you hadn't mentioned me,' Janson said.

'Why?'

'No one except you knows who it was on that game-fishing boat. Now you've gone and told this guy Lynch.'

'Lynch is OK,' Rayner said. 'Anyway, so what? Your job's done, isn't it? You know how the guns are moved, and you know who's doing it.'

'Someone still has to stop the delivery, and stop another load from being shipped from somewhere else.' Janson lit his third cigarette of the morning. 'Lynch won't give two fucks about guns going into South Africa. Nor will his friends in Washington. My job's not over yet. Do you want to give me a hand to finish it?'

'No,' Rayner said. 'I've got something else to do.'

'You'd be better off leaving that alone.' Janson went to the coffee pot for a refill. 'Lynch told you she'll be OK. Let him sort it out. What can you do?

'Find somewhere safe to stay; talk to the local police; check out the Kinshasa Copper office; have a look at their warehouse at Hung Hom and tell the guy who I rented the sampan from where he can find it. I don't want him causing trouble.'

'Is that all?' Janson said caustically. 'You don't want to call Wu Kinwah to say you'd like to have lunch with him. It's time you woke up. You're not dealing with people who think the same way as you do. If you believe you can go head to head with these guys, you're crazy. Do you know what Kinshasa Copper is?'

'What?' Rayner said.

'It's the first African-based crime syndicate that there's ever been. And it isn't like anything else you've come across. These guys have Africanized what they've learned from the West, mixed it up with a few ideas from the Far East Triads and formed the equivalent of an African Mafia.'

Rayner was thinking of something Lynch had said to him in New York.

'What's the matter?' Janson said. 'Don't you believe me?'

'Sure I do. Lynch used the same words – when he was talking about Kabinda.'

'Lynch was guessing. I'm not.' Janson stubbed out his cigarette. 'How about I come along with you for the ride today?'

'I can manage, thanks.' Rayner held out his right hand and moved his fingers.

'Two good hands,' Janson said. 'And a head full of shit.'

Rayner was in no mood to argue. 'OK,' he said. 'We'll do my hotel first. Then we can pick up my rental car – if it's still there.'

'One more thing,' Janson said. 'Forget the police.'

'Why?'

'What are you going to tell them? That they've got ivory coming in to Hong Kong and guns going out. For a start you can bet they know already – and if they don't, what evidence have you got? No photos, no ivory, no guns.'

'And no Cris,' Rayner said. 'I don't care about the rest of it.'

'Well, you'd better start caring. Stop being so pig-headed.' Janson paused. 'There's something else as well.'

'What?'

'Unless you put on some clean clothes real soon, I'm not going anywhere with you. I can smell you from here. Is it a deal?'

'It's a deal,' Rayner said.

The girl behind the hotel desk recognized him at once. 'Well, there you are, Mr Rayner,' she said. 'Have you and Miss

Castela been away somewhere?'

'Three-day cruise.' Rayner made sure he didn't stand too close to her. 'Your name's Janine, isn't it?'

'That's right.' She smiled. 'Can I get your key for you?'

'Please.' He slid a credit card across the counter. 'I'm afraid we're checking out. Is it OK to charge our accounts to that while I go up and collect our luggage?'

'Of course. What room numbers are they again?'

'421 and 238.' He waited to see if she would hand over both keys.

'Here you go.' She gave them to him. 'I'll have everything ready by the time you come down.'

Rayner was relieved. 'Look,' he said, 'sorry to be a nuisance, but could you arrange to have this delivered for me?' He gave her an envelope addressed to the owner of the sampan. 'Put the charge on my account.'

'There'll be no charge, Mr Rayner.' She smiled again.

Rayner thanked her, then went to join Janson at the elevator.

'No trouble?' Janson said.

'Not so far.'

'I don't understand why you want to clean her room out.'

'She's not here to do it herself, is she?'

'Suppose someone's expecting you to call by?'

'Let's wait and see.' As well as being on edge, Rayner didn't want to talk about it.

The need for caution was unnecessary. Chamber-maids were pushing linen trolleys along the corridor, guests were vacating their rooms and there was a crowd of people waiting for the elevator.

The instant Rayner let himself into Cristabel's room he knew he shouldn't have come. Besides the lingering smell of perfume, everywhere there were reminders of her – her clothes, her handbag, the enamel WOPES badge she wore and the doll she'd bought one evening on the waterfront.

He started bundling things into a suitcase, ramming them in one on top of the other until all evidence of her having been here had been removed. He gave the case to Janson. 'Come on. I'll grab my stuff and then we can get going.'

In Rayner's room there were more reminders. Lying on the coffee table were the notes she'd brought from New York; a pair of her ear-rings were clipped onto the lampshade above the bed, and on top of the fridge where she'd left them stood the bag of strawberries and the empty honey carton. Rayner threw the bag and the carton into a rubbish bin, nearly tipping it over.

'Did you two really have something going?' Janson asked.

'I haven't ever met anyone like her before.' Rayner wasn't annoyed. Expecting Janson to comprehend was as unrealistic as believing the South African could imagine what it had been like to make love to her. Rayner wished he'd shut up.

'Did she know how her sister died?' Janson asked. 'Or did she get the story from you?'

'I told you. She saw the photos. Felix sent them to WOPES in New York. It was Felix who started off this whole mess.' Rayner stopped packing. 'How did he know you were in Angola?'

'I half-way told him before I went up there. He knew I worked for SAMI.' Janson took out his cigarettes but put the packet back in his pocket without opening it. 'I wonder if it was Felix who dropped you in the shit?'

'What do you mean?'

'Those goons who came after you in the States – who told them where you were?'

'Felix didn't know I'd be at Sandy Neck,' Rayner said. 'All he had was Wendy's phone number and her address.'

'Same thing.'

'OK. So it was Felix. What difference does it make?'

'It makes a lot of difference. Who told Kabinda you took those photos? Why did Kabinda believe Felix had the film?'

'I don't know.' Rayner had considered the question before, but without coming up with an answer that made any sense. 'Maybe your friend Charlie told him.'

'Charlie didn't know you were working for De Beers.'

To stop himself from thinking about Cristabel or Felix, Rayner made himself stop thinking altogether. He put on clean clothes, dropping his sweat-stained shirt and trousers in the rubbish bin to cover up the honey carton. Then he went to the lampshade, unclipped the ear-rings and put them in his pocket.

'All done?' Janson inquired.

'Yes.' Rayner stood on the lid of his case and flipped over the catches with his foot. 'Let's see if my car's still there.'

It was, parked in the basement lot where he'd left it, covered in a light film of dust. He waited while Janson opened the hood of the Toyota to check for surprises.

'You're paranoid,' Rayner said. 'How would Wu know I had a rental car?'

'How did he know you'd turn up at the village on a sampan?'

'Because someone saw us following the goddamn junk. Or because we were the only Europeans for five hundred square miles. I'll wear a disguise next time.'

Janson grinned. 'Next time don't take a girl with you.' He shut the hood. 'Do you want me to drive?'

'No, it's OK. I know where I'm going more or less.' Rayner slid behind the wheel and started the engine. He was anxious to be doing something instead of talking about it.

At the exit of the underground carpark he pushed the Toyota out into the traffic and forced himself to concentrate on his driving until they reached the Kinshasa Copper office in Sham Shui Pu. It was a small glass-fronted building sandwiched between two others.

'Not much to look at.' Janson wound down the car window. 'I suppose you want me to check it out.'

'Do you mind?'

'No.' Janson climbed out. 'I don't mind. Pick me up back here as soon as you see me.'

Although it took Janson the best part of fifteen minutes to complete his reconnaissance, the expression on his face told Rayner that they'd wasted their time.

'Are you certain?' Rayner said.

'I'm telling you. It's one room and a toilet. There isn't the space for anything else. Unless she's locked in the bathroom, she isn't there. I went into the buildings on both sides. One of them's a factory making plastic flowers, the other is some kind of mail order depot.'

'We'll try the warehouse, then.'

'Tonight,' Janson said. 'When we can do it properly. There're some things I have to see to – calling South Africa for a start. If you want to keep going you'd better drop me off.'

'Have you got any ideas?'

'Take a drive around the waterfront. You never know, you might just see Wu's launch tied up somewhere. It's a long shot, but what do you have to lose?'

Rayner was past considering what he had to lose. In the absence of any leads, he was beginning to realize the impossibility of what he was trying to do. Which meant it all rested with Lynch, he thought. On how quickly the *Coloane* could be traced, and whether Cris was on board or whether she was already dead.

Had it not been for a light in an upstairs window at the rear of the building, Rayner would have been tempted to abandon the whole thing. He studied the street again, trying to decide if anyone lived here and whether the area was as deserted as it appeared to be.

The warehouse itself was lost in shadows, flanked by the railroad on one side and by an equally featureless brick building on the other. Just a warehouse? he wondered. Or could Cris really be inside somewhere?

'How do we do it?' Janson asked. He was sitting behind the wheel of the Toyota with an unlit cigarette hanging from his lips. Tonight, for reasons known only to himself, he was wearing a pair of dirty shorts and a black singlet with holes in it.

'Roller door.' Rayner pointed. 'Those things are locked by metal tangs that slide out into the door frame. They stop the door from being forced up and are supposed to take the shock of a car ramming into it from the outside.'

'Piece of cake, then,' Janson said dryly.

'Why do you think I brought the hook and rope? You can bend the tangs – just so long as you pull the door outwards from the middle. We'll use the car. It'll make a bit of noise, that's all.'

'What about the alarms?'

'If they're motion sensors we're out of luck. If they're infra-red beams we're OK.' Rayner got out and started looping the rope around a spring shackle at the rear of the car.

Janson came to help, carrying the free end of the rope over to the door before he attached the steel hook.

Rayner kicked the hook into the gap under the door, making sure that the curved tip of the hook would bite into the metal when the load came on. 'First gear,' he said. 'Nice steady pull. The minute you hear the tangs pop out, stop right away – unless the alarms go off.'

'What if they do?'

'Give it hell. Rip the whole door out of its guides. I'll just have to be quick.'

'You'd better have this.' Janson produced an automatic. 'You're not as quick as you think you are.'

Rayner put it in his pocket without saying anything.

'Do it now?' Janson queried.

'Might as well.' Rayner waited for Janson to restart the car, then he checked the hook and moved well to one side as the rope grew taut.

Although the street was still empty, Rayner wasn't sure how long it would remain empty if the lock proved stubborn. Already the door was creaking, bulging outwards under the strain. It continued to bulge until the steel plates buckled. Rayner heard one of the tangs snap. A moment later the tip of the hook burst through the sheet metal, and the second tang tore free.

After Janson had reversed the car and disconnected the rope, he came to inspect the damage. 'No alarms,' he said.

Rayner was already on his knees, easing up the door, using his flashlight to check for sensors.

He could see two sets – both infra red – one of them throwing an invisible beam across the doorway about two feet off the floor.

'Looks OK,' he said. 'There's a mezzanine floor at the back with a catwalk. That's where the room is.' He withdrew his head and stood up. 'If there's another beam across the stairs I might have to find some other way to get up there.'

Janson had been recoiling the rope. He handed it to Rayner.

'Take the car round the back and keep the engine running,' Rayner said. 'Park it in the alley. If I trigger the alarms, we'll be coming out through the window.'

'She's not here,' Janson said quietly. 'You know that, don't you? You're doing this for nothing.'

'Maybe.' There was a familiar taste in Rayner's mouth and he was nervous – mostly because, if she wasn't here he didn't know what else to do.

Once the car had gone, the street was lonely. Although no lights had come on in the neighbouring buildings and the warehouse remained in darkness, he could feel his confidence draining away.

Keeping his arms by his side, he wormed his way under the door on his back, pulling the rope behind him. When he was clear of the beam he stood up.

It was extremely dark inside and the air was hot and humid. There was also a powerful smell of diesel oil, coffee beans and sisal.

Rayner switched on his flashlight, directing the beam first

at the line of trucks parked along the south wall, and then at the stairs which led up to the catwalk. As far as he could determine, the stairway was free of sensors. All he could see was the light coming under the door of the room above him.

He resisted the impulse to shout, to call her name, but couldn't prevent himself from taking the stairs two at a time until he reached the catwalk. Half-way along it he stopped suddenly, certain that he could hear voices.

Listening more carefully, he heard them again, two men talking quietly in Chinese. They were in the room, one of them laughing now.

Rayner stayed where he was, refusing to believe that the occupants hadn't been alerted by the noise of the door being forced open. If they were guards, who were they guarding? And what was keeping them here after all the disturbance downstairs?

He remembered the snipers on the ridge, recalling how a shot from one of them had driven him to take shelter among the rocks where the other had been waiting. Another trap? Rayner wondered. Because someone was expecting him?

Gripping Janson's automatic, he inched along the catwalk toward the light. Outside the door he waited for a second before cautiously pulling it open.

The source of the voices was obvious immediately, but he nearly missed the trip-wire, a single strand running across the doorway at ankle height. Rayner stepped over it, looking everywhere for other signs of danger.

There was nothing – just a table supporting the tape recorder and a wooden chair with a hand-grenade taped to one of its legs. The pin was already partly withdrawn from the grenade, connected to the free end of the trip-wire. He unfastened the wire, trying to blank out the continuous drone of voices. They were mocking him, telling him Janson had been right. Cris wasn't here and she had never been here.

He slammed the gun into the tape recorder to stop it, and was on the point of leaving when the lights in the warehouse all came on at once.

Rayner didn't hesitate. Pulling the pin on the grenade, he threw the whole chair through the door. Then he kicked out the window. Twenty feet below in the alleyway outside, Janson was standing beside the car smothered in broken glass. As he looked up, the grenade exploded downstairs in the warehouse.

How much damage it had done Rayner didn't know. Nor did he know how much time he had. He lashed the end of his rope to the table, cleared away the rest of the glass with the gun barrel, and climbed out on to the windowsill.

Janson had moved away from the Toyota, watching now from a safer distance.

'Back up,' Rayner yelled. He tossed the gun into the darkness.

Janson managed to catch it. He crouched behind the car, covering the building while Rayner clambered down the rope to join him in the alleyway.

'You didn't have to drop the whole goddamn window on me.' Janson shook more glass out of his hair. 'How many men?'

'No idea.'

'Do you want me to nail one if they stick their head out?'

'No. We can be gone before they get upstairs.' Rayner was more concerned about being trapped in the alley.

Janson stood up, holding the automatic in both hands. 'You drive,' he said. 'Soon as you're ready, give me a blast on the horn.'

His eyes on the corner of the building, Rayner slipped behind the wheel and hit the horn button.

There was the sound of three shots before Janson appeared. 'Thought I'd send a message,' he explained. 'To stop them getting too excited.'

Rayner put his foot down hard, keeping the Toyota in second gear until he reached the main road. Although there was no sign of pursuit, and no other cars that he could see, he increased his speed, heading south now toward the lights of the Kowloon waterfront.

'Take it easy.' Janson was endeavouring to light a cigarette. His face was beaded in sweat and his hands were shaking.

Rayner was not entirely surprised. He could remember Janson's hands shaking like this before – in the diamond area – before Kabinda had arrived.

'She wasn't there, then?' Janson said.

'Just a tape recorder and a trip-wire.'

'What does that tell you?'

Even if he could have found a way to avoid the question, Rayner knew he would only be deceiving himself. He slowed the car, allowing it to coast to a halt on a hill overlooking the water before he started putting everything together – adding one piece of information to another, recalling scraps of conversation in New York and remembering what he'd said to Lynch on the phone.

'Jesus.' Rayner's hands tightened on the wheel.

'Do you want to go through it now?' Janson blew smoke out of the window. 'See if it all fits while you're still angry.'

Rayner wasn't angry. He was trying to think.

'Come on,' Janson said. 'Get the shit out of your system. Who knew you were going to the warehouse?'

'Lynch,' Rayner muttered.

'Who knew you photographed Kabinda in Angola?'

'Felix,' Rayner said. 'And Felix sent those photocopies to Lynch. That's what set everything off. It was Lynch who told Kabinda about the film.'

'And what got Felix killed,' Janson said. 'Because he'd seen the pictures and because no one would believe him when he said he didn't have the negatives.'

'And what do I do?' Rayner was bitter now. 'As soon as the photos and negatives arrive in the mail I rush off and give them to Lynch.'

Janson shrugged. 'You didn't know then. It was exactly what Lynch wanted you to do. All he was worried about was whether you'd taken a set of prints for yourself. Do you remember if he asked you?'

Rayner nodded. 'Wu asked me the same thing. He must have been checking to make sure.'

'Nice little club.' Janson threw his cigarette away. 'Kabinda, Wu and Marle, with Lynch handling the US end for them. I wouldn't hold your breath waiting for WOPES to contact the Angolan Government now.'

'Lynch has got that covered,' Rayner said. 'He sent me a fax saying there'll be a delay while Washington sorts out a human-rights issue with Luanda.'

'He's had you covered all along. Now you know how those guys found you in the States, don't you? Once Lynch got Wendy's address from poor old Felix he put your friend Cristabel on the job. He used her to track you down.'

Rayner pushed open the car door, and went to stand by himself on the roadside where he could see the city lights sparkling and glittering under a sky that was just beginning to lighten. Soon it would be dawn, he thought, the end of another night, and the end of a fruitless search for Cris.

Janson came to stand beside him. 'Proper downer,' he said. 'We should've figured all this out before.'

'How did you guess Lynch was involved?' Rayner continued staring at the lights.

'I wasn't sure. I tried to get some information this afternoon, but it'll be a while before the answers start coming in.'

'Through your English friends in Hong Kong?' Rayner said.

'Yeah. The people who lent me the game-fishing boat. I'll fix it so you can stay with them until you can get a flight back home. You're not going to do any good hanging around here.'

'What about you?' Rayner looked at Janson. 'Won't your people want to know where the *Coloane*'s going?'

'Maybe. But Kabinda won't risk landing the guns in South Africa after this. He'll have already been told you've seen his torpedoes and that you're on the loose somewhere. If he's got any sense he'll unload the guns in Angola or Namibia and truck them south from there.'

'Why don't you try and trace the freighter anyway?' Rayner picked up a stone and threw it out into space.

'Might be easier to find Kabinda. That's where I came in. We know he operates out of some place in Zaire – in the jungle somewhere. If we can knock the bastard out where he lives, we'll have fixed the problem permanently.'

'Which leaves Lynch,' Rayner said. 'I can't see why the hell he talked me into coming here to start with.'

'Because you gave him the idea you were going to be real trouble. Once you told him that, he figured the smart thing to do was to sidetrack you on a hunt for ivory he knew damn well you'd never find.'

'I did find it,' Rayner said.

'You weren't supposed to. How was Lynch to know you'd seen cocaine torpedoes operating in the Persian Gulf? He fouled up, that's all.' Janson hesitated. 'He might even have figured you wouldn't bother much, because you'd have your hands full with the Castela girl. You know – because he knew you had the hots for her.'

'It didn't start off like that,' Rayner said. 'You don't understand.'

'Do you want to tell me about it?'

'No.'

'You're not giving-up on her, are you?'

Rayner threw another stone. 'What am I supposed to do?'

'I don't know. But if you don't want to tell me who she is or where she comes from, I'm not going to be a lot of help, am I?'

'She's Portuguese,' Rayner said. 'Her father was a conservationist in Angola.' He stopped abruptly.

'Go on.' Janson took out his cigarettes. His hands were steadier, but he still fumbled with the packet.

Rayner began again, providing a brief outline of what he knew about Cris, telling Janson what she'd said about her sister, but omitting all mention of how his relationship with her had developed.

The South African listened in silence until Rayner could think of nothing more to say.

'Great story,' Janson said. 'With a lousy ending. Let's go and find out if there's any news yet.'

'From your friends?'

'You're going to like them. They're sort of in your line of business.'

Rayner was unwilling to leave. He remained where he was for several minutes before returning to the car, aware that his thoughts had been drifting back to Wendy. Someone to run to? he wondered. The surrogate sister he should have listened to before a bad dream about another sister had turned into something that was rapidly becoming a nightmare.

Seven

A year ago, as a guest in the homes of some of Africa's wealthiest people, Rayner had seen what real money could buy. Before that, in Saudi Arabia, he had been inside homes that cost a fortune. But none of the houses had been as gracious as this one, and in none of them had he felt quite so out of place.

From the balcony outside his room he could see a number of equally expensive residences. They were sprawled over the headland with their estates either stretching down to Repulse Bay on one side or Deep Water Bay on the other. He could see clusters of swimming pools as well, and tree-lined driveways leading up from a forest of wrought-iron gates along the coast road. An area that reeked of affluence, Rayner thought, a place where only the richest Hong Kong families could afford to live.

Because Janson had provided the directions for their early morning drive across the island, Rayner had paid little attention to where they were going, not imagining for a moment that Janson's friends would live anywhere like this. Only when they reached the house did Rayner begin to realize what he was walking into.

Even now, after two hours of wondering how Janson could possibly know anyone in the rarefied, upper strata of Hong Kong society, Rayner was still without an answer. Another surprise, he thought, but one that was a good deal more pleasant than the others he'd experienced of late.

A knock on his door made him leave the balcony. A member of the household staff had come to see him, an elderly Chinese lady who had shown him to his room earlier this morning.

'Sir Anthony asks if you would care to join him,' she said.

'Yes, I would. Thank you.' Rayner picked up his jacket. 'Where is he?'

'Please, I will take you.'

Rayner followed her downstairs and out through some French windows into a tiled courtyard. At the far end of it by the pool, Sir Anthony Carmichael was seated at a table reading a newspaper.

He stood up to greet Rayner. 'Well, well,' he said. 'You didn't fall asleep after all then.' He offered a chair. 'I was hoping we'd be able to have a chat.'

Rayner sat down feeling vaguely that he should be somewhere else. On their arrival here shortly after dawn, Sir Anthony had introduced himself only briefly, and because Janson had gone straight to his room in the guest wing, until now Rayner had spoken to no one except the housekeeper. He wondered if this was going to be difficult and how much Janson had said about Cristabel.

Sir Anthony folded his newspaper and poured himself a glass of orange juice. Although Rayner guessed he was probably no older than sixty, the Englishman's face was so heavily lined that it was hard to read his expression. His manner, though, was unaffected and he seemed genuinely pleased to have company for breakfast.

'Bacon and eggs?' he inquired. 'Is that all right?'

'Fine,' Rayner said. 'Anything at all.'

Sir Anthony waved toward the house. 'I must say you seem to be having an interesting time of it,' he said. 'But I imagine interesting is hardly the right word in the circumstances. Not from your perspective anyway.'

Rayner smiled. 'I don't have a perspective any more.'

'No. Very sensible of you. Ross has filled me in on the background, and explained why the pair of you have been chasing your tails around Hong Kong. And he's told me about this friend Cristabel of yours, of course.' Sir Anthony drank some juice. 'Grim business all round, but perhaps not as grim as you think it is.'

'Janson had an idea you might be able to help,' Rayner said. 'But I don't know why he thought that.'

Sir Anthony paused while a waiter delivered Rayner's breakfast to the table. 'Ross hasn't mentioned our little operation here then?' he said.

'No.'

'In that case you'd better eat while I talk. I'm sure you

understand that what I say is in confidence.'

Rayner nodded.

'Let me start by saying that Hong Kong is in something of a mess if you hadn't noticed. The place is more like a damn pressure cooker than a British Crown Colony – mainly as a result of the '89 Tiananmen Square massacre. Sixty-two thousand people left here last year alone, and God knows how many more will pull out on the run up to 1997.'

'When the Chinese take over,' Rayner said.

'Yes, indeed. The British Government is doing its best to guarantee some sort of local autonomy after that happens, but talking with Beijing generally means we take two steps back for every one we make forward. Discussing anything with the Chinese is never simple, but over the last eighteen months or so the British have failed rather badly.' Sir Anthony peered over his glasses. 'If you haven't guessed already, my job is to rectify matters by providing the British Government with a negotiating advantage.'

'By doing what?' Rayner said.

'This and that. We have a small daytime staff who intercept radio transmissions, analyse reports from the mainland, interview people who have recently been in China – you know the sort of thing – Ross calls it an eyes-and-ears operation.'

'Why wouldn't he call it British Intelligence?' Rayner stopped eating.

'Because that would be an exaggeration. We're an information gathering centre – nothing more – a sort of quasi-diplomatic service.'

'But you're not a diplomat.'

Sir Anthony smiled. 'Not any more. Just an old colonial hand seeing out his time, I'm afraid – officially anyway. Unofficially, I run this place to support the Governor and the bright young men from London who believe the acquisition of information is only marginally less important than the pursuit of happiness.' He paused. 'I imagine that doesn't explain why we should be in a position to help you.'

'No,' Rayner said. 'It doesn't explain why you're helping Ross Janson either. Why are you?'

'Because the British Government has other interests besides Hong Kong. We have substantial investments in South Africa – investments that must be protected while apartheid is dismantled and the new South African Government sorts itself out. If the Azanian Peoples

Liberation Army and the Pan-Africanist Congress create a bloodbath in South Africa, Britain stands to lose billions of dollars. We're as anxious to prevent guns from falling into the wrong hands as the South African Government is.'

'Does that mean you can get information on the *Coloane?*' Rayner said slowly.

'We already have. We have information on a number of things – including some encouraging news for you, Mark.' Sir Anthony raised a hand to shield his eyes from the sun. 'You don't mind me calling you Mark, do you?'

Rayner shook his head. He'd been unprepared for this, never thinking that the British could be involved.

'Life is extraordinary, isn't it?' Sir Anthony remarked. 'Here you are, an American in Hong Kong searching for an Angolan born Portuguese girl, while Ross is here at the same time doing his best to stop the export of Chinese guns to South Africa. Sometimes I think the world has become too small.'

'Mix in ivory and diamonds,' Rayner said. 'And Kinshasa Copper.'

'To say nothing of a gentleman sitting in the WOPES headquarters in New York. Although in confidence I think we can assume his days are numbered, don't you?'

'Tell me about the *Coloane*,' Rayner said. 'In confidence.'

'I can do better than that.' Sir Anthony was amused. 'I'm sorry. I should have explained before. You see, in the last forty-eight hours while you've been out and about, we've received communications from Pretoria, from Zaire and from London. Things have changed quite quickly – not just in regard to the *Coloane.* Part of this change relates to another phonecall we had from a young lady in Massachusetts.'

'Wendy? Why?'

'To say that she'd just been speaking on the telephone to someone called Cristabel Castela.'

Rayner was stunned. 'Cristabel called Wendy?' he said. 'How? Where from?'

'All I can tell you is that Miss Castela isn't on board the *Coloane*. She's with her uncle in Macau.'

Rayner knew it wasn't true. She could no more be in Macau than she could be in Hong Kong. He knew she couldn't be because it was impossible. 'Have you spoken to her?' He tried to think. 'Do you have her number?'

Sir Anthony's smile widened. 'Miss Armitage said she'd prefer to give it to you. Would you like to phone the States?'

He waved again toward the French windows.

This time, instead of the waiter, a pretty Chinese girl hurried out across the courtyard carrying a telephone. She placed it on the table and plugged the cord into a socket in the ground.

'I think Mr Rayner would like to make a call to the United States,' Sir Anthony said. 'Perhaps you'd be kind enough to get it for him.'

'Certainly.' The girl gave Rayner a notepad and a ballpoint pen. 'May I have the number please?'

Pushing away his feelings of doubt and disbelief, he scribbled down the number for her then waited while she pushed buttons on the phone.

'It's ringing for you now, Mr Rayner. Here you are.' She handed the receiver to him.

'Do you mind if I listen?' Sir Anthony remained seated while the girl returned to the house.

Rayner shook his head. A click on the line was followed by a short delay. Then he heard Wendy say hello.

'It's me,' he said.

'Mark, are you all right?' She sounded concerned. 'My mother had a call the other day from someone in Hong Kong asking where you were. As soon as I heard I called back, but I didn't know what it was all about. Then this afternoon that Castela woman from WOPES called me. She says she's in Macau. For heaven's sake what's going on?'

'Didn't she tell you?'

'No. All she said was that it was terribly important for her to get hold of you. That's why I phoned again. Why doesn't anyone know where you are? Why does she want to see you? Are you still in Hong Kong?'

Rayner couldn't think of anywhere to start.

'Mark, are you still there?'

'Yeah, I'm here. It's a hell of a story. I can't tell you now. What did Cristabel say?'

'Nothing – well nothing much. She just gave me her phone number in Macau. Do you want it?'

'Please.' Rayner wrote it down.

'What's she doing there?' Wendy asked. 'You didn't say anything about her in your note. Is it about the ivory?'

'Sort of.'

'Which means you don't want to tell me.'

'It'd take all day,' Rayner said. 'Listen, I don't want you to stay at Sandy Neck.'

'Why? I only came home two days ago.'

'Because it's dangerous. And don't talk to that guy Lynch at WOPES if he calls you. Just hang up. Can you go back to Salem?'

'I suppose I could. Mark, you have to tell me what's happening.'

'I will. When I get home.'

'When will that be?'

'I'm not sure,' Rayner said.

'Give my love to the lovely Miss Castela then, won't you?'

The line went dead before he could say goodbye. He hung up the receiver, wishing he could have found a way to explain the unexplainable.

Sir Anthony had been immersed in his newspaper again. He glanced at Rayner over the top of it.

'Look,' Rayner said, 'could I ask you something? Before I phone Macau?'

'You might do better talking to my wife. I'm not very good at these sort of things.'

'It's not that.' Rayner grinned. 'If this doesn't turn out to be some kind of mistake, I was wondering if I could bring Cris here – just until we get on a plane.'

'Do you think she's still in danger?'

'Maybe. I don't know.'

Sir Anthony put down his paper. 'You haven't asked me about the news we have from Africa and Europe, or about the *Coloane*.'

'No.' Rayner hesitated. 'I'm sorry. I need to check on Cris first.'

'Of course you do. Silly of me. Call her, please. And naturally you're both more than welcome to stay. It'll be nice to have some young people around for a change. We can talk about those other things later.'

'OK.' Rayner used the phone again, trying unsuccessfully to tell himself that she would be there.

She answered at once, speaking quietly in Cantonese.

'Hi,' Rayner said. 'Is that really you?'

'Oh God.' There was a long pause before she spoke again. 'I've been waiting all night – just hoping.'

'Are you OK?' The disbelief had gone. In its place was urgency, a need to be with her as quickly as he could.

'I am now. I've been so worried.' There was another pause.

'Now I'm talking to you I don't know what to say.' Her voice faded.

'What the hell happened?' he said.

'Everything. Then it all went wrong. Right up until now.'

The questions could wait, Rayner decided. 'I can be there in an hour,' he said. 'What's the address?'

'You mustn't come here. In case someone's watching the house. Hold on while I check something.' She was out of breath when she came back to the line. 'Mark, I can be at the Hong Kong ferry pier at eleven-fifteen. There's a jet-cat leaving here in twenty minutes time. My uncle says he'll send someone with me.' She hesitated. 'Can you find somewhere safe for us to go?'

'I already have.' Rayner checked his watch.

'You'll meet me, won't you?'

'Just get on that jet-cat,' he said. 'Just do it.'

'I will. I'll be there soon, I promise I will.'

This time when Rayner put down the phone, the events of the last four days seemed peculiarly unimportant. The sunset off Sai Wan; his cell with its frozen wall; the snipers; Janson's destruction of the landing-stage and the raid on the warehouse – all of them a blur, a past whose only purpose had been to make him sweat out the days and nights until he found her. That she was alive was more than he'd hoped for. That she was on her way to join him seemed so unlikely that he couldn't bring himself to imagine what it would be like to see her again.

'Well?' Sir Anthony interrupted his thoughts. 'Everything all right?'

'She's leaving in twenty minutes.'

'Did she explain how she ended up in Macau?'

'No,' Rayner said. 'God knows how she got there. You know, a couple of times, I even decided she was dead.'

'Like her sister.'

Rayner nodded. 'I don't think I could've handled Cris as well.'

'Yes, indeed. Mary and I lost one of our daughters in a yachting accident some years ago. That was bad enough, but nothing like you saw in Angola, of course. Now, what about some coffee?'

'No thanks,' Rayner said. 'I'll head off to town. I can check on the flights out of here before I meet the jet-cat.'

'You don't believe there's a risk of her being followed?'

'Her uncle's sending someone to ride shotgun. She'll be OK.'

'Keep an eye open for Ross,' Sir Anthony said. 'He was intending to visit a travel agent, I think.'

A hint, Rayner realised. Because he still hadn't asked about the *Coloane.* 'Janson isn't going back to Africa, is he?' he asked.

'Good Lord no. I wish he was. He's off to Taiwan, and arranging a flight out of Luanda for a friend of his – someone called Charlie.'

'I haven't been listening to you properly, have I?' Rayner said slowly. 'I've only got half the damn story. What's this about Taiwan and Charlie?'

'Why don't we wait until you're back and Ross is here? Then we can all have a look at the satellite photographs together.' Sir Anthony smiled. 'I hope that doesn't sound too mysterious.'

'It does,' Rayner said. 'How many signposts have I missed?'

'Most of them.' Sir Anthony was amused again. 'Ross did warn me that you were a bit preoccupied.'

'With Cris?'

'Well, yes. But I'm certain that once you've collected her and brought her back here, you'll be more relaxed and able to concentrate better.'

Sir Anthony didn't understand either, Rayner thought. How could he? How could anyone understand if they'd never kissed her, or made love to her, or seen her wake up beside them still sleepy from the night before?

Excusing himself, he walked back across the courtyard to the house, unable to prevent himself from wondering what she would look like and what she would be wearing. In his mind's eye he could picture her already – not an imaginary Cris standing with Wendy and her sister on the deck of the freighter, but the real Cris, alone, with the innocent eagerness in her eyes that Rayner knew he would never have been able to quite forget.

The jet-cat maintained speed until congestion in the harbour forced the captain to throttle back. There was time for Rayner to see the bows dip and the twin hulls settle deeper into the water before one of the outgoing Star ferries blocked his view. The ferry was overflowing with people taking photographs or waving to friends, while another equally packed tour boat was preparing to berth in front of him.

He was trying to find somewhere better to stand when the jet-cat slid alongside the pier.

She was the third passenger off, scanning the crowd anxiously for him, but looking in the wrong direction.

Rayner called her name and saw her turn. A moment later she was in his arms. Although there were people all around them, pushing and jostling their way along the pier, she wouldn't let him go. She clung to him, refusing to release him until he pushed her away so he could see her. Tears were rolling down her face, and she was unable to speak.

'Hey.' He wiped the tears away. 'You're supposed to be happy.'

'I am. It's not what you think.'

'What isn't?'

'Nothing. I'm sorry. I'm so mixed up.'

'We'll soon fix that,' Rayner said. 'Come on. The car's over there.'

She remained where she was. 'It's you,' she said. 'I wasn't going to say anything, but now you're here it's all come back again.'

Rayner kept quiet, too pleased to see her to be concerned.

'It's been going round inside my head ever since we were on the sampan,' she said. 'I don't know how much I'm pretending or how much is real. All I do know is that we made love – over and over like two crazy people. But that's all we did. You never said if it meant anything. Don't you see?'

'One-night stands.' Rayner grinned at her. 'You're too wound up to know what you're talking about.'

'Oh.' She attempted to regain her composure. 'Aren't you going to say hello?'

'No.' He began to lead her away. 'Where's this minder of yours – the guy who came with you?'

'He's going back on the jet-cat. I've told him I'll be all right. Don't you want to know what happened to me?'

'You haven't given me much of a chance.' He tightened his grip around her waist, conscious of her being close to him, aware of the texture of her dress against his arm.

'Stuart told me you thought I was on the freighter,' she said.

Rayner stopped walking. 'Have you been in touch with Lynch?'

'Of course I have. I phoned him before I phoned Wendy. I

thought he'd be the best person to help me find out where you'd gone.'

He waited until they were in the car before he spoke again. Because of her outburst, and her uncharacteristic lack of confidence, he was unwilling to rush her.

'Talk to me.'

'Aren't we going somewhere?'

'In a minute.' He took her hand.

'I tried so hard,' she said. 'God I tried – for both of us.'

'What do you mean?'

'With Wu. After he'd finished asking me questions.' She shivered. 'He kept stroking my hair.'

'Questions about me?'

'Mm. Over and over and over.'

Rayner could feel her trembling. 'You should've told him whatever he wanted to know,' he said.

'I did.' She paused. 'I had to. He said it was the only way I could keep you alive.'

'Did you tell him the truth?'

She nodded. 'I said you were working for WOPES and that you'd guessed how the ivory was being brought into Hong Kong.'

'Did he ask if I'd taken a set of prints of the negatives I shot in Angola?'

'Lots of times. I just answered his questions. I didn't know what else to do. Then he started asking how much I knew about the guns, but I didn't know what he was talking about.'

'Do you know now?'

'No. What guns?'

'Never mind.' He squeezed her hand. 'If you'd seen them you probably wouldn't be here. Even so, I still can't figure out why he let you walk away.'

'He didn't. Mark, he didn't. My uncle arranged it. I told Wu my uncle would give him money. Wu was paid to let us go. That was three days ago.'

'Oh Jesus.' Not for a moment had Rayner considered a payoff. 'How much?' he said.

'Two hundred thousand Hong Kong dollars.' She flushed. 'Half of it for you.'

He was disconcerted now, as much by her embarrassment as by the size of the payment. 'You shouldn't have bothered,' he said quietly. 'Wu was all set to double-cross us. He had other plans for me. When did your uncle hand over the money?'

'Yesterday morning. They kept me locked up in that warehouse until then.'

'I just missed you.' He smiled. 'I called by.'

'And I just missed you at the hotel. I went to collect my things and found out you'd already been there. That's how I knew you were all right.'

'But you figured it was because of your uncle's money.'

'Mm.' She nodded. 'All I had to do then was find you.'

'So you phoned Lynch.'

'Yes. He was terribly confused at first because when you contacted him you said I'd been taken on board the *Coloane*. Eventually we got things sorted out, but it didn't help because he had no idea where you were.'

'Did he explain about Janson?' Rayner asked.

'Not properly. Only that he thought that Janson had somehow helped you get away. Stuart asked me why on earth Janson was in Hong Kong, but, of course, I didn't know.' She paused. 'I still don't.'

'Lynch didn't mention the guns?'

She shook her head. 'Why should he? I don't understand.'

'You will,' Rayner said. 'Trust me.'

'Is that a way of saying I've been stupid? Have I made a mess of things?'

'No. If you hadn't phoned Wendy we'd still be looking for each other. That was pretty smart.'

'She's worried about you.' Her expression brightened. 'How does it feel to have both of us worrying about you?'

Rayner chose the safest option. He didn't answer.

Leaning across she brushed her lips against his cheek. 'Wendy's not here,' she said. 'But I am. And you have to find a way to pay back all my uncle's money, haven't you?'

Her breath was on his face and he could taste the residue of her tears. He started to speak, but before he could say anything she had crushed herself against him, closed her eyes and fastened her mouth on his.

Lady Carmichael was cutting flowers outside in the garden. As soon as the Toyota pulled up in the driveway she came over to introduce herself.

For a woman in her mid-fifties she was well preserved with a good figure and rather fine features. She was also very smartly dressed.

'Well, there you are,' she said. 'I'm so sorry I missed saying hello this morning. You must be Mark, and this young lady is your friend Cristabel.' She removed her gardening gloves to shake hands.

'It's kind of you and Sir Anthony to let us stay here,' Rayner said. 'We'll be out of your hair in a day or so.'

'Oh, don't say that.' Lady Carmichael smiled. 'Stay as long as you like.'

Rayner picked up a flower that she'd dropped. 'Do you know if Janson's back yet?' he asked.

'No, I'm sorry, I don't.' She took the flower from him. 'Why don't you forget about him for a little while? I'm sure there'll be plenty of time later to talk about African terrorists and heaven knows what else. Now then, Cristabel, do you have any luggage?'

'No. I'm afraid I haven't.' She looked awkward. 'I haven't brought anything at all.'

'Your stuff's in the car,' Rayner said. 'I picked it up yesterday – remember?'

'You bring it inside then, Mark, and I'll have someone show Cris to her room.' Lady Carmichael marched off into the house leaving him to unload the suitcase from the trunk.

'I had no idea we'd be staying anywhere like this,' Cristabel whispered.

'I told you we were.'

'I wasn't listening.'

'Because you're still mixed up?' Rayner walked with her up the steps.

'No. Because I haven't had time to catch up with things. You've been talking at me non-stop ever since we left the waterfront. I don't know what to think about first. I'm all muddled up with Stuart Lynch and Janson, and guns going to South Africa, and people shooting at you in the hills.'

'It's going to get worse,' he said. 'For some reason or another Janson's off to Taiwan, and Sir Anthony wants to show us some satellite photos.'

'Mr Rayner.' The elderly Chinese housekeeper was waiting for them in the hall. 'Please give me the luggage.'

'It's OK.' Rayner couldn't imagine her struggling with a case that was very nearly as large as she was. He carried it upstairs, followed Cris into one of the guest rooms, and waited while the woman pulled back the curtains and opened the windows.

When she'd gone, Cris went out onto the balcony. 'What a marvellous view,' she said. 'My uncle's house looks out over the sea, but it's nothing like this.'

'Do you want to have a wander round? We can probably get some lunch if we ask someone.'

'I'd rather stay and freshen up. Do you mind?'

He shook his head. 'Bang on my door when you're ready. It's the next one along.'

'I'll only be a minute.' She stood on tiptoe to kiss him. 'Thank you for bringing me here.'

Rayner reached into his pocket for her ear-rings. 'You left these on my lampshade back in the hotel,' he said.

Her reply was interrupted by the arrival of Lady Carmichael. She was holding an armful of towels and had brought a vase in which she'd arranged the flowers.

'Oh thank you.' Cris took the vase from her. 'These are lovely. Where shall I put them?'

Rayner left them to it, retreating to his own room where he lay down on the bed to examine the airline brochures he'd brought from town. He chose the Cathay Pacific timetable, going through it half-heartedly, marking flights from Kai Tak to New York before his thoughts drifted back again to Cris, to Angola, to Felix, and inevitably to Wendy. Was it this easy to override the decision he'd made at Sandy Neck? he wondered. Would being with Cris really allow him to forget what had brought them together to begin with? Or was he only fooling himself?

His speculation was short-lived. Whatever he'd been searching for, Cristabel herself had come to provide an answer. Somehow she had managed to unlock the internal door that connected his suite to hers. She was standing barefoot just inside his room, dangling the key from her hand, trying to keep a straight face. Her hair was down and the top four buttons of her dress were undone.

'Guess where I got this?' She threw the key to him.

'Tooth fairy.' Rayner could hardly bear to look at her.

'Lady Carmichael thought it would be nice for me to have it.' She burst out laughing. 'She said I seemed to be a very sensible young lady and that she wanted me to feel at home here.'

He remained silent.

'I just came to say hello,' she said.

'No, you didn't.'

'No.' She compressed her lips. 'No, I suppose I didn't.'

He went to her, picked her up and carried her over to the bed in his arms.

'Happy ending?' she said softly.

Rayner wished he could be sure. 'Beginning,' he said. 'Just the beginning.'

Janson was clearly taken with Cristabel. Instead of being off-hand or surly as Rayner had half expected him to be, the South African had been talking to her easily and had even insisted on going to fetch her another glass of wine.

While they were waiting for him to return she took Rayner's arm and made him walk along beside the pool with her. Despite their afternoon together, in the dusk he found her more desirable than ever, either because the afternoon hadn't been long enough, or because of the way she kept touching him as though she was frightened he might suddenly disappear.

She pointed out into the bay. 'That's Lamma Island,' she said. 'You can just see it. Isn't it wonderful? I could stay out here all night.'

'We're supposed to be talking to Sir Anthony.'

'About the guns?'

'Either that or about Janson going to Taiwan.'

She rested her head against his shoulder. 'Janson's nicer than you said he was.'

'But not as nice as me.'

'I don't know.' She laughed. 'Shhh. Here he is.'

This evening Janson had abandoned his shorts and singlet in favour of long trousers, a clean white shirt and one of Rayner's ties. He handed Cristabel her drink.

She took a sip from the glass. 'I haven't thanked you, have I?' she said. 'For trying to save my sister's life. Mark told me what you did.'

Janson shrugged. 'She shouldn't have been in Lunda Norte.'

'Francesca might have been trying to play Kabinda at his own game. She wasn't the kind of person people thought she was.'

'Yeah,' Janson said. 'I heard. No one can play games with

these bastards. You're lucky Wu didn't do for you what Kabinda did for her. Still, maybe this time we've got a leg over them – Marle too.'

'Is that what Sir Anthony wants to talk about?' Rayner asked. 'Or is he worried about Lynch?'

'To hell with Lynch.' Janson drank from his can of beer. 'Sir Anthony hopes you'll talk me out of my trip to Taiwan.'

'Shouldn't be hard,' Rayner said. 'Seeing as how I don't know why you're going or why you're meeting Charlie, or what day it is today.'

'Whose fault's that?' Janson grinned. 'You've been too busy to stick your head up and sniff the wind. Have you seen the set-up here?'

'Not yet.'

'Come on then. I'll show you.' Janson put his beer can on a table. 'If there were a few places like this sprinkled around South Africa, we'd have been able to bite the heads off these Pan Africanist bastards before they got big ideas.' He headed off across the courtyard towards the house.

Cristabel hung back, holding on to Rayner's arm. 'Does Ross believe you're going to help him?' she asked.

'Who knows?' Rayner was unwilling to discuss the possibility. 'Are you coming to look?'

She nodded. 'It's in the basement. Lady Carmichael told me.'

Janson was waiting for them. He led them down two flights of stairs and ushered them into a small airconditioned room crammed with telecommunication equipment. Radio receivers were perched on top of television monitors; cables littered the floor; and in the gap between racks supporting transmitters, fax machines and telephones a number of document shredders were at work. Rayner had never seen such a concentration of electronics in such a small space.

'Want to listen to the North Koreans directing troop movements?' Janson asked. 'Or find out if the Cambodians are still running drugs across the new bridge into Laos?'

'Not right now, thanks.' Rayner was watching the television screens. Two of them were displaying a newscast covering a rail disaster somewhere while others showed pictures of Chinese soldiers on manoeuvres. He was trying to make sense of the commentary when a fax machine began beeping.

Janson made no attempt to read the message. Instead he pointed at an aluminium cable duct coming in through the ceiling. 'Satellite dishes and radio aerials on the roof,' he said. 'Everything but a direct line to God.'

'Do the people here really listen to radio signals from countries like Korea?' Cris asked.

'Bet your life they do. So do the Americans.' Janson fitted a fresh roll of paper to the fax machine. 'Mostly the Brits are after stuff from China, though. Because of 1997. They're scared they're going to lose their shirts in South Africa and Hong Kong at the same time. Why do you think I'm allowed to poke around in here?'

Cristabel smiled. 'Sir Anthony told Mark this morning.'

'But he didn't mention Taiwan?'

'No.' Rayner answered for her. 'I'm getting tired of hearing about Taiwan.'

'So is Sir Anthony.' Janson grinned. 'We'd better go and see where he is.'

On the way back upstairs Rayner decided that the South African was being evasive. Because this wasn't the right opportunity to talk? he wondered. Or because he was reluctant to explain in front of Cris?

'Hello there.' Sir Anthony met them in the hall. 'Has Ross been twisting your arm?'

'No.' Rayner said. 'Guided tour.'

'Ah, I see. Perhaps we can get this over with then – so you can give us the benefit of your advice. I'm rather hoping you'll be able to think of something that we haven't – although I realize that might be difficult now we've quite literally missed the boat.'

'The *Coloane*?' Rayner said.

'Indeed. Still, you never know, do you?' Sir Anthony led them into an annexe off the library. It was windowless, and unlike the rest of the house, furnished inexpensively with a table and chairs that were more functional than ornamental.

After switching on the lights and closing the door he crossed the room to slide back the cover of a wall-mounted white-board. It was covered with a network of coloured lines connecting the names of countries, individuals and products to a central rectangle in which the name Taiwan had been written in capital letters.

'Right.' Sir Anthony used a wooden pointer to identify Kabinda's name at the top of the board. 'Maximilian Kabinda. Lufthansa flight 431 from Zaire to Bombay, followed by British Airways flight 39 to Bangkok and Taipei. According to

Ross's people in Pretoria arrival time is 0730 hours on June 13th.'

Cristabel touched Rayner's arm. 'That's tomorrow,' she whispered.

'Wu Kinwah.' Sir Anthony relocated his pointer. 'Cathay Pacific flight 21 to Taipei on June 10th from Hong Kong. Wu is already in Taiwan – has been for two days.'

Janson walked over and put his finger on the board. 'And here we have director number three,' he said. 'Our friendly European diamond broker from Antwerp. Arrives in Taipei tonight if Sir Anthony's information from London is correct.'

'Do we know why they're meeting in Taiwan?' Rayner asked.

'Got a pretty good idea.' Janson lit a cigarette. 'What would you say if I told you that Kinshasa Copper has chartered an aircraft to fly a shipment of ivory out of Zaire and into Taipei?'

'They can't,' Cristabel said. 'No one can. It's against international law. They'd never be allowed to take the ivory out of Africa.'

Janson grinned. 'What if each tusk is engraved with an identification number and accompanied by an export certificate from its country of origin?'

'Legal ivory?' She was surprised. 'Do you mean they're tusks from deceased animals or legal culls?'

'Hundred per cent above-board.' Janson blew out a stream of smoke. 'On paper anyway. There might be a twist, though. I don't think Marle would be making the trip unless there were diamonds on their way as well – smuggled diamonds that is.'

'Smuggled inside the tusks?' Rayner said.

Janson nodded. 'It's been done before. Because of the trade ban. Kinshasa Copper knows damn well that Customs will check the number of each tusk against its certificate. That makes ivory a perfect carrier. It's like smuggling heroin in with a load of dangerous chemicals or prescription drugs. Customs get all excited about the main cargo and forget to look for anything else.'

Sir Anthony spoke again. 'From our point of view, what's coming in is unimportant,' he said. 'It's what the aircraft might be carrying on the way back that interests us.'

'Do you know?' Rayner asked.

'Officially, twelve tons of milk powder and eight tons of rice. Sourced by Kinshasa Copper through their agents in Taiwan and packaged on steel pallets with built-in impact resistance.

The trade commissioner here received an enquiry for the pallets three days ago. Government House telephoned me to see what I thought.'

'Air-drop pallets,' Janson said. 'This is probably a deal that's been jacked up with some aid outfit in Africa. It could even be a Government contract or something to do with the United Nations. The Namibians were air-dropping medical supplies and food all last winter. It made bugger-all difference to the people in the hills but it looks good internationally.'

Sir Anthony tapped his pointer against the board. 'So what do we have?' he said. 'An aircraft flying into Taipei with ivory on board and leaving again with a cargo of rice and milk powder that can be air-dropped to remote areas of Africa. A splendid arrangement, don't you think?' He glanced at Rayner. 'But perhaps not an arrangement that would necessitate the presence of Kinshasa Copper's three directors in Taipei.'

'Which brings us to the *Coloane*,' Janson grunted. 'And the satellite pictures.'

Sir Anthony tipped the contents of a large envelope on to the table. 'Have a look at these,' he said. 'They're high-altitude photographs of the Pacific showing an area off the Chinese coast between the latitudes of twenty and thirty degrees north.'

Rayner picked one up. 'How did you get hold of them?' he asked.

'Through the British Foreign Office in London. They were taken by one of the US Interstat satellites and kindly transmitted on to us from Washington.'

While Rayner was endeavouring to find his bearings, Cristabel pointed over his shoulder. 'There,' she said. 'Look.'

Among what seemed to be hundreds of tiny vessels dotted on the artificially yellow surface of the ocean, she had picked out one. Except for being almost off the bottom of the picture, to Rayner's eyes it appeared indistinguishable from any of the other dots.

'Can't you see it?' she asked.

'Yeah, I can see it.' He inspected the photograph more closely. 'What's so special?'

'That.' She used her fingernail to show him. 'The shadow at the end of the wake – those little dark lines.'

It was the torpedoes. Barely visible below the surface, but on a bright, sunny day, visible nonetheless. He could see both of them now, tiny smudges contrasting with the brighter streak of colour which was the freighter's wake.

'Sailing south,' Sir Anthony remarked. 'As you can see.' He handed Rayner another photograph. 'Then, two days later.'

This time Rayner didn't have to search for the right dot. Someone had ringed it with a marking pen. They had also drawn an arrow beside it to indicate a new direction of travel. In this photograph, at the head of its two smudges, the *Coloane* was sailing north.

Sir Anthony smiled. 'It seems the captain had a change of heart,' he said. 'Or that for some reason or another he received new instructions.'

'After Mark got away from the village,' Cristabel said. 'Because Wu knew he'd seen the torpedoes being loaded.'

'I believe so. The dates all tie in rather nicely. Now you understand why Ross is champing at the bit.'

'Doesn't look like the Namibians are going to see too much rice or milk powder,' Janson said. 'Nor is anyone else. They're more likely to get flattened by a pallet-load of assault rifles. If we're right – and I'm bloody sure we are – that aircraft's going to leave Taiwan stuffed with guns. Kabinda and Wu know they're in trouble so they've come up with a new game plan. How do you like it?'

Rayner was thinking. 'Have you tried picking up radio signals from the *Coloane?*' he asked.

Sir Anthony nodded. 'On and off. But we can't monitor all the frequencies all the time. The photographs are our best lead, I think – at least until the freighter enters coastal waters. After that we'll be guessing because the torpedoes won't show up if there's any silt or mud around. And, of course, we're only getting a picture every twenty-four hours from the satellite.'

'There's another problem,' Rayner said. 'The torpedoes have fixed fins. If the *Coloane* slows down they won't travel so close to the surface.'

'Yes, I see.' Sir Anthony's expression changed. 'I hadn't considered that.'

'I can't take the damn plane out,' Janson said. 'I have to nail the bastards before they start unloading the torpedoes. It doesn't matter if they tow them up an estuary or dump them on a beach just so long as I know where.'

'Look for boxes of rice or milk powder,' Rayner said. 'Trace them and you'll know where they're going to make the transfer.'

'How the hell am I going to do that in Taiwan?'

Cristabel had been thinking too. 'Can't you tell the Taiwanese what's going to happen?' she said.

'Why should they care?' Janson lit another cigarette. 'They've beaten the Japanese and Hong Kong ivory carvers to a whole load of legally imported tusks, and they've signed a contract with Kinshasa Copper to supply milk powder and rice. Then this mad South African turns up rattling on about guns from the Chinese mainland being flown out to a bunch of terrorists in Africa somewhere. Naturally he hasn't got any proof – just a half-baked story about torpedoes and some rusty old freighter. Who the hell's going to listen to a story like that?'

'So you're going to play cowboys in Taiwan,' Rayner said. 'You and Charlie – to fix what you should've fixed when the *Coloane* was here in Hong Kong. Is that the idea?'

'How much do you want to give me a hand?' Janson coughed on his cigarette smoke. 'I've already got approval from Pretoria. Rand, US dollars or British pounds. Give me a figure.'

'You'll never pull it off,' Rayner said. 'What about the lecture you gave me on being out of my depth and how smart these guys are?'

'Maybe they won't be so smart outside of their own territory. My guess is that they've never done this before. It's a one-shot deal because you fouled things up for them.'

'Have you ever been to Taiwan?' Rayner asked.

'No. That makes it a level playing field.'

'You're mad,' Rayner said.

'I've already told him.' Sir Anthony stopped cleaning the white-board. 'Particularly when we can't offer any support. If the guns were still inside Hong Kong territorial waters it would be a different matter altogether, but unfortunately, of course, they're not.'

'Shouldn't have let myself get sidetracked when they were here, should I?' Janson was grinning.

'So you figure it's my fault,' Rayner said. 'And I'm supposed to go with you.'

'Sure. You owe me. You got two nice diamonds for taking me to Malanje so we're even on that. But you'd be face down in the tide if I hadn't rammed a hole through that landing-stage up the coast.'

'I'll send you a check from WOPES,' Rayner said. 'As soon as I persuade Lynch to pay me a little bit extra. He's not going to mind.'

'Oh for goodness sake stop it,' Cristabel interrupted. 'You're both mad.'

Janson ignored her. 'There's something else,' he said. 'How about phoning the States and telling Lynch I've gone back to Angola or somewhere? Now he knows Cris is OK he'll be expecting you to call him.'

Sir Anthony removed his glasses and started polishing them with a handkerchief. 'Perhaps Mark feels this is none of his business any more,' he said. 'One way or the other it might be better if we gave ourselves more time to consider the problem, don't you think? Let's all go and have a drink and forget about it until tomorrow.'

Instead of following Janson and Sir Anthony from the room, for the second time this evening Cristabel remained behind.

'Don't ask,' Rayner said. 'I don't owe Janson anything.'

She toyed with the belt of her dress. 'Are you still having that bad dream about my sister?'

'No.' The question had caught him wrong-footed.

'Has it really gone?'

'I've told you it has.'

'Do you think Janson might go after Kabinda as well as the guns?'

'No – yes. I don't know.' Rayner wasn't at all sure where this was leading. 'Why?'

'It's the way you've been talking. As if I wasn't here. I don't think you need me any more. You don't know whether to go to Taiwan, or run home to Wendy, do you?'

'For Christ's sake,' Rayner said. 'I'm not going anywhere with Janson and I don't want to run home to Wendy.'

'Why did you write to her then? She told me you had when I spoke to her on the phone. You wrote to her from the hotel. While you were sleeping with me.'

'It was a note.'

'Do you want her more than you want me?'

'No,' Rayner said. 'Look, this isn't the right time.'

'No, it isn't, is it?' She smiled tightly. Then, before he could do anything to stop her, she kissed him on the cheek and walked away.

Eight

Janson was not accustomed to seeing Cristabel in a bikini. The South African was where Rayner had left him, slumped in a chair watching her swim tirelessly from one end of the pool to the other.

'Well?' Janson enquired. 'Was Lynch pissed off because you hadn't called him before?'

'Fairly.'

'Has he guessed we're on to him?'

'I don't think so. I didn't tell him what happened at the warehouse and he didn't mention it. All he wanted to know is whether I'd managed to locate Cris and where the hell we are.'

'In case someone wants to have another go at you,' Janson said. 'Nice of him to ask.'

'I said Cris was staying on at the hotel and that I was heading back to the States today. I told him you'd already left for Johannesburg.' Rayner paused. 'I can't see him worrying about us anymore – not if Kinshasa Copper's going to fly the guns out.'

'Don't kid yourself. Once the guns are moving, they'll want to tie up the loose ends. You're still a nuisance to them. So am I – because you went and told Lynch I was in Hong Kong.'

'But I can make up for that, right?'

'What?' Janson wasn't listening. Instead his attention was on the pool again.

'Great day for it,' Rayner said.

'For flying guns out of Taiwan?'

'Watching Cris.' Rayner grinned. 'Go ahead. I don't mind if she doesn't.'

'Yeah.' Janson dragged his eyes away and drank some

coffee. 'Maybe if she was sleeping with me I wouldn't be going anywhere either.'

'When do you have to be at the airport?'

'Couple of hours. I'm on an early flight so I can meet Charlie off his plane. He'll be mad about the whole thing. He was on vacation.'

Last night, there had been cause for Rayner to remember the day he'd first met Charlie on the diamond field – a day when it would have been as easy to retreat from the confrontation with the *garimpeiros* as it had been to bluff his way past them with a loaded rifle. Then, because it was Charlie who'd been bluffing, Rayner had lost his chance of turning back and avoiding everything that had happened since. Now, he knew there was another chance – either to forget the mistakes, or make one more by going with Janson in an attempt to straighten out the past.

'How long's Charlie been working for South African Intelligence?' he asked.

'Three years. He was a weapon technician in the army before he got ambitious. Charlie thinks that working undercover is a big deal. No one's told him how he'll wind up.'

'Did anyone tell you?' Rayner said.

'No.' Janson held his hands out in front of him. They were shaking, but only slightly. 'Fifteen years,' he said. 'Once you're in, you stay in.'

'You don't have to chase those guns. What difference are they going to make?'

'Not a lot.' Janson lowered his hands. 'But you tell me how often anyone's going to find Kabinda, Wu and Marle all wrapped together in one place.'

Rayner looked at Cristabel. She was at the far end of the pool, standing on the diving board, silhouetted against a cloud-free sky and the blue haze of Repulse Bay.

'Why don't you give it a rest?' Janson grunted. 'You're going to screw yourself to a standstill. I need you more than she does. Just for a week.'

'I'll sort Lynch out for you. I've got friends in Washington – in the Security Council.'

Janson shook his head. 'Lynch is small time. Don't bother with him.'

'Tell that to Susan Osterman,' Rayner said. 'It was Lynch who sent those guys after me in Sandy Neck.'

'He was doing what Kabinda told him to do.' Janson levered

himself out of his chair. 'Will you come and look at something with me?'

'Sure.' Guessing this would be Janson's final attempt to solicit help, Rayner accompanied him across the courtyard and into the house.

'In here.' Janson opened the door to the library annex.

Taped to the white-board, five of the satellite photographs had been arranged in chronological sequence. On each of them, the past and the predicted future of the *Coloane* was shown by a series of solid and dotted red lines.

Janson went to the most recent photo dated June 15th and drew a circle around the freighter. It was located close to the east coast of Taiwan about a third of the way down the island from its nothernmost tip. 'Check the picture from the day before,' he said.

Now Rayner understood why Janson was in a hurry. In the last twenty-four hours, the freighter had hardly moved at all. There were no smudges behind it, nor was there any evidence of a wake.

'It's anchored,' Janson said. 'Or the torpedoes have been dropped off somewhere.'

'They're more likely hanging in deep water off the stern,' Rayner said. 'What are you going to do if they start moving again?'

'Depends if I'm in time. Sir Anthony's given me the name of some people in Taipei who import explosives. If I can lay my hands on some magnetic mines they might do the job.'

'To hammer the freighter or the torpedoes?'

Janson glanced at him. 'What's the difference?'

'For a start, the torpedoes look as though they're made from stainless steel, and stainless steel isn't necessarily magnetic. On top of that they could be a couple of hundred feet down. How's your scuba diving technique?'

'So I go for the cable,' Janson said. 'And hope the bloody things sink out of sight.'

'Good luck.'

'I don't need luck, I need another pair of hands.'

'Get more people,' Rayner said. 'Phone home.'

'You're joking.' From his pocket Janson produced a crumpled sheet of paper and began reading aloud from it. 'Additional funds transferred through British channel today. Support arrives 1420 hours Taipei, June 16th.' He looked up briefly. 'Charlie's the support. It's the rest of it that'll give you the idea of how Pretoria thinks.'

'I don't want to know how Pretoria thinks,' Rayner said.

'Just listen.' Janson continued reading. 'Remind you SAMI will not in any circumstances acknowledge presence in Taiwan. Strongly recommend you consider alternative means of satisfying primary objective. Request for additional support denied. Irrespective of opportunity, do not, repeat do not attempt secondary objective on Chinese mainland or in Republic of Taiwan. Message ends.'

'What's the secondary objective?'

'Use your imagination.' Janson lit a cigarette. 'Sir Anthony's fixing up a radio link from here, but he doesn't know if I'll be able to pick up a signal five hundred miles away on the east coast of the island. So it's me and Charlie and a communications hook-up that might or might not work.'

'Tough break,' Rayner said.

'Stop being such a prick. Are you suffering from a fucking loss of memory or something? Susan Osterman; that hole in Wendy's shoulder; a whole bunch of people spraying bullets at you down the beach; a present for you in the warehouse; those Angolan soldiers along the river.' Janson paused for breath. 'You're not going to forget what Kabinda did to Cris's sister any more than I can. Cris told me you have this dream.'

'Anything else?' Rayner said.

'Yeah, there is. If she didn't have a rich uncle in Macau, she wouldn't be out there jumping around with no clothes on. And if that's how it had turned out, you'd have been asking me to give you a hand instead of the other way round. Get your mind off what's hanging between your legs and have a good think about that.'

Rayner had been thinking for two days. He'd been thinking of something else as well – about Janson's secondary objective.

The South African began ripping the satellite photographs from the board. 'I've got to go,' he said. 'If you change your mind, give me a call on the radio. I'll only be five hundred miles away sitting on a beach somewhere.'

'I'll run you to the airport.'

'It's OK. Lady Carmichael's going shopping with Cris. They're dropping me off.' Janson hesitated. 'Long time since we had that scotch together in my tent, isn't it? Funny how things turn out.'

'Say hello to Charlie.'

'Yeah.' Janson shook hands awkwardly before he went to the

door. 'I'll say hello to Kabinda for you too.'

It was almost midnight when Rayner said goodnight to Sir Anthony and headed for bed. The evening had been less than a success. In the absence of the South African, as if by mutual consent, the conversation over dinner had revolved around incidentals, and it wasn't until Lady Carmichael and Cristabel had retired that Rayner had felt inclined to mention his discussion with Janson. It was a mistake. In an attempt to rationalize his intention to book flights home in the morning, he'd been conscious of sounding defensive and, by the time he'd left the table, he was morose and annoyed with himself for believing that it was necessary to justify his decision either to Cristabel or to Sir Anthony.

He let himself into his room, slammed the door behind him then made more noise in the bathroom, deliberately knocking over a bottle of aftershave so she would know he was back. When there was no response he went to the adjoining door and opened it.

She'd fallen asleep with the light on. A magazine lay on her pillow and there was an empty glass of milk on the table beside the bed. While he was wondering whether to wake her she opened her eyes. 'Hi,' he said.

'What time is it?'

'Late.'

'Oh.' She struggled to sit up. 'I gave up on you. Where have you been?'

'Talking.'

'Are you just going to stand there, or can I go back to sleep?'

'You can go back to sleep.'

She patted the sheets. 'Come here.'

Rayner sat down close to her. 'I came to say hello,' he said.

'That's my line. You didn't come to say hello. You want me to tell you we're doing the right thing.'

'I already know we are.'

'So why have you woken me up?'

'No reason.' He picked up the magazine.

'Leave that.' She tried to take it from him, accidentally tearing off the front cover and allowing some loose pages to fall out onto the floor.

Rayner gathered them up, realizing that they weren't pages

from the magazine at all. They were black and white pictures – the photocopies Felix had sent to WOPES.

'What are you doing with these?' he said.

'Janson saw them when he helped you collect my things from the hotel. He asked if he could look at them again this morning before he left. I think he wanted to make himself – you know – to make it easier if – ' She stopped abruptly.

Rayner's eyes were on the pictures, seeing the image of her sister for the hundredth time, remembering how Kabinda's men had held her legs apart, remembering how she'd kicked and for how long she'd screamed. He folded the pictures in two and began systematically tearing them to pieces.

'You didn't have to look,' she said.

'Nor did Janson. Did he say anything about me?'

'Only that I have to make sure you're not silly about Lynch. Ross understands why you haven't gone with him. Is that what you're worried about?'

'No.'

She was wide awake now. 'Has Sir Anthony made you change your mind?'

'Not exactly.'

'You said you don't owe Janson anything. And it won't bring Francesca back, will it?'

'It's not for Janson, or your sister. It's for me.' Rayner put the magazine on the table. 'If I go will you stay here? So I know you'll be OK?'

'I'd rather be at my uncle's place. But I won't be going there because you're not going to Taiwan.' She smiled. 'I won't let you. You cost a hundred thousand dollars, Mark Rayner. You're not going anywhere without me, and I'm not going anywhere without you.'

'It'd only be for a few days.' Rayner knew that until now she hadn't been taking him seriously.

Her expression changed. 'Well that's fine, then. What about us? What if something goes wrong?'

'If it does, I don't want to spend the next five years wondering if I could have made the difference. You don't understand.'

'Am I part of this five-year plan? Or do I just fit in between Wendy and some imagined threat to your masculinity?'

In his present mood Rayner had no intention of putting up with another inquisition about Wendy. And if she wanted an argument, this seemed to be as good a time as any to have one.

'You don't ever learn, do you?' he said. 'This has nothing to do with Janson or Wendy. And I sure as hell don't need any help from you to make up my mind about Taiwan. Let me tell you something.'

'Mark, don't.' She interrupted him. 'I'm sorry. I shouldn't have said that.'

In the past, by being contrite she had invariably managed to disarm him and make him feel as though he was being unreasonable. But on this occasion there was a difference; Sir Anthony's scotch, the photocopies of her sister and the mention of Wendy had tipped Rayner over the edge. He didn't have a five-year plan – he had a five-day plan – a plan that satisfied the only two damn things that mattered. The uncertainty was gone, and for the first time in a week, he knew exactly what he wanted and what he had to do.

Removing his left shoe, he used a thumbnail to prise the one remaining diamond from the cavity in the heel.

'Right,' he said. 'Now you listen to me. However you think it is between Wendy and me, you're wrong. If I wanted to be in her bedroom instead of yours, I'd be there. She's never told me where I can go or when I can go, and you're not going to tell me either. Have you got that?'

She nodded tight-lipped and apprehensive.

'This is for your uncle.' Rayner gave her the diamond. 'I don't know how much it's worth, but if it's not enough I'll get a couple more. Thank him for what he did, and tell him that as things turned out you didn't need the money after all.'

'Mark, please,' she said. 'My uncle won't want your diamond. I don't want it either. For God's sake it was a joke. And I wasn't trying to tell you what to do. Don't talk to me like this, please.'

'I haven't finished. There's something else.'

She stared at the bedclothes. 'What?'

'I've got a message for you to deliver. Tell your uncle that while I'm clearing up some business in Taiwan, he's to keep you locked up somewhere safe until I come for you.'

'Oh.' Her expression turned to relief. 'I thought you were going to – '

'Any more smart remarks?'

She shook her head.

'You're the one who wanted a happy ending,' he said. 'This is how we get it.'

'Suppose you run into trouble. You still can't use your hand properly. I've seen the way you try to hold things.'

'I'm not going rock climbing.'

'Let me see.' Taking his hand she examined it for a moment, then carefully guided it under the sheet and placed it on her breast.

Rayner could feel her breathing. And he could feel her nipple against his palm.

'You frightened me,' she murmured. 'Promise you'll never do that again.'

'Or what?'

She smiled. 'Or I won't let you have your diamond back. I've hidden it somewhere.'

Rayner didn't want the diamond. He wanted her. Despite his ultimatum, despite his decision, nothing had changed. Choosing to go to Taiwan might have eased the doubts about himself, but the desire for her was greater than ever.

Almost without knowing what he was doing he slid his hand down over her stomach, feeling her body rise as he searched gently for the diamond. By then her eyes had closed in expectation and she was whispering urgently, as eager to help him retrieve it as he was to take it from her.

He was still searching when she started fumbling to unfasten his belt. Rayner couldn't wait. He stripped, pulled the sheet away and knelt over her on the bed. For a second her eyes flickered open, then she arched her back, forced his face down to hers and opened her mouth to kiss him.

Over the next hour, on what was to be their last night together in Hong Kong, the enjoyment he shared with her was to be unlike any of the times before. To say goodbye she led him into a whirlpool of dissolute sensual indulgence while he responded by teasing her until she had to plead with him for her release. The experience was of intense physical pleasure – one that left him drained but wide awake with his heart pounding and the blood rushing in his ears. As a result, long after she'd fallen asleep, Rayner was still unable to relax.

He lay unmoving on his back, listening to her breathing, aware that his thoughts were already of tomorrow, of another place far away from Hong Kong and far away from the sleeping figure of the girl beside him. Not for another two days in very different circumstances would he remember her whispers of tonight and wonder how he could ever have been so stupid as to risk leaving her behind.

Nine

The terraces of the Cuango River had been pockmarked ridges of silt and gravel. Here, on the other side of the world, flanking the banks of another river, the terraces were of a different kind – curved stairways of fertile land leading uphill from the rice fields behind the monastery. The river too was different, as muddy as the Cuango, but much wider where it spread out to meet the sea, and instead of being yellow, the water was stained a light-brown colour.

From the hilltop where he stood, Rayner could see that the tide had turned. Small waves were washing into the river-mouth, breaking on the beach where the aboriginal labourers were still sitting beside their boat. Unlike yesterday the men appeared to be alone. Of the Taoist monks there was no sign, and apart from water-buffalo and pigs wandering around the monastery building, nothing was moving in the heat. Which probably meant it would happen today, he decided. When they were least expecting it; before Charlie returned and before Janson had got any answers over the radio.

For three days it had been like this, seventy-two hours of watching and waiting with nothing but the 4wheel drive Pajero parked under the trees by the monastery to warrant Janson's confidence that they were in the right place. Not that there was any other damn place, Rayner thought. To the north the road ran along the top of cliffs which dropped vertically into the sea, while to the south the shoreline was equally formidable – a twenty mile stretch of the Taiwanese east coast as inhospitable as it was deserted.

He inspected the map, searching again for anywhere they might have overlooked – another river, another beach, or even mud-flats where the *Coloane* could perhaps drop off the torpedoes. There was nothing, just as Janson had said. Nothing but gorges, rock-faces and the huge Chungyang range of mountains. Which was precisely why the *Coloane* was here, Rayner thought. And why, if it was going to happen, there was nowhere it could happen except here.

The lack of movement on-shore was being matched by similar inactivity on board the *Coloane*. It was riding at anchor a quarter of a mile out on an almost flat sea, swinging with the tide, but otherwise more lifeless than the monastery appeared to be. This afternoon there were no men on deck doing their laundry, and instead of the usual ring of garbage floating round the hull, there was only a slight trail of oil leaking from the stern.

Deciding it was pointless continuing the surveillance, Rayner retreated to the shade of the trees and sat down to consider how long he was prepared to stay. Although the radio link with Hong Kong provided some contact with civilization, he felt cut-off from Cristabel and increasingly worried about Janson's unwillingness to admit that, without the right hardware, they might as well abandon the whole idea.

He was endeavouring to think of an alternative approach to the problem of the torpedoes when the South African reappeared.

'Did you get through?' Rayner asked.

'More or less.' Janson was sweating heavily and out of breath. 'I've taken the aerial right up to the top of that bloody tree. It's made a bit of difference, but the signal's still lousy and there's still interference coming in on our frequency.'

'So what did you find out?'

'The charter plane was supposed to have arrived in Taipei yesterday morning. That's about it. Not a lot of help, is it?'

'Is Cris still in Hong Kong?'

'Don't know.' Janson slapped at a mosquito on his arm. 'Anything going on at the monastery?'

'No. The Pajero hasn't moved and those guys with the rowing boat haven't gone anywhere either.'

'I asked Sir Anthony about them. He said there are aboriginal reservations all over Taiwan.'

'They don't look Chinese,' Rayner said.

'They're not. They're indigenous natives who were in Taiwan before the Chinese took over the island. They do the work while the monks do the praying.'

'Maybe someone's made them a better offer.'

'Like Kabinda, you mean?' Janson went to the edge of the trees and looked out over the terraces. 'If the bastard's down there, why the hell haven't we seen him yet?'

Rayner didn't reply. To the north where the dirt road from the monastery joined the main highway, a cloud of dust was rising through a gap in the forest.

'Charlie,' Janson said.

'It's not a car. Listen.'

The noise of engines was followed by a glimpse of two trucks. They were in low gear, winding their way between the trees on the steep descent to the river-flats.

'Got them.' Janson was using his binoculars. 'What do you bet this is Marle and Wu with the rice and milk powder?' He watched the trucks emerge from the forest, scattering pigs and chickens before they drew up partly out of sight behind a line of cedar trees.

The arrival of the vehicles seemed to be a signal. Where a minute ago nothing had been happening anywhere, there was already much more activity. Men on the beach were uncoiling lengths of rope on to the mud and dirty smoke was issuing from the *Coloane*.

'Shit.' Janson swung his binoculars onto the freighter.

'It's too early,' Rayner said. 'No need to get excited yet.'

'Suppose they do it now – in daylight.'

'You're guessing,' Rayner said. 'They'll wait for high tide – or somewhere near to it.'

'Yeah,' Janson grunted. 'We're going to look pretty bloody stupid if they don't.' He glanced at his watch. 'How much longer do you figure Charlie might be?'

'Depends how often he has to fill up the radiator of that crummy car you rented.' Rayner grinned. 'We might never see him again.'

Janson ignored the remark. 'The *Coloane*'s going to drop the torpedoes on the bottom,' he said. 'The ropes are for pulling them up on to the shore.'

'With what? You're talking about a dead weight of at least a couple of tons for each torpedo. No one's going to pull them anywhere without a winch – a big winch.'

'Maybe they've got one.' Janson put down the binoculars and lit a cigarette. 'They could always hook up a team of water-buffalo.'

'Or a hundred aboriginals.'

'If you don't give a shit how they're going to do it and how we're going to stop them, what did you come here for?'

Rayner had stopped wondering what he was doing here, but Janson's comment about the water-buffalo still raised a number of questions. If Kinshasa Copper had done this before on beaches in Africa, how had they dragged fully loaded torpedoes from the water there? Were the torpedoes more buoyant than he thought? Could they even perhaps be unloaded out at sea?

'Hey look.' Janson pointed. 'I told you.'

On the mud-flats, teams of men were feeding ropes into the water behind the rowing boat. The boat itself was already twenty or thirty feet off-shore, heading out toward the *Coloane* through the choppy water at the river-mouth. And for the first time in three days, the *Coloane* had changed position, moving very slowly, but unquestionably underway.

'They'll never do it,' Rayner said. 'Even if they've got a winch on the beach they'll need a steel cable not a couple of skinny manila ropes like those.'

Janson checked his watch again. 'How long did it take us to get here after I'd picked you up from the airport in Taipei?'

'Just over three hours,' Rayner said. 'Once we'd stopped driving around town chasing these people who are supposed to be supplying you with explosives.'

'So where the hell is Charlie?'

'Perhaps he can't find them either.'

'If he doesn't hurry it's not going to matter, is it?' Janson stubbed out his cigarette against a tree. 'They'll have the guns out of the torpedoes and on to those trucks while we're standing up here scratching ourselves.'

'Sabotage the trucks,' Rayner said. 'Then we won't have to worry about the torpedoes.'

'Great idea. Do you want to ask the drivers to hang on while I let their tyres down?'

'Later.' Rayner grinned. 'When it's dark.'

Less than two hundred yards off-shore the *Coloane* had dropped anchor again. From the stern, members of the crew were shouting encouragement to the men in the rowing boat who were tiring in their efforts to drag out the ropes. Half submerged behind the boat, both ropes were being carried away in a curve by the incoming tide.

Rayner watched through the binoculars until the boat

disappeared behind the hull of the freighter. Although his doubts about being in the right place had gone, the mystery of how the torpedoes were to be brought ashore was beginning to bother him. Janson's impatience was bothering him too.

'That's it then,' Janson announced. 'We're fucked. You can go now – catch a plane back to Hong Kong and pick up Cris.'

'She's probably in Macau by now.' Rayner didn't want to think about her. 'Why don't you give it a rest?'

'Give what a rest?'

'Talking yourself into a corner. Even if they can land them it'll take a while to unload the guns and repack them ready for the trucks.'

'I thought you'd decided they couldn't do it at all.'

'Look,' Rayner said, 'let's just see how things turn out.'

'Does that mean you've changed your mind about staying?'

'I haven't got much option unless I walk, have I?'

It was another four hours before Charlie's return gave Rayner the choice of spending another night fighting mosquitoes on the hilltop, or of heading back to Taipei in a car with a leaking radiator. But by then, if he'd ever had any intention of leaving, all thoughts of it had been forgotten.

Two months ago, framed in the viewfinder of his camera he had watched Maximilian Kabinda cut the binding from the wrists of a naked and terrified girl before she died. Now, in the fading light of evening, Rayner was looking at him again through the binoculars.

Despite the poor light, Kabinda was unmistakable, the good-looking, well-dressed African who had stood by and watched while his men had gang-raped Francesca Castela – the same man who had shot and killed her. He was standing with his hands in his pockets, leaning against one of the carved pillars on the monastery's verandah.

'You sure?' Janson said.

'I'm sure.' Rayner steadied the binoculars. 'Wu's there too,' he said. 'And a little fat guy with a beard.'

'That's Marle. What are they doing?'

'I don't know. Talking. They've got people lifting crates off the trucks.'

'How many men to each crate?'

'Four.' Rayner gave the binoculars to Janson. 'Why?'

'The crates are still full then. I figured someone might have dumped the milk powder and rice before they got here.'

Charlie's curiosity had got the better of him. Balancing a

pair of semi-automatic pistols on top of three cartons of dynamite, he came over from the car to join the discussion. In his free hand he carried a container of semtex plastic explosive.

'Where do you want this stuff?' he asked.

'Down there.' Janson pointed at the monastery. 'Unless you're smart enough to swim out and blow a hole in the *Coloane*.'

Charlie lowered the boxes to the ground. Except for his white teeth and muscled forearms he bore no resemblance to the shirtless *garimpeiro* from the diamond field. Portuguese and broken English had been replaced by a broad South African accent, and as far as Rayner could make out, instead of waiting for instructions, the real Charlie went about his business exhibiting a cheerful disregard of almost everything Janson said to him.

'How much did this little lot cost?' Rayner picked up one of the automatics. It was a .357 Israeli-made Eagle with an extended barrel, an unusual gun he'd encountered only once before outside the Middle East.

'The dynamite and detonators were free.' Charlie smiled. 'The guns, the semtex and the timers cost an arm and a leg. Just as well SAMI's paying. I ought to have bought a car while I was about it. I had to stop four times for water on the way back.'

'Did you bring anything else?' Janson asked. The delivery of the explosives seemed to have improved his mood.

'Toilet paper, canned food, Chinese cigarettes and a couple of packs of Australian beer.'

'OK.' Janson lit a cigarette. 'This is how we play it. Rayner's decided they haven't got the grunt to drag the torpedoes on to the beach. I think he's full of shit. They've got a couple of ropes out to the freighter and they wouldn't have bothered to do that if they weren't going to try. If they try tonight, I want to hit the torpedoes as soon as we see them. That means while they're on the beach and before anyone starts unloading them. The guns are packed in those suckers like sardines in a can. The longer we wait, the more people we'll have to deal with and the more likely it'll be that the guns'll be all crated up in a nice cushion of rice and milk powder.' He paused. 'Any questions?'

'Secondary objective,' Rayner said.

Janson glanced at him. 'I don't want anyone screwing up

while we're busy with the torpedoes,' he said.

'And I don't need anyone to say hello to Kabinda for me.'

'One thing at a time,' Janson said. 'You got a problem with that?'

'No.' Rayner handed him the automatic. 'You decide who's going to do what. I'll figure out how Kabinda's going to use two pieces of string and a water-buffalo to land four tons of guns.'

Janson was suspicious. 'If you've already got it figured out, I want to know now,' he said.

'I'll tell you when I get back. I need to look at something first.'

'Are you going right now?'

'Sure. I won't be long.' Rayner turned his back on Janson and walked to the edge of the trees to check the monastery for observers.

Behind him now, except for a wisp of cloud glowing high above the hills, there was no light in the sky. The terraces, the rice fields and the river were as featureless as the mud-flats, and the *Coloane* was nothing more than a dirty shadow against a sea from which all the colour had been leached.

He waited for another ten minutes, then crawled over a ledge on to the highest terrace and began slithering downhill on his stomach. To begin with he was able to make good progress; but, as he drew closer to the monastery, Rayner became more cautious. In the dusk it was impossible to see whether the crates were still being unloaded, and although from time to time he could hear voices, they were muffled and too far away for him to be sure where they were coming from.

On the bottom terrace, thirty feet from the north wall of the building, his hand touched something soft. It was a Taoist monk lying face down on a patch of freshly-tilled soil. Because the body was cold, and because it looked as though some of the pigs had been attracted to the smell coming from it, Rayner gave it a wide berth, concerned now that there might be other bodies lying around.

There were none that he could see, nothing but cedar trees, an unbroken area of grassland and the outlines of the trucks and the Pajero.

Keeping on the terrace, he crawled inland until he reached an irrigation ditch carrying river water to one of the rice fields. This was low-lying territory, shielded from the hilltop by the cedars, a strip of partly cultivated land bordering the river. From here his view of the monastery was obstructed by the trees, but he was further away from the building than he had been before, and in the dusk, he knew there was little chance of being able to see anything worthwhile from ground level.

While he was wondering whether to risk standing up, one of the trucks burst into life. Caught by surprise, Rayner just beat the flash of headlights by scrambling headfirst into the ditch. He stayed there, immersed in water, hearing the other truck start up a moment before a second set of headlight beams swept over the top of him. Not until the ditch was again in darkness did he raise his head above the bank to see where the trucks had gone.

They hadn't gone anywhere. Instead of heading for the monastery road as he'd expected them to do, they had simply been repositioned with their lights facing the river-mouth. Further out to sea at the extremity of the headlights, Rayner could pick out the shape of the *Coloane* now. And now he understood how the torpedoes were to be brought ashore.

Sixty or seventy feet away from the 4wheel drive Pajero, the directors of Kinshasa Copper were attaching a steel pulley block to the base of one of the largest trees. Kabinda was doing most of the work, looping lengths of rope around other trees to reinforce the attachment point while Wu and Marle held the block at waist height off the ground.

It wasn't only the pulley block that had caught Rayner's attention. Nearby, on the east side of the monastery building, was a bamboo pig run. Inside it, packed like animals in a cage, a dozen or more monks were squatting on the ground, either staring blankly into the lights or with their heads lowered as if in prayer.

The original occupants of the building, Rayner realized, caught up in something they had no hope of comprehending let alone preventing – men who were still alive, but imprisoned because this was the only place along the coast where the guns could be landed and repacked ready for their cargo flight to Africa.

How long the monks might remain alive was another matter. Rayner closed his mind to the problem. One thing at a time, Janson had said. Words from someone who was unlikely to worry about a few monks until he'd finished trying to change the world with two hand guns, a bucket of plastic explosive and some sticks of dynamite.

Forcing himself to ignore the complication, Rayner clambered dripping from the ditch, crawled away from the rice field and began the slow return climb to inform Janson.

Charlie was waiting on the hilltop. He stuck out a hand to assist Rayner over the ledge from the last terrace.

'You smell like a water-buffalo,' he said.

'I know.' Rayner stood up smothered in partly dried mud. 'Where's Janson?'

'Fixing up the timers and the detonators.'

'Does he know what he's doing?'

'Sort of.' Charlie grinned. 'He's getting jumpy.'

Janson had heard them talking. He wandered out from the trees with an unlit cigarette drooping from his lips. 'What were all those lights?' he asked.

'Just the trucks.' Rayner was still recovering his breath.

'Well, seeing as they've turned the lights off again you'd better get ready to go back. We need to be on the beach in plenty of time.'

'We've got plenty of time,' Rayner said. 'Wait until the *Coloane* starts up its diesel.'

'Why?'

'Because nothing's going to happen until then. The freighter's going to do all the work. Those two skinny ropes we saw were the ends of a single one. It's looped round a pulley block down by the monastery.'

'So what?' Janson said.

'So the crew of the *Coloane* are going to use the ship's winch to haul in one end of it. That way they'll be able to use the other end to pull a steel hawser on to shore, around the pulley block and out to sea again. Once they've done that they're in business.'

Janson frowned, but said nothing.

'Forget the rope,' Rayner said. 'It's just a way to thread the hawser around the pulley.'

'I don't see how that helps.'

'Think about it. If the *Coloane* heads straight out to sea with one end of the hawser tied to its stern, what happens to the other end?'

'It winds up on the beach.' Janson stopped frowning. 'With the torpedoes shackled to it.'

'Right,' Rayner said. 'There's a freighter out there with enough horsepower to pull over the monastery. The *Coloane*'s towed those torpedoes all the way from Africa. Now it's going to do the last little bit.'

'You didn't guess, did you?' Janson grunted. 'You remembered how that lighter dragged the torpedoes into the water when they were up at the fishing village.' He paused. 'I still want us down on the beach before the moon gets too high.'

'There's another problem.' Rayner sat down and took off his shoes. 'There's a bunch of monks shut up in a bamboo cage by the east wall.'

'Why's that a problem?'

Rayner wondered if it would be worthwhile reminding Janson about the Angolan soldiers on the plateau, but decided that it was probably a waste of time.

'We do the torpedoes first,' Janson said. 'The minute they hit the beach. Everything else we worry about afterwards. Now listen up. This is the game plan.'

Rayner only half listened, thinking less about the guns than he was about his reason for being here. If there had ever been reason, where was it now? he wondered. What was this for? Retribution for something he'd witnessed months ago on another continent? To prove something to himself about himself? Or was this for Cris – a way to show her that he hadn't forgotten her sister's death?

He tried to picture her in Macau, but tonight, because the image of her was clouded, he pushed it away, knowing that she wasn't the reason he was here. There wasn't one – just some half-baked idea invented by someone he could hardly recognize. He remembered what Felix had said in Johannesburg and how Wendy had told him to look in a mirror. Had he really become that much of a stranger to Felix and to her? And if he had, who was it Cristabel had taken for her lover?

There were more questions, but the opportunity to answer them had long since passed. Tomorrow would be the time to look in a mirror, he decided. By then some of the questions would have answered themselves, and by then perhaps the stranger would be gone.

Apart from a broad band of moonlight on the surface of the ocean, everything was grey – the rice fields, the river-mouth and the mud-flats, all the same dull grey colour that made it difficult to pick out detail. Only the *Coloane* was conspicuous.

It was no more than a thousand yards away, stern on to the beach with water boiling from its propellor and the noise of its engine throbbing in Rayner's ears.

'There.' He pointed to the high-watermark.

'Can't see it.' Janson lay the binoculars down. 'Are they both coming?'

'Just the first one so far. Look over there where the waves are breaking.' There was something menacing about the emerging torpedoes, Rayner thought. At the fishing village he'd watched them disappear in bright sunshine. Here, 500 miles away, the first of them was sliding from the sea, glinting in the moonlight with seaweed trailing from its fins. Barely moving, it was leaving a water-filled groove behind in the mud, travelling toward them at less than walking speed.

Charlie hoisted the rucksack of explosives onto his shoulder. 'If they don't go any faster than that I can do them on the run,' he said. 'They won't tip over on me, will they?'

'No reason why they should,' Rayner said. 'They're too heavy. Just keep your feet away from the fins.'

'And don't rush it,' Janson said. 'Set the timers for six minutes on the first bastard. That ought to be OK.'

'What setting do you want for the other one?' Charlie looked at him.

'Depends how long it'll take you to get back here. If you figure it's a three minute trip, set them for two and run like hell.' Janson grinned. 'Don't slip over.'

Charlie took a deep breath, wiped the sweat off his hands against his shirt and started walking toward the beach.

In the distance now, both torpedoes were visible, the second of them following in the groove cut by the one ahead of it. Out of the water and travelling uphill, the increased resistance was having an effect. They were approaching even more slowly, 200 yards away with the towing cable no longer sagging, but stretched taut for as far as Rayner could see in the moonlight.

'I don't want anything going wrong.' Janson gave Rayner one of the automatics. 'You watch the monastery. If you see anyone coming to have a look, don't mess around.'

'No one's going to come down here.' Rayner put the gun in his pocket. 'They won't bother checking anything until the first torpedo's right up to the pulley.'

'Unless they see Charlie,' Janson said. 'Look at that moon.'

Rayner was unconcerned. Except for the gleaming metal

cylinders at the river-mouth nothing was moving out there, and against the uniform greyness of the mud-flats and the sea, Charlie was all but invisible. As long as he didn't hang around, Rayner thought. And as long as he wasn't having trouble attaching the semtex to the wet steel.

It was some minutes before the lead torpedo slid close enough for Charlie to be seen more clearly. He was sitting on the rear of it, straddling the cylinder while he set the last of the timers. When he'd finished, he swung his leg over, stood upright on one of the fins and jumped off. As he did so, the torpedo rolled onto its side, travelling now with the fin tip dragging through the mud.

Rayner's surprise turned to doubt, then to alarm. Either Charlie hadn't noticed, or the implication had yet to dawn on him.

'Jesus bloody Christ.' Scrambling to his feet Rayner tried to decide whether to risk shouting over the noise of the freighter's engine.

'What's the matter?' Janson's face was blank.

'We have to get him back – right now.' Rayner threw the gun to Janson. 'I'll go.'

'What the hell do you mean – get him back?'

'It's a set-up,' Rayner said. 'The torpedoes are empty.' Ignoring Janson's protests, he sprinted down the beach heading for the tow cable. Twenty feet further on he was mired ankle-deep in mud, his progress reduced to almost nothing.

Only with enormous effort was he able to keep going. Laboriously, one step at a time he fought his way seaward trying not to think of all the other mistakes – the snipers, Lynch, and the trip-wire in the warehouse. But this time, if it was a set-up, the deception had been more subtle, and this time it was Charlie who was at risk.

A hundred yards from the second torpedo, Rayner started yelling. He saw Charlie climb off it, lose his footing then begin to retreat.

The torpedoes were still moving, gliding across the mud like two amphibian missiles homing on some distant, unseen target. Rayner watched them, too exhausted to take another step, knowing that, if it was a trap, by going on he was only walking further into it.

Charlie too was losing his strength. He slithered the last few yards gasping for breath.

Rayner didn't bother with explanations. 'Trouble,' he said. 'Get the hell out of here.'

Charlie nodded.

'Move.' Rayner seized the rucksack and threw it away.

But no sooner had they begun the trip back to the beach than they were blinded by headlights from the trucks. Simultaneously another more concentrated beam of light flared out from the bridge of the *Coloane*.

Rayner stopped with his heart thumping. 'Freeze,' he said. 'Don't even blink.'

Charlie didn't blink. Instead, very carefully, he wiped the face of his watch and started counting.

Bathed in light from two directions and with nowhere to go, Rayner tried to estimate how long it would be before the lead torpedo drew level with them.

'How many minutes?' he said.

'Just over two.' Charlie spat. 'It's going to be close.'

'We're not going to make it by standing here,' Rayner said. 'What do you reckon – dig a hole or run?'

They had no opportunity to do either. The first bullet caught Charlie in his leg an instant before another tore away part of his left shoulder.

He fell to his knees moaning.

Grabbing him under the arms, Rayner turned him on to his back and started dragging him away from the tow line.

There were no more shots, just the sound of the *Coloane*'s engine as Rayner used what strength he had left, slithering and sliding across the mud while he counted off the time. At 110 seconds he rolled Charlie face down and lay on top of him, waiting with his arms wrapped around his head.

The initial explosion was worse than he expected, a wall of flame and a hammering shock-wave that left him insensitive to the one that followed.

It was some seconds before he was able to persuade himself that it was over. He sat up, temporarily deaf, seeing nothing but the pure white light coming from the *Coloane*. The beam was overpowering, boring into his eyes, driving away the pain from the flame burns on his neck and arms.

With difficulty he managed to pull Charlie over and clear the mud from his mouth so he could breathe. By then Rayner's mind was functioning well enough for him to know exactly what he had to do next.

He remained where he was, holding Charlie's head out of

the water while Kabinda's men struggled out across the mud to get him.

The rain was keeping Charlie alive. It was beating into the monastery's verandah where he lay unmoving at the base of the pillar to which Rayner's hands and neck were tied. Since daybreak when the storm had first swept up the coast, Charlie had neither spoken nor opened his eyes. He was crumpled on the boards, limp and breathing far too quickly. Only the blood seeping through his shirt told Rayner that he was still somehow hanging on.

On the river-bank, still attached to the tow cable, the remains of the torpedoes were a testimony to the failure of Janson's plan – two twisted metal cylinders that had served so well as a decoy. But the real evidence of failure lay downriver, fifty yards behind the torpedoes where the guns were being unloaded from the fishing-net. Working in a snowstorm of polystyrene beads, men were removing the rifles from their waxed-sealed tubes before bringing them up to the monastery for repacking.

Last night, shortly after the men had found him, the fishing-net had slid past Rayner, trailing behind what was left of the torpedoes on their way inland to the pulley block. Then, he hadn't been sure what the net contained. But at dawn this morning it had been easy to see how complete the deception had been. How or when the plastic tubes had been transferred from the torpedoes to the net, he didn't know. Nor did he have any idea why Kabinda had taken the precaution. All he did know was that the trap had worked, and that unless Charlie received medical attention soon, he was going to bleed to death.

The rain had made Rayner's wrists slippery but not slippery enough for him to free his hands. More seriously, each time he tried to find the knot or break the binding, the loop around his throat became much tighter. Leaning back against the pillar he tried not to panic. But faced with the prospect of watching Charlie die in front of him, Rayner found that the only way to get a hold on himself was by pretending Janson could still do something.

From his position on the verandah he could see the terraces and the hilltop where he imagined the South African might be watching through his binoculars. Was he there? Rayner wondered. The same Janson who'd risked his life to save Francesca Castela? Or had he already gone, now there was nothing more he could do to destroy the guns?

Out at sea, between rain squalls, the horizon was as grey as it had been in the moonlight. There were no gulls, no game-fishing launch, and of the *Coloane* there was no trace. Its job complete, overnight it had disappeared, bound either for a new destination known only to the men who had brought it here, or to collect fresh torpedoes somewhere off the coast of Africa. All that remained was what Rayner could see – the guns; the air-drop pallets and dozens of wooden crates – the magic boxes in which milk powder and rice for Africa's needy had already been turned into assault rifles for South Africa's leading terrorists.

He could smell the milk powder. It was being poured into the river, discolouring the water for fifty or sixty yards downstream along the northern bank. He could see the trucks as well, both of them being loaded by the team of aboriginal labourers from the reservation. Like the Chinese at the fishing village, these too were small men, working barefoot and wearing straw hats sodden by the rain. Twice in the last hour, when Rayner had endeavoured to attract their attention, they had either hurried away or stared at him as if he wasn't there, and twice Rayner had sworn at them for their disregard of a dying man. Now he tried again, yelling for someone to come and look at Charlie.

Disturbed by the noise, Charlie started groaning. He struggled to sit up, either too weak or in too much pain to recognize his name when Rayner spoke to him.

'Charlie,' Rayner said. 'For Christ's sake. Open your eyes.'

There was no response, only the sound of footsteps on the verandah as Kabinda came to stand in front of the pillar.

For the first time, Rayner was face to face with the man he'd photographed in Angola. But his impression of Kabinda had been wrong. On the plateau, the African had been relaxed and confident, trading diamonds for ivory in an environment that he controlled. This was a different man, someone in a hurry and ill at ease.

'Do you know who I am?' Kabinda asked the question in perfect English.

'Yes, I know.' Rayner kept his voice level. 'You have to do something about my friend here. He's been losing blood ever since your people dragged him up here from the beach.'

'Where's Janson?'

'No idea. Last I heard he was in Brazzaville.'

Kabinda used his shoe to push Charlie over on to his back.

'Leave him alone,' Rayner said quietly. 'If you don't want to help him, let me do it.'

'I understand there are no copies of the photographs you took.'

'Ask Lynch and Wu. I've already told them.'

'I'm asking you.'

'Go to hell,' Rayner said.

'Where was Janson last night?' Reaching into his pocket, Kabinda withdrew a revolver.

Rayner had seen it before, the same small calibre gun with ivory grips he remembered from Angola.

'Well?' Kabinda wiped raindrops off the barrel with his finger.

'Look,' Rayner said, 'Lynch has the prints and the negatives, and you've got what you came here to get. By tomorrow you won't even be in Taiwan. I don't give a damn about your guns, and Charlie isn't about to do anything to stop you flying them out, is he?'

'I don't think you understand. Now please tell me where Janson has concealed the radio transmitter.'

'It's up the river. On the west side of the reservation.' Rayner clenched his teeth.

'When you seem so willing to change your mind about Janson's whereabouts, how can I be sure you are telling me the truth about the radio?'

Driving inland from the sea, another squall was coming. Rayner waited for the rain to arrive, hearing it hammering on the verandah roof, feeling it wash warm across his face while he grasped for answers that weren't there. Nothing was going to work. With no lies that Kabinda would believe, and in the absence of anything with which to bargain for Charlie's life, Rayner knew he not only needed a miracle but that he needed it right now.

Kabinda had stopped looking out at the hill. 'Can I persuade you to be more precise in describing where the radio is located?' he said.

'I've told you where it is.'

'I see.'

'I'll show you,' Rayner said. 'I can take you there.'

'I think not. Perhaps I should return later when you've had the opportunity to reconsider.'

Too late Rayner realized he had misread the signals. Struggling in a last attempt to free his hands, he saw Kabinda stoop, put the gun to Charlie's head and pull the trigger.

Rayner didn't hear the gun go off. The coldness of the execution had left him without feeling. There was no outrage, no revulsion – nothing but an emptiness so severe that it took several seconds to realize what he had done to himself.

By fighting against the cord he had tightened it around his neck to the point where he was being strangled.

Only by twisting his head sideways could he prevent it from biting into his windpipe. As a result, when at last the anger came it was overwhelmed by his urgent need for air. He stood very still, choking, unable to turn his head when two other men came out onto the verandah. One was Marle, the other was Wu Kinwah. Neither of them spoke.

Even after Kabinda had gone, they remained silent as if disinterested in what had happened. Eventually, either to demonstrate his indifference or his contempt, Marle glanced at Rayner before pushing Charlie's lifeless body off the boards with his foot. Wu was even less inquisitive. He ignored Rayner and the body, concentrating his attention instead on the trucks where Kabinda had started paying off the gang of aboriginals.

Five minutes, Rayner thought helplessly. In five minutes the trucks would be leaving. And with them would go the guns, Marle, Wu and Kabinda. He strained his eyes, searching the rainswept hillside for the rescue that he knew would not now come. If Janson was out there he would have acted long ago, either overnight in the dark, or at dawn while the guns were being unloaded from the net.

So this was how it ended, Rayner thought. The final irony – the end of all the futile expectations and the last of the mistakes that had cost so many lives. Already he found it difficult to believe that the long journey from Angola to Taiwan had been programmed to end in any other way.

Alone now on the verandah, he waited unconcerned for Kabinda to return, accepting the mistakes as though they had somehow always been inevitable. Even when he saw the flash and heard the roar of an explosion, for a few seconds he remained detached, not yet appreciating that he had misjudged Janson's determination.

Blasted from its position above the terraces, the rental car commenced its downward journey by ploughing nose-first through the soil fifty feet below the hilltop. On fire, trailing a fountain of burning gasoline, it bounced and became airborne before hitting a lower terrace on its roof.

The cord around his throat forgotten, Rayner watched the car continue its fiery downhill run, sliding first on its wheels, then on its side. It reached the rice fields rolling fast with three of its tyres burning like torches in the rain. A second later another explosion ripped through the bodywork, hurling one of the doors thirty feet into the air.

As a diversion, the spectacle had only partly worked. Some of the aboriginals had backed away, but a half a dozen or more were still standing around nervously beside the trucks.

Kabinda, though, was shouting, urging the men to finish loading the last of the crates. They started work again only to be interrupted by another roar, this one dangerously close to the west wall of the monastery.

Rayner felt the verandah shake and saw the blast drive a bamboo pole through a fence not more than six feet away from Kabinda's Pajero.

This time the effect was more dramatic. A frightened water-buffalo was joined in its flight for the river by pigs, chickens and men. By himself now, Kabinda was shouting not at the retreating aboriginals but at Wu and at Marle.

It was only when Marle climbed into the cab of the leading truck that Rayner realized that the directors of Kinshasa Copper were going to cut their losses.

The next blast was less severe and further away, a report from what Rayner guessed was a single stick of dynamite buried in the mud beside the empty fishing-net. How many more sticks and timers Janson had hidden, Rayner didn't know. Dizzy from lack of oxygen, no longer able to hold himself upright against the pillar, he was gradually becoming weaker.

The trucks were leaving. In the second of them, Wu was behind the wheel, driving with the door open, shouting something to Kabinda. But Kabinda wasn't listening. He had his back to the departing trucks, staring at the edge of the rice field where the figure of a man was emerging ghost-like from the rain. It was Janson, walking slowly toward the monastery, a gun held loosely at his side.

Although he was in easy sprinting distance of the Pajero,

Kabinda seemed to be uncertain. He ran first for the car, then veered off to the building, disappearing into the east entrance.

Janson continued walking, approaching the verandah until he was close enough for Rayner to see his face. It was without expression, the face of a man under such control that he barely looked at Charlie's body.

Without saying a word he used a knife to cut the cord from Rayner's throat and to saw through the binding around his wrists.

Through a spasm of coughing that drove him almost to his knees, Rayner tried to speak.

'Keep out of this,' Janson instructed. 'Stay here.'

'Give me a gun.' Rayner reached for the one in Janson's belt.

'Don't be so fucking stupid.' Janson knocked his hand away. 'You can't even stand up.'

'Give it to me,' Rayner said.

'If you don't stay here I'll blow your legs off.'

Rayner believed him. 'Kabinda's inside,' he said.

'Yeah.' As if he was expecting Kabinda to reappear, Janson left the verandah and moved closer to the Pajero.

The African did reappear. But not alone. He was using Cristabel as a shield. One of his hands was knotted in her hair pulling her head back while with his other hand he was forcing the muzzle of his revolver into her mouth.

Disbelievingly, Rayner saw her dragged kicking to the car. She was terrified, holding her arms away from her body like a doll.

Neither comprehending nor caring how things could have ever come to this, he managed to call out her name.

'Shut up.' The answer came from Janson. In a grip that had never been steadier, his gun was levelled at Kabinda.

Rayner couldn't stand it. Without any idea of what he was going to do, he pushed himself away from the pillar. But before his foot touched the ground, half a mile away on the monastery road, the trucks exploded in a tremendous ball of flame. And at that instant, in the tenth of a second that Kabinda lost attention, Janson shot him dead.

The bullet entered above his left eye, slamming him backward against the Pajero, his gun unfired.

Only by the narrowest of margins had Cristabel survived. When the chance for error had been so great, she had escaped unharmed not because of Janson's accuracy, but because of luck. Rayner knew it, just as he knew how crazy Janson had been to take the risk.

She stumbled once, recovered and began to walk toward Rayner, but stopped when Janson raised his gun again.

Rayner saw her put out her hands to protect herself. Then, in slow motion, he saw the bullet smack into her chest.

In his dream of her sister, her skin had been warm to touch. In this dream too, when he knelt beside her to unbutton her blouse, the warmth of her was as familiar as the single bead of blood leaking from the same, tiny puckered hole between her breasts.

Yet unlike the other dreams, this one was different, he realized – the version he'd been waiting for – the one at last in which he had the opportunity to save her.

There was no accusation in her eyes when they flickered open, and no reproach in her voice when she whispered his name for the last time.

He cradled her in his arms, knowing now with awful certainty that the dream had been a dream, and that just as the rain had dissolved away the bead of blood, so had all his hopes been washed away to nothing.

Still kneeling, he turned and hurled himself at the man who had taken her from him.

Janson was ready. Unhurriedly, without compunction, he kicked Rayner in the head.

Ten

Wakes from yachts and pleasure craft were flecks of white paint on the hazy blue of Repulse Bay. Further out to sea, where the shadows from clouds drifting over Lamma Island had turned the water a deeper blue, other boats were dotted about, some moving too slowly to form wakes at all. Rayner watched a junk crawl across the seascape, its sails glowing in the sun as though they were on fire. There were gulls all around it, scooping up something that had been thrown over the side.

'It's just how things are, you see.' Lady Carmichael spoke in a matter-of-fact way. She was cutting late roses from a bush that had already lost most of its blooms. 'Did Sir Anthony tell you about our daughter?'

'Yes.' Rayner continued staring out to sea.

'She drowned not more than five miles from here. I know it's not the same, but I don't believe you can ever be sure of everything really.'

'You tried to find Cris in Macau, didn't you?'

'Well, yes. But I'd rather you spoke to my husband about it.' Lady Carmichael stepped out of the flower bed. 'He'll be home soon. I'm so sorry you've had to wait like this. You have spoken with him, though, haven't you?'

'Sort of.' Rayner corrected himself. 'Only about the message he sent to Janson over the radio. That's all I know for sure. Janson and I talked about Cris on the drive back to Taipei and on the flight back here, but he only had half the story and I was in pretty bad shape.'

Lady Carmichael smiled slightly. 'I'm afraid you don't look very much better now.' She inspected the bruise on his head and the weal marks around his neck.

'It's the burns that hurt.' Rayner held out his arms. 'I was real close to the first bang.'

'So I understand. Ross said you were lucky. But it's not the bruise and the burns, is it?'

Rayner shook his head. 'Look, would you tell me what her uncle said to you? I'd like to know.'

'Shall we walk? I find it's always better to walk at times like this.'

'Why did you go to see her uncle?' Rayner said.

'Because of the diamond. The housekeeper found it in Cristabel's bed the morning after she'd left.' Lady Carmichael glanced at him. 'If it hadn't been for that, heaven knows what might have happened.'

'And you thought the diamond belonged to Cris?'

'It didn't occur to any of us that it might not. Fortunately, when you were here last, you'd written down her uncle's number on a notepad so we were able to ring her to say the diamond was in safe hands.' She paused. 'Tried to ring her, I should say.'

'That's when you discovered she wasn't there,' Rayner said.

'No, not at all. I was judging at a flower show in Macau on the Thursday afternoon so I took the diamond with me in case I could drop it off. You see there was no answer from her uncle's phone. When I got to Macau I looked up the address in the phone directory and realized we'd been ringing the wrong number. Naturally I imagined we'd copied it down incorrectly or something. I thought nothing of it really.'

'Until you went to the house.'

'Well, yes. Her uncle was there. He's a charming man with an absolutely lovely Chinese wife. After I'd introduced myself, I explained that Cristabel had been staying with us and told him why I'd called round.'

Rayner was having trouble. Up to now it had been the bitterness he couldn't handle. But talking about her had brought back the other feelings – the excruciating knowledge that she'd deceived him from the beginning and that everything she'd told him had been lies or half-truths to gain his confidence.

'Are you sure you're all right?' Lady Carmichael looked concerned.

'I'm fine. Go on. I want to hear the whole thing.'

'There's not a great deal more to say. I think you can guess the rest.' She started walking again. 'Of course, I never did see Cristabel.'

'Because she'd gone straight to Taiwan,' Rayner said slowly. 'To tell Kabinda what we were planning to do. She probably wasn't even at her uncle's the time before when she phoned Wendy.'

'No, I'm afraid she wasn't. She hadn't been in Macau for over a year.'

Rayner kicked at a stone on the path. 'Her uncle must have thought you were mad,' he said.

'I don't believe so. He seemed to have a very clear idea of the kind of person she was. If you want me to, I can tell you what he said.'

'Please.' Rayner had some idea of what was coming.

Lady Carmichael compressed her lips. 'He told me about both his nieces – how pretty they were and how different they were. Apparently, Cristabel was still quite young when her father realized he had a problem with her. She started stealing things when she was ten and became sexually active before she was fourteen. According to her uncle, she was sleeping with men on the game reserve while she was still at school.'

'What about her sister?'

'Mr Castela said Francesca was nothing like that – just as full of life, but completely caught up with what her father was doing in Africa and then later with her job for WOPES. It's strange, isn't it? How the two girls were such opposites, I mean.'

Rayner was elsewhere – back in a hotel room listening to Cristabel describing her sister, remembering the picture of Francesca that she had painted for him – hearing her tell the story of a teenager so sexually promiscuous that her father had kicked her out of his house. Not Francesca, Rayner thought despairingly. Even that had been a lie. To add authenticity to her whispered secrets – to more thoroughly seduce him and manipulate him – she had described a sister who was in reality herself.

'Mark.' Lady Carmichael's voice broke in on his thoughts. 'You're not blaming yourself for any of this, I hope.'

'For Felix, for Charlie or for Francesca Castela?'

'You're being melodramatic. Feeling sorry for yourself isn't going to help. You have to try to forget what's happened.'

'How?' Rayner said. 'How the hell can I forget?'

'I can't answer that for you. It's something you have to work out for yourself. Anyway, if anyone's to blame, it's Ross. He never suspected Cristabel was working for Kinshasa Copper. None of us did. We all liked her.'

'I didn't just like her.'

'No, I suppose not. But somehow you have to find a way to understand who she was.'

'I know who she was,' Rayner said. 'It doesn't help. I can't get her out of my head.'

'Well you have to.' Lady Carmichael spoke more firmly. 'I hardly like to say so, but in the circumstances I think it's as well that things have turned out as they have done.'

'You don't understand,' Rayner said.

'Yes I do. But that doesn't change anything. Ross believes it was Cristabel who warned Kabinda about the army raid in Angola. If it's true, she was directly responsible for the death of her own sister.'

'And we thought it was Lynch,' Rayner said. 'God, how could I have ever been so stupid?'

'Because she was an extraordinarily attractive and provocative young woman who knew exactly what she wanted.' Lady Carmichael rearranged the roses in her hand. 'Once Kinshasa Copper had learned about the photos you'd taken and realized how dangerous they could be, I'm sure it was easy for her to find out what your intentions were. Most men would have been as taken with her as you were.'

Not taken, Rayner thought. Overwhelmed. He struggled to dispel another image of her, this time seeing her smiling at him, lying on the bed naked with the strawberry crushed between her breasts and with the honey running down warm and sweet between her thighs. He started cursing under his breath, unable to forgive himself for taking the pleasure she had been so willing to provide. A long hedonistic ride to nowhere, he thought, a ride he had been no more able to resist than he was able to forget.

Over the island now the clouds were thinning, no longer casting shadows on the sea, but dissipating into thin air as though they'd never been there to begin with. He watched them vanish one by one, willing himself to pretend that when they had all gone the memories of her would have disappeared as well.

Lady Carmichael said nothing, reluctant to reopen the conversation because of the expression on his face.

'For nothing,' Rayner said. 'All the things she said and all the things she did – just a goddamn job for that son of a bitch Kabinda – just to make sure I didn't have copies of the photos. She slept with me for that.'

'And to make sure you weren't a nuisance,' Lady Carmichael said quietly. 'She'd already attended to the negatives, of course.'

'How?'

'You can ask my husband.' She pointed to a black BMW coming up the driveway. 'He'll be able to explain about Thursday night.'

'After we blew the torpedoes, you mean? The evening after you'd been to Macau.'

'That's right. ' Lady Carmichael waved to her husband. She seemed relieved to see him.

Janson was in the car as well. He accompanied Sir Anthony across the courtyard and out into the garden.

'Where the hell have you been?' Rayner said.

'Government House.' Janson gave him an envelope. 'I picked up your airline tickets while we were in town. You're booked business class tomorrow night.'

'To hell with the tickets. Have you forgotten we've got some talking to do?'

Sir Anthony intervened. 'It's my fault,' he said. 'Bad manners, I know. I had every intention of being here to answer your questions but the damn diplomats are nervous. They insisted on a briefing in case of repercussions from Taipei. You must appreciate their position – particularly as you left something of a trail behind you.'

'They're worried about the Pajero,' Janson said. 'I shouldn't have told them we left it at the airport. If I'd said we'd shoved it off a cliff somewhere they'd have been happy.'

'It's more a question of the people at the monastery,' Sir Anthony remarked. 'Despite what Ross thinks, they may not be wholly co-operative or supportive. Their gratitude may not offer you and Ross much in the way of insulation if the Taiwanese decide to carry out some kind of witch hunt.'

'We'll be long gone before then,' Janson said. 'Anyway, it's only the Brits who've got themselves excited, and they wouldn't know shit from clay – I'm sorry.' He glanced at Lady Carmichael. 'You know what they're like.'

'Yes, I do.' She smiled. 'Why don't I have some coffee sent out – then you can try and cheer up Mark.'

'Good idea.' Sir Anthony marched off toward the courtyard.

'Hang on.' Rayner caught him up. 'I need a proper run down – not from Janson – from you.'

'How much has my wife told you?'

'We've only been talking about Cristabel.'

'Ah.' Sir Anthony sat down at a table beside the swimming pool. 'I suppose we'd better see what we can do to gather in the loose ends then.'

The loose ends didn't matter, Rayner thought. All that mattered was finding a way to handle the emptiness and the disillusionment.

'Rotten business altogether,' Sir Anthony said. 'Last thing we expected, really. Still, that doesn't make it any easier for you, I imagine.'

'I heard about Lady Carmichael's visit to Macau.'

'Yes, well that was the beginning of it. But we weren't too concerned until later that night when Ross started trying to raise us on the radio.'

Janson came over to join them at the table. 'You're lucky I even got to the radio,' he said. 'I had to climb back up that goddamn hill in the moonlight.'

'Tough,' Rayner said caustically.

'What do you think it was like? Easy – when I didn't know whether it was you who'd shafted us or whether it was Cristabel.'

'You knew it wasn't me.' Rayner was surprised. 'Didn't you?'

'How? After what happened I didn't know what the hell to think.'

Sir Anthony leaned back in his chair. 'Nor did I quite,' he said. 'So I told Ross to sit tight while I tried to make some sense out of what we did know.'

'That's when you decided to call New York,' Rayner said. 'You decided to call Lynch.'

'Indeed. As I recall it was gone midnight before I managed to get hold of him on the phone. But things progressed fairly quickly after that.'

'Did you explain about the guns?'

'Let's say we had a rather frank discussion.' Sir Anthony met Rayner's eyes. 'For about an hour.'

'About Cristabel?'

'Yes. You see Lynch had never asked her to help you trace

the ivory shipment. It was her idea. He said she was insistent to the point where he concluded that you were having an affair with her. The real reason never occurred to him, of course.'

'Go on,' Rayner said.

'Naturally it wasn't just that. There was a lot more to it. Four days before I telephoned him, WOPES received official US Government approval to alert Luanda to the activities of Kinshasa Copper in Angola. But when Lynch went to retrieve the negatives and the prints of your photographs from his file, he couldn't find them.'

'Clean-up job,' Janson grunted. 'Your pretty friend took care of them before she came out here to join you. All she had to do then was check that you didn't have copies and make sure you didn't get too ambitious hunting down the ivory.'

'She helped with the ivory,' Rayner said. 'To begin with.'

'Sure. But she never bargained on you being tricky enough to start looking for cables hanging over the back of freighters. If you hadn't done that she wouldn't have had to warn Wu about your visit to the fishing village. Think about it – if you'd never rented that sampan you could've carried on screwing her silly until she got tired of it.'

Rayner didn't want to think about it. He ignored Janson, directing his attention back to Sir Anthony. 'What else did Lynch say?' he asked.

'He offered to check the WOPES telephone accounts – he rang me back.'

'Guess where she'd been calling,' Janson said.

'Where?'

'Zaire and Hong Kong – the Kinshasa Copper offices. The little bitch had probably been working for Kabinda ever since she started the job in New York.'

The use of the word bitch had a peculiar effect on Rayner. For the first time anger was welling up inside him – not the vindictiveness or hatred he remembered seeing in Janson's eyes, but anger that was real enough to make him break out in a sweat.

'Hey.' Janson glanced at him. 'You OK?'

'Yeah. I'm OK.'

'She had you by the balls.' Janson lit a cigarette. 'Then you got away from Wu at the village and she had to start all over again. She had one hand between your legs and the other one round your throat. If you hadn't brought her here so she could get a fix on what we had in mind for the guns, you'd be dead.'

Through Rayner's anger, the contradictions were piling up too fast for him to separate them – their nights together, the journey on the sampan, the tripwire at the warehouse and the way she'd fallen into his arms at the ferry pier – carefully orchestrated events to help lead him from her bed to the fishing village and then back to her bed again. There was the raid on the cottage too, he thought, and the night before he'd left for Taiwan when she'd made him search for the wretched diamond – days and nights no more real than the dream he'd once had of her sister.

Janson blew out a stream of smoke and coughed. 'I still can't figure out one thing,' he said. 'Why didn't she try to talk you into going with me to Taiwan? Kabinda must have told her he wanted all three of us there.'

'I talked myself into it,' Rayner said. 'She hadn't put away those photocopies Felix sent to WOPES – the ones you asked her for. I started going through the damn things and got to thinking about Angola and Felix – you know how it is.'

Janson raised his eyebrows. 'So did she,' he said.

'Listen, leave it alone, will you?' As quickly as it had come, Rayner's anger had gone, leaving him with nothing but the bitterness.

'I didn't ask to see the photocopies,' Janson said. 'She made sure you saw them, though. She knew you better than you know yourself. All she cared about was burying you, me and Charlie out there on those fucking mudflats.'

Rayner didn't care any more. He watched a girl bring the coffee out from the house. She was about nineteen, slightly built with long black hair tied back behind her head. And she had small, pointed breasts pushing out against her blouse.

When she put the tray down and smiled at him, Rayner couldn't look at her. He left the table, walked across the courtyard and back out into the garden.

It wasn't going to go away, he realized. Not ever. That he couldn't find a way to hate her was unimportant. Whoever she had been, whatever she had been, the pleasure of making love to her had been an experience so extreme that just as his anger had been unable to drive away the bitterness, he knew hate could never quite replace the memories of her.

Walking slowly he followed the pathway through the garden down to the wrought-iron gates beside the coast road. The gate was warm to touch and heat was shimmering off the road in waves. For a long time he stayed there looking through the waves, sheets of rippled glass distorting not only his view of the bay, but of everything he could see, and everything he imagined he might ever see again.

This year the leaves of the cherry tree were falling early. They were everywhere, spoiling the neatness of the lawn that he had laboured to mow over the last week. There were leaves in the gutter too, blocking the downspout. Although the rain had stopped before daybreak, water was still overflowing from the guttering, leaving a wet streak on the wall of the cottage nearest to the wood-pile.

And there was the axe, half buried under a log where he'd left it, the mark from the bullet still shiny on the otherwise rusty head.

Rayner made a conscious effort to ignore it. Like his camera, the cherry tree and the wood-pile, the axe was connected with a past that was difficult enough to accept without searching for things to remind him of it.

Only the fishing-rod was safe. Because it had more to do with Wendy than it did Cristabel, so far the rod's association with the past seemed to be benign. Which was more than he could say about the weather, Rayner thought. Last night's rain had been the worst reminder yet, hammering on the roof so hard that twice when he'd woken up, the cottage had been the monastery and Sandy Neck had been the rain-drenched mud-flats of Taiwan.

Knowing he'd missed the best of the tide, he locked the front door, put the rod over his shoulder and started off for the beach by foot.

There were no cars in the car-park and no one on the foreshore, just an empty beach, an ocean full of fish and the sun rising into a cloudless and haze-free sky. Home? Rayner wondered. Was this home? The place Felix had told him he'd forgotten, where summers never ended and where the promises he'd made to Wendy were supposed to have lasted forever?

She found him sitting on the sand, his eyes fixed on the horizon.

'Hi.' He didn't look at her.

'You didn't call me,' she said.

'No.'

She sat down beside him. 'When did you come back?'

'Week and a bit. I can't remember. Monday I think.'

'Was it bad? Really bad?'

'She died the same way as her sister did – more or less.'

'Like that girl in your dream?'

Rayner couldn't answer. He was nervous – too scared to turn his head in case Wendy wasn't there. 'Janson shot her,' he said.

'I know,' she said quietly. 'Stuart Lynch phoned – not just to tell me, to ask if I'd seen you. That's how I knew you were home.'

'What did he want?'

'I think he wants to talk to you about a job in Africa somewhere. I said you'd be in touch.'

Rayner remained silent.

'Mark, it's me – remember. I don't care about you and her.'

He turned now, seeing her as if for the first time. She too was beautiful – perhaps even more so. Her hair was across her face and her cheeks were wet with tears, not for herself but for him.

He wiped them away, trying to believe that if he couldn't bring the summers back, she would be able to do it for him. 'You didn't have to come,' he said.

She smiled through her tears. 'Yes I did.'

'I'm not looking for a sister to run to.'

'You haven't got a sister. All you have is me. I'm all you'll ever have, and all I'll ever have is you. Don't you understand that yet?'

'Maybe we were smarter than we thought,' he said.

'Making the pact?'

'Why else would either of us be here? I can't see that anything else matters much.'

'You look dreadful,' she said. 'Except for your eyes. They're not funny any more.'

'I know they're not.' He wondered if it was a good sign.

'What am I going to do with you then?'

'Nothing. Not yet.' He stood up. 'There's something I have to do first. You stay here.'

In his pocket was the diamond from Cristabel's bed, the last reminder of a past that, if he was careful, it might just be possible to leave behind.

Standing at the water's edge, he threw the diamond out to sea, watching it sparkle briefly in the sunlight before it disappeared.